WITH DEATH IN HIS CORNER

My second match had flickered out, so I struck another and went down the hall, my footsteps echoing in the emptiness. The walls were discolored by dampness and ancient stains, no doubt left by the first settler.

A door at the end of the hall stared blankly back at me. My fist lifted, and my knuckles rapped softly. Suddenly, I had that strange and lonely feeling of one who raps on the door of an empty house. My hand dropped to the knob, and the door protested faintly as I pushed it open. A slight grayness from a dusty, long-unwashed window showed a figure on the bed.

"Rocky?" I spoke softly, but when there was no reply, I reached for the light switch. The light flashed on, and I blinked. I needed no second look to know that Rocky Garzo had heard his last bell. . . .

Bantam Books by Louis L'Amour

NOVELS
Bendigo Shafter
Borden Chantry
Brionne
The Broken Gun
The Burning Hills
The Californios
Callaghen
Catlow
Chancy
The Cherokee Trail
Comstock Lode
Conagher
Crossfire Trail
Dark Canyon
Down the Long Hills
The Empty Land
Fair Blows the Wind
Fallon
The Ferguson Rifle
The First Fast Draw
Flint
Guns of the Timberlands
Hanging Woman Creek
The Haunted Mesa
Heller with a Gun
The High Graders
High Lonesome
Hondo
How the West Was Won
The Iron Marshal
The Key-Lock Man
Kid Rodelo
Kilkenny
Killoe
Kilrone
Kiowa Trail
Last of the Breed
Last Stand at Papago Wells
The Lonesome Gods
The Man Called Noon
The Man from Skibbereen
The Man from the Broken Hills
Matagorda
Milo Talon
The Mountain Valley War
North to the Rails
Over on the Dry Side
Passin' Through
The Proving Trail
The Quick and the Dead
Radigan
Reilly's Luck
The Rider of Lost Creek
Rivers West
The Shadow Riders
Shalako
Showdown at Yellow Butte
Silver Canyon
Sitka
Son of a Wanted Man
Taggart
The Tall Stranger
To Tame a Land
Tucker
Under the Sweetwater Rim
Utah Blaine
The Walking Drum
Westward the Tide
Where the Long Grass Blows
West of Dodge
With These Hands
Yondering

SACKETT TITLES
Sackett's Land
To the Far Blue Mountains
The Warrior's Path
Jubal Sackett
Ride the River
The Daybreakers
Sackett
Lando
Mojave Crossing
Mustang Man
The Lonely Men
Galloway
Treasure Mountain
Lonely on the Mountain
Ride the Dark Trail
The Sackett Brand
The Sky-Liners

SHORT STORY COLLECTIONS
Beyond the Great Snow Mountains
Bowdrie
Bowdrie's Law
Buckskin Run
The Collected Short Stories of Louis L'Amour (vols. 1–7)
Dutchman's Flat
End of the Drive
From the Listening Hills
The Hills of Homicide
Law of the Desert Born
Long Ride Home
Lonigan
May There Be a Road
Monument Rock
Night Over the Solomons
Off the Mangrove Coast
The Outlaws of Mesquite
The Rider of the Ruby Hills
Riding for the Brand
The Strong Shall Live
The Trail to Crazy Man
Valley of the Sun
War Party
West from Singapore

THE HOPALONG CASSIDY NOVELS
The Riders of High Rock
The Rustlers of West Fork
The Trail to Seven Pines
Trouble Shooter

NONFICTION
Education of a Wandering Man
Frontier
The Sackett Companion: A Personal Guide to the Sackett Novels
A Trail of Memories: The Quotations of Louis L'Amour, compiled by Angelique L'Amour

POETRY
Smoke from This Altar

LOST TREASURES
Louis L'Amour's Lost Treasures: Volume 1 (with Beau L'Amour)
No Traveller Returns (with Beau L'Amour)
Louis L'Amour's Lost Treasures: Volume 2 (with Beau L'Amour)

THE HILLS OF HOMICIDE

Stories

Louis L'Amour

Postscript by Beau L'Amour

BANTAM BOOKS • NEW YORK

2019 Bantam Books Mass Market Edition

Published in the United States by Bantam Books, an imprint of Random House, a division of Penguin Random House LLC, New York.

BANTAM and the HOUSE colophon are registered trademarks of Penguin Random House LLC.

Originally published in the United States by Bantam Books, an imprint of Random House, a division of Penguin Random House LLC, in 1983.

ISBN 978-1-984-81789-1
Ebook 978-0-593-15636-0

Cover art: Gregory Manchess

Printed in the United States of America

randomhousebooks.com

2 4 6 8 9 7 5 3 1

Bantam Books mass market edition: November 2019

This book is dedicated to honesty in publishing.

CONTENTS

FOREWORD

One evening in the Brown Derby on Vine Street in Hollywood I was introduced to a former convict who had written a book. Several of us were talking but I believe it was that gentleman who told the story of a man who had been arrested a number of times for petty crimes. For each he served but a few weeks or months in jail.

Someone got the idea that if this man were taught to read and write he would then get a job and live a decent life.

He was taught to read and write, became an excellent penman and within months was back in jail, for forgery!

Only that time he got three years.

THE HILLS OF HOMICIDE is a special collection that I have put together of my detective and crime stories.

They were written in the so-called "hard-boiled" style for magazines that also featured the work of writers like Dashiell Hammett, Raymond Chandler, and Cornell Woolrich. Although I am best known for my fiction about the American frontier, there's no reason why a person who is known for stories about one area cannot write successful stories in another. Good storytelling can be applied to any area at any time.

The detective genre fascinated me right from the beginning of my professional writing career. I had travelled around cities a good deal all over the world and of course one of the major differences between the detective story and the frontier story is that the former generally takes place around a city. I've also known many police officers through the years from whom I learned a great deal, I met a lot of characters through my professional prizefighting days, and of course, during recent years, I suppose everybody has become increasingly familiar with crime since it's happening everywhere. In beginning to do detective stories, I just applied the situations that I knew and with which I had made myself familiar through experience or research.

One of the questions most often asked of an author is: Where do you get your ideas?

The obvious reply is that one must have ideas if one is to become a writer, but that would be only half the truth.

Story ideas can come from anywhere and everywhere, but one must be quick to perceive them. They can be derived from a chance remark, a happening, a word, a place, or a person. To become successful as a writer one must become story-minded, that is, he must become able to perceive the story value of what he sees, hears, or learns. An idea that offers riches to one might be useless to another. Hence the idea is less than what the writer brings to the idea.

Each writer brings to his profession his personal viewpoint and experience. Ten persons given the same idea would come up with ten entirely different stories. Hence it is what one does with the idea that matters.

When I wrote the original magazine versions of the stories in this volume there were times when I might be working on a detective story in the morning and a western story in the afternoon or vice versa. As I mentioned above, there are differences in the approach to the two kinds of writing. The detective protagonist does not usually come to fear the land as much as the characters in a frontier story. A man travelling in the West finds himself off the beaten track many times and away from any help or any aid that he couldn't devise for himself. When he was lucky, he could find a few other people like himself.

In detective stories, the characters come to fear the *people* they have to associate with in the city. Of course, the character strengths that the men and women in these detective stories draw upon to resolve their conflicts would stand them in good stead in the struggles of survival that I write about in my frontier stories in previous collections like BOWDRIE, BUCKSKIN RUN, and THE STRONG SHALL LIVE. For that matter, Chick Bowdrie, the Texas Ranger featured in all of the stories in BOWDRIE would have the skills to solve many of the cases in this book with surprisingly few adjustments for the difference in period. I've been encouraged to put this collection together from many of the readers who responded favorably to my only previous collection of essentially non-frontier stories, YONDERING.

I hope you enjoy THE HILLS OF HOMICIDE.

Louis L'Amour
Los Angeles, California
July 1983

THE HILLS OF HOMICIDE

THE IMPOSSIBLE MURDER

The station wagon jolted over a rough place in the blacktop, and I opened my eyes and sat up. Nothing had changed. When you are in the desert, you are in the desert, and it looks it. We had been driving through the same sort of country when I fell asleep, the big mesa that shouldered against the skyline ahead being the only change.

"Ranagat's right up ahead, about three, four miles." Shanks, who was driving me, was a thin-faced little man who sat sideways in the seat and steered with his left hand on the wheel. "You won't see the town until we get close."

"Near that mesa?"

"Right up against it. Small town, about four hundred people when they're all home. Being off the state highway, no tourists ever go there. Nothin' to see, anyway."

"No boot hill?" Nearly all of the little mining towns in this section have a boot hill, and from the look of them, shooting up your neighbors must have been the outstanding recreation in the old days.

"Oh, sure. Not many in this one, though. About fifteen or twenty with markers, but they buried most of them without any kind of a slab. This boot hill couldn't hold a candle to Pioche. Over there they buried seventy-five before the first one died of natural causes."

"Rough place."

"You said it. Speakin' of guys gettin' killed, they had a murder in Ranagat the other night. Old fellow, got more money than you could shake a stick at."

"Murder, you say?"

"Uh-huh. They don't know who done it, yet, but you needn't worry. Old Jerry will catch him. That's Jerry Loftus, the sheriff. He's a smart old coot, rustled a few cows himself in the old days. He can sling a gun, too. Don't think he can't. Not that he looks like much, but he could fool you."

Shanks put a cigarette between his lips and lit it with a match cupped in his right hand. "Bitner, his name was. That's the dead man, I mean." He jerked his cigarette toward the mesa. "Lived up there."

"On top?" From where I sat, the wall of sheer, burnt-red sandstone looked impossible to climb. "How'd he get up there?"

"From Ranagat. That's the joker in this case, mister. Only one way up there, an' that way is in plain sight of most of Ranagat, an' goes right by old Johnny Holben's door. Nobody could ever get up that trail without being seen by Johnny.

"The trail goes up through a cut in the rock, and believe me, it's the only way to get on top. At a wide place in the cut, Johnny Holben has a cabin, an' he's a suspicious old coot. He built there to annoy Bitner because they had it in for each other. Used to be partners, one time. Prospected all this country together an' then set up a company to work their mines. 'Bitner and Holben,' they called it. Things went fine for a while, and they made a mint of money. Then they had trouble an' split up."

"Holben kill him?"

"Some folks think so, but others say no. Bitner's got him a niece, a right pretty girl named Karen. She came up here to see him, and two days after she gets here he gets murdered. A lot of folks figure that was a mighty funny thing, her being heiress to all that money, an' everything."

So there were two other suspects, anyway. That made three. Johnny Holben, Karen Bitner, and my client. "Know a guy named Caronna?"

"Blacky Caronna? Sure." Shanks slanted a look at me out of those watchful, curious eyes. I knew he was trying to place me, but so far hadn't an inkling. "You know him?"

"Heard of him." It was no use telling Shanks what I had come for. I was here to get information, not give it.

"He's a suspect, too. An' in case you don't know, mister, he's not a nice playmate. I mean, you don't get rough with him. Nobody out here knows much about him, an' he's lived in Ranagat for more than ten years, but he's a bad man to fool with. If your business is with him, you better forget it unless it's peaceful."

"He's a suspect, you say?"

"Sure. Him an' old Bitner had a fight. An argument, that is. Bitner sure told him off, but nobody knows what it was about but Caronna; an' Blacky just ain't talkin'.

"Caronna is sort of a gambler. Seems to have plenty of money, an' this place he built up here is the finest in town. Rarely has any visitors, an' spends most of his time up there alone except when he's playin' poker.

"The boys found out what he was like when he first came out here. In these Western towns they don't take a man on face value, not even when he's got a face like Blacky Caronna's. Big Sam, a big miner, tangled with him. Sam would weigh about two-fifty, I guess, and all man. That's only a shade more than Caronna.

"They went out behind The Sump, that's a pool hall an' saloon, an' they had it out. Boy, was that a scrap! Prettiest I ever seen. They fought tooth an' toenail for near thirty minutes, but that Caronna is the roughest, dirtiest fighter ever come down the pike. Sam was damn near killed."

"Big guy, you say?"

"Uh-huh. Maybe an inch shorter than you, but wide as a barn door. And I mean a big barn! He's a lot heavier than you, an' never seems to get fat." Shanks glanced at me. "What do you weigh? About one-eighty?"

"Two hundred even."

"You don't say? You must have it packed pretty solid.

But don't you have trouble with Caronna. You ain't man enough for it."

That made me remember what the boss said before I left. "His money is as good as anybody's money, but don't you get us into trouble. This Caronna is a tough customer, and plenty smart. He's got a record as long as your arm, but he got out of the rackets with plenty of moola, and that took brains. You go over there and investigate that murder and clear him if you can. But watch him all the time. He's just about as trustworthy as a hungry tiger."

The station wagon rolled down the last incline into the street and rolled to a halt in front of a gray stone building with a weather-beaten sign across the front that said Hotel on one end and Restaurant on the other.

The one street of the town laid everything out before you for one glance. Two saloons, a garage, a blacksmith shop, three stores, and a café. There were two empty buildings, boarded up now, and beyond them another stone building that was a sheriff's office and jail in one piece.

Shanks dropped my bag into the street and reached out a hand. "That will be three bucks," he said. He was displeased with me. All the way over I had listened, but he had no more idea who I was than the man in the moon.

Two thistle-chinned prospectors who looked as if they had trailed a burro all over the hills were sitting on the porch, chewing. Both of them glanced up and stared at me with idle curiosity.

The lobby was a long, dank room with a soot-blackened fireplace and four or five enormous black leather chairs and a settee, all looking as if they had come across the plains fifty or sixty years ago. On the wall was a mountain lion's head that had been attacked by moths.

A clerk, who was probably no youngster when they opened the hotel in '67, got up from a squeaky chair and shoved the register at me. I signed my name and, taking the key, went up the stairs. Inside the room I waited just long enough to take my .45 Colt out of the bag and shove it behind my belt under my shirt. Then I started for the sheriff's office. By the time I had gone the two blocks that comprised the full length of the street, everyone in town knew me by sight.

Jerry Loftus was seated behind a rolltop desk with both feet on the desk and his thumbs hooked in the armholes of his vest. His white, flat-crowned hat was shoved back on his head, and his hair and mustache were as white as the hat. He wore cowboy boots with spurs, and a six-shooter in an open-top holster.

Flipping open my wallet, I laid it in front of him with my badge and credentials showing. He glanced down at them without moving a hand, then looked up at me.

"Private detective? Who sent for you?"

"Caronna."

"He's worried, then. What do you aim to do, son?"

"Look around. My orders are to investigate the crime, find evidence to clear him, and so get you off his back. From the sound of it"—I was fishing for information—

"he didn't seem to believe anybody around here would mind if he was sentenced or not. Guilty or not."

"He's right. Nothing against him myself. Plays a good hand of poker, pays when he loses, collects when he wins. Maybe he buys a little highgrade once in a while, but while the mine owners wish we would put a stop to it, we don't figure that what gold ore a man can smuggle out of a mine is enough to worry about.

"All these holes around here strike pockets of rich ore from time to time. Most of the mines pay off pretty well, anyway, but when they strike that wire gold, the boys naturally get away with what they can.

"The mines all have a change room where the miners take off their diggin' clothes, walk naked for their shower, then out on the other side for their street clothes, but men bein' what they are, they find ways to get out with some gold.

"Naturally, that means they have to have a buyer. Caronna seems to be the man. I don't know that, but I never asked no questions, either."

"Would you mind giving me the lowdown on this killing?"

"Not at all." Loftus shifted his thumbs to his vest pockets. "Pull up a chair an' set. No, not there. Move left a mite. Ain't exactly safe to get between me an' that spittoon."

He chewed thoughtfully for a few minutes. "Murdered man is Jack Bitner, a cantankerous old cuss, wealthy as all get-out. Mine owner now, used to be a prospector. Hard-headed as a blind mule and rough as a chapped lip. Almost seventy, but fit to live twenty years more, ornery as he was. Lived up yonder on the mesa."

Loftus chewed, spat, and continued. "Found dead Monday morning by his niece. Karen Bitner. Killed sometime Sunday night, seems like. Stabbed three times in the back with a knife while settin' at the table.

"Only had two visitors Sunday night. Karen Bitner an' Blacky Caronna. She went up to see the old man about five of the evenin', claims she left him feelin' right pert. Caronna headed up that way about eight, still light at that hour, an' then says he changed his mind about seein' the old man without a witness, an' came back without ever gettin' to the cabin.

"Only other possible suspect is Johnny Holben. Those two old roosters been spittin' an' snarlin' for the last four years, an' both of them made threats.

"Johnny lives on the trail to the mesa, an' he's got ears like a skittish rabbit an' eyes like a cat. Johnny saw those two go up an' he seen 'em come back, an' he'll take oath nobody else went up that trail. Any jury of folks from around Ranagat would take his word for it that a gopher couldn't go up that trail without Johnny knowin' it. As for himself, Johnny swears he ain't been on the mesa in six years.

"All three had motives, all three had opportunity. Any one of the three could have done it if they got behind Bitner, an' that's what makes me suspect the girl. I don't believe that suspicious old devil would let any man get behind him."

"Caronna can't clear the girl, then? If he had gone up

to the house and found the old man alive, she'd be in the clear."

"That's right. But he says he didn't go to the house, an' we can't prove it one way or another. The way it is, we're stuck. If you can figure some way to catch the guilty man, you'd be a help." Jerry Loftus rolled his quid in his jaws and glanced at me sharply. "You come up here to find evidence to prove Caronna innocent. What if you find something to prove him guilty?"

"My firm," I said carefully, "only represents clients who are innocent. Naturally, we take the stand that they are innocent until proved guilty, but we will not conceal evidence, if we believe it would clear anyone else. If we become convinced of a client's guilt, we drop out of the case. However, a good deal of leeway is left to the operative on the case. Naturally, we aren't here to convict our clients."

"I see." Loftus was stirring that one around in his mind.

"Mind if I look around?"

"Not at all." He took his feet down from the desk and got up. "In fact, I'll go along. Johnny might not let you by unless I am with you."

When we started up the trail, it took me only a few minutes to understand that unless Johnny Holben was deaf as a post it would be impossible to get past his cabin without his knowledge. The trail was narrow, just two good steps from his door, and was of loose gravel.

Holben came to the door when we came alongside. He was a tall, lean old man with a lantern jaw and a handlebar mustache that would have been a dead ringer for the sheriff's except for being less tidy and more yellowed.

"Howdy, Loftus. Who's the dude with you?"

"Detective. Caronna hired him to investigate the murder."

"Huh! If Caronna hired him, he's likely a thief himself." Holben stepped back inside and slammed the door.

Loftus chuckled. "Almost as bad as Old Bitner. Wouldn't think that old sidewinder was worth a cool half-million, would you. No? I guessed not. He is, though. Bitner was worth half again that much. That niece of his will get a nice piece of money."

"Was she the only relative?"

"Matter of fact, no. There's a nephew around somewheres. Big game hunter, importer of animals, an' such as that. Hunts them for shows, I hear."

"Heard from him?"

"Not yet. He's out on the road with a show of some kind. We wired their New York headquarters."

"Wouldn't be a bad idea to check and see where his show is playing. It might not be far away."

Loftus glanced at me. "Hadn't thought of that. Reckon I'm gettin' old. I'll do that tonight."

"Does the girl get all the money? Or does he get some?"

"Don't know. The Bitner girl, she thinks she gets it. Says her uncle told her she would inherit everything. Seems like he had no use for that nephew. So far we haven't seen the will, but we'll have it open tomorrow."

The path led along the flat top of the mesa over the sparse grass and through the scattered juniper for almost a half-mile. Then we saw the house.

It was built on the edge of the cliff. One side of the house was almost flush with the edge, and the back looked out over a natural rock basin that probably held water during the winter or fall, when it rained.

It was a three-room stone house, very carefully built and surprisingly neat. There were a few books and magazines lying about, but everything else seemed to have its place and to be kept there. There was a dark stain on the tabletop that identified itself for me, and some more of the same on the floor under the chair legs. Looking at the dishes, I figured that Bitner was alone and about to begin eating when death had struck.

The one door into the house opened from a screened-in porch to the room where he had been sitting. Remembering how the spring on the door had screamed protestingly when we opened it, there was small chance that anyone could have entered unannounced.

Moreover, a man seated at the table could look out that door and down the path almost halfway to Ranagat.

The windows offered little more. There were three in the main room of the house, and two of those opened over that rock basin and were at least fifteen feet above the ground. Nobody could have entered quietly from that direction.

The third window appeared to be an even less probable entrance. It opened on the side of the house that stood on the cliff edge. Outside that window and about four feet below the sill was a cracked ledge about two feet wide, but the ledge dwindled away toward the back of the house so it was impossible to gain access to it from there. At the front, the porch ran right to the lip of the precipice, cutting off any approach to the ledge from that direction.

Craning my neck, I could see that it was fifty or sixty feet down an impossible precipice, and then a good two hundred feet that was almost as steep, but could be scaled by a daring man. The last sixty feet, though, made the way entirely impracticable.

The crack that crossed the ledge was three to four inches wide and about nine or ten inches deep. In the sand on the edge of a split in the rock was a track resembling that of a large gila monster, an idea that gave me no comfort. I was speculating on that when Jerry Loftus called me.

NIGHT WALKER

At the door I was confronted by three people. Nobody needed to tell me which was Blacky Caronna, and I had already seen Johnny Holben, but it was the third one that caught me flat-footed with my hands down and my chin wide open.

Karen Bitner was the sort of girl no man could look at and ever be the same afterward. She was slim and lovely in whipcord riding breeches and a green wool shirt that didn't have that shape when she bought it. Her hair was red-gold and her eyes a gray-green that shook me to my heels.

Caronna started the show. He looked like a bulldozer in a flannel shirt. “You!” His voice sounded like a hob-nailed boot scraping on a concrete floor. “Where have you been? Why didn’t you come and look me up? Who’s payin’ you, anyway?”

“Take it easy. I came up here to investigate a murder. I’m doing it.”

Caronna grabbed me by the arm. “Come over here a minute!” He had a build like a heavyweight wrestler and a face that reminded me of Al Capone with a broken nose.

When we were out of earshot of the others, he thrust his face at me and said angrily, “Listen, you! I gave that outfit of yours a grand for a retainer. You’re to dig into this thing an’ pin it on that dame. She’s the guilty one, see? I ain’t had a hand in a killin’ in—in years.”

“Let’s get this one thing straight right now,” I said. “I didn’t come up here to frame anybody. You haven’t got money enough for that. You hired an investigator, and I’m him. I’ll dig up all I can on this case and if you’re in the clear you’ll have nothing to worry about.”

His little eyes glittered. “You think I’d hire you if I were guilty? Hell, I’d get me a mouthpiece. I think the babe did it. She stands to get the old boy’s dough, so why not? He’d had it long enough, anyway. Just my luck the old billygoat would jump me before he gets knocked off. It’s inconvenient, that’s what it is!”

“What was your trouble with him?”

He looked up at me and his black eyes went flat and deadly. "That's my business! I ain't askin' you to investigate *me*. It's that babe's scalp we want. Now get busy."

"Look," I said patiently, "I've got to have more. I've got to know something to work on. I don't give a damn what your beef was, just so you didn't kill him."

"I didn't," he said. He hauled a roll from his pocket and peeled off several of the outer flaps, all of them showing a portrait of Benjamin Franklin. "Stick these in your kick. A guy can't work without dough. If you need more, come to me. I can't stand no rap, get me? I can't even stand no trial."

"That's plain enough," I told him, "and it answers a couple of questions I had. Now, one thing more. Did you actually stop before you got to the house? If I knew whether the old man was alive or dead at that hour, I'd know something."

A kind of tough humor flickered in his eyes. "You're the dick, you figure that one out. On'y remember: I didn't stick no shiv in the old guy. Hell, why should I? I could have squeezed him like a grape. Anyway, that wouldn't have been smart, would it? Me, I don't lose my head. I don't kill guys for fun."

That I could believe. His story sounded right to me. He could arrange a killing much more conveniently than this one had happened, and when he would not have been involved. Mr. Blacky Caronna, unless I was greatly mistaken, was an alumnus of the old Chicago School for Genteel Elimination. In any rubout job he did he would have a safe and sane alibi.

Yet, one thing I knew. Whether he had killed Bitner

or not, and I doubted it, he was a dangerous man. A very dangerous man. Also, he was sweating blood over this. He was a very worried man.

Loftus was talking to Holben, and Karen Bitner stood off to one side, so I walked over to her. The look in her eyes was scarcely more friendly than Caronna's. "How do you do?" I said. "My name is—"

"I'm not in the least interested in your name!" she said. "I know all about you, and that's quite enough. You're a private detective brought up here to prove me guilty of murder. I think that establishes our relationship clearly enough. Now if you have any questions to ask, ask them."

"I like that perfume you're wearing. Gardenia, isn't it? By Chanel?"

The look she gave me would have curdled a jug of Arkansas corn. "What is that supposed to be—the psychological approach? Am I supposed to be flattered, disarmed, or should I swoon?"

"Just comment. How long has it been since you've seen your uncle? I mean, before this trip?"

"I had never seen my uncle before," she said.

"You have a brother or cousin? I heard there was a nephew?"

"A cousin. His name is Richard Henry Castro. He is traveling with the Greater American Shows. He is thirty-nine years old and rugged enough to give you the slapping around you deserve."

That made me grin, but I straightened my face. "Thanks. At least you're concise. I wish everyone would give their information as clearly. Did you murder your uncle?"

She turned icy eyes on me. Just like the sea off Labrador. "No, I did not. I didn't know him well enough to either murder him or love him. He was my only relative aside from Dick Castro, so I came west to see him.

"I almost never," she added, "murder people on short acquaintance—unless they're detectives."

"You knew you were to inherit his estate?"

"Yes. He told me so three years ago, in a letter. He told me so again on Saturday."

"I see. What's your profession?"

"I'm a secretary."

"You ever let anybody in to see your boss?" I asked. "No, don't answer that. How many times did you visit your uncle on this visit?"

"Three times, actually. I came to see him on the day I arrived and stayed approximately two hours. I went to see him the following day, and then the night he was killed."

"How did he impress you?"

She glanced at me quickly. "As a very lonely and tired old man. I thought he was sweet."

That stopped me for a minute. Was she trying to impress me? No, I decided, this girl wouldn't try to impress anyone. She was what she was, for better or worse. Also, with a figure like that she would never have felt it necessary to impress anyone.

For almost an hour we stood there, and I asked the questions and she shot back the answers. She had met her cousin, a big, handsome man given to many trips into the jungle after his strange animals, up to a few years before. He had his own show traveling as a special exhibit with a larger show. They made expositions and state fairs, and followed a route across country, occasionally playing carnival dates or conventions.

Her short relationship with her uncle had been friendly. She had cooked lunch the day before he was killed, and he had been alive when she had left him on her last visit. He had said nothing to her about his trouble with Caronna, but she knew he was very angry about something. Also, he kept a pistol handy.

"He did? Where is it?"

"In the sideboard, on the shelf with some dishes. He kept a folded towel over it, but it was freshly oiled and cleaned. I saw it when I was getting some cups."

Then Bitner had been expecting trouble. From Caronna? Or was it someone else, someone of whom we had not learned?

That night, in the café, I sat at my table and ran over what little I knew. Certainly, the day had given me nothing. Yet in a sense it had not been entirely wasted. The three suspects were now known to me, and I had visited the scene.

The waitress who came up to my table to get my order was a sultry-looking brunette with a figure that needed no emphasis. She took my order, and my eyes followed her back toward the kitchen. Then I saw something else. She had been reading a copy of *Billboard*, the show business magazine. It was spread out on the counter now.

Bitner's nephew, Castro, was in show business. It was something to think about.

Caronna came in. He was still wearing the wool shirt that stretched tight over his powerful chest and shoulders, and a pair of tweed trousers. He dropped into the chair across from me and leaned his heavy forearms on the table. "You got anything?" he said. "Have you got anything on that broad?"

I cut a piece of steak, then looked up at him. "A couple of things. I'm working on them."

He was in a pleasanter mood tonight, and I noticed his eyes straying around, looking for somebody, something. I even had an idea who he was looking for. "They got nothing on me," he said, not looking at me. "The old man an' me, we had a fuss, all right. They know that, an' that I went up the trail to see him. That wasn't smart of me. It was a sucker's trick, but despite that they've got less on me than on that Bitner babe.

"Nobody can prove I went in the house or even went near it. Holben can testify that I wasn't gone long. Your job is to dig up something that will definitely put me in the clear."

"Maybe I've got something."

He leaned back in his chair, looking me over. It was the first time he'd taken a good look. This Caronna was nobody's fool. He had more up his sleeve than a lot of muscle, but I couldn't see him killing Jack Bitner. Not that way.

Murder was not new to Caronna, but he knew enough about it so he would have had an out. He was in this, up to his neck. That much I believed, and I was sure there was more behind the killing than there seemed. That was when I began to get the idea that Caronna had a hunch who had done the job, and somehow figured to cash in.

The waitress came over, and while I couldn't see their expressions, and she only said, "Anything for you, Mr. Caronna?" I had a hunch they were telling each other a thing or two. She dropped her napkin then, and Caronna picked it up for her. Where did they think I was born? I caught the corner of the paper in my glance as they both stooped, but the paper was palmed very neatly by Caronna as he returned the napkin to the waitress.

Caronna left after drinking a cup of coffee and rambling on a little. When I went over to pay my check, the *Billboard* was still lying there. Deliberately, although I had the change, I sprung one of Caronna's C-notes on her. I was praying she would have to go to the kitchen for change, and she did.

This gave me a chance at the *Billboard* and I glanced down. It was right there in front of me, big as life:

GREATER AMERICAN
PLAYING TO BIG CROWDS
IN NEVADA

When I got my change I walked outside. The night was still and the stars were out. Up at the mine I could hear the pounding of the compressor, an ever-present sound wherever mines are working.

I really had my fingers on something now, I thought.

If Greater American was playing Nevada, then Castro might have been within only a few miles of Ranagat when Bitner was killed.

If Loftus knew that, he was fooling me, and somehow I couldn't picture that sheriff, smart as he was in his own line, knowing about *Billboard*. There was a telephone booth in the hotel, so I hurried over, and when I got the boss in Los Angeles, I talked for twenty minutes. It would take the home office only a short time to get the information I wanted, and in the meantime I had an idea.

Oh, yes. I was going to check Karen Bitner, all right. I was also going to check Johnny Holben. But all my mind was pointing the other way now.

There were several things I had to find out.

Where had Richard Henry Castro been on the night of the murder at the hour of the crime?

What was the trouble between Caronna and Old Jack Bitner?

What was the connection between that walking hothouse plant in the café and Caronna? Or between her and Castro? Or—this was a sudden thought—*both* of them?

Had either Holben or Karen seen anything they weren't telling?

It made a lot to do, but the ball was rolling, and in the meantime I had a few definite things to work on. From the sign, I saw that the restaurant closed at ten o'clock, so I strolled back again to the hotel and dropped into one of the black leather chairs in the lobby and began to think.

Not more than an hour after my call went in, I got the first part of an answer. The telephone rang, and it was Los Angeles calling me. The Great American, said the boss, had played Las Vegas the day before the murder . . . and its next date had been Ogden, Utah!

In a rack near the desk were some timetables, and some maps put out by filling stations. I picked up one of the latter and glanced over the map. Something clicked in me. I was hot. It was rolling my way, for there was one highway they *could* have followed, and probably did follow that would have carried them by *not over a mile from the mesa!*

Studying it, I knew I didn't have such a lot, although this did bring another suspect into the picture, and a good hot one. One thing I wanted to know now was the trouble between Caronna and Bitner. I walked restlessly up and down the lobby, racking my brain, and only one angle promised anything at all. Loftus had hinted that Caronna was buying highgrade ore from miners who had smuggled it out of the mines.

Then I looked up and saw Karen Bitner coming down the stairs from her room.

Somehow, the idea of her staying here had never occurred to me, but when I thought about it, where else in this town could she stay?

Our eyes met, and she started to turn away, but I crossed over to her. "Look," I said, "this isn't much of a town, and it's pretty quiet. Why don't we go have some coffee or something? Then we can talk. I don't know about you, but I'm lonely."

That drew a half smile. After a momentary hesitation, she nodded. "All right, why not?"

Over coffee our eyes met and she smiled a little. "Have you decided that I'm a murderer yet?"

"Look," I said, "you want your uncle's murderer found, don't you? Then why not forget the hostility and help me? After all, I'm just a poor boy trying to get along, and if you aren't guilty, you've nothing to fret about."

"Aren't you here to prove me guilty?"

"No. Definitely not. I was retained by Caronna to prove him innocent. Surprising as it may seem, I think he is. I believe the man has killed a dozen men, more or less, but this isn't his kind of job. He doesn't get mad and do things. When he kills it's always for a good enough reason, and with himself in the clear.

"Also, from what he has said, I have an idea that he wants anything but publicity right now. Just why, I don't know, but it will bear some looking over."

"Do you think old Mr. Holben did it?"

That brought me up short. After thinking it over, I shook my head. "If you want my angle, I don't think those old reptiles disliked each other anywhere near as much as they made it seem. I've seen old men like that before. They had some little fuss, but it probably wore itself out long ago, only neither one would want the other to know. Actually, that fuss was probably keeping both of them alive."

"Then," Karen said, "with both Caronna and Holben eliminated, that leaves only myself. Do you think I did it?"

"I doubt it," I said. "I really do. If you were going to kill a man, you'd do it with words."

She smiled. "Then who?"

"That, my dear, is the sixty-four-dollar question."

She smiled, and then she asked softly, "Who is the Siren of Ranagat? An old flame of yours? Or a new one you've just fanned into being? She scarcely takes her eyes off you."

"My idea is that the lady is thinking less of romance and more of finance. Somewhere in this tangled web somebody started she is weaving her own strands, and I don't think my masculine beauty has anything to do with it."

Karen studied me thoughtfully. "You do all right, at that. Just remember that this is a small town, and you'd be a break here. Any stranger would be."

"Uh-huh, and she has a lot of fancy and obvious equipment, but somehow I doubt if the thought has entered her mind. I've some ideas about her."

It was cool outside, a welcome coolness after the heat of the day. The road wound past the hotel and up the hill, and we walked along, not thinking much about the direction we were taking until we were standing on the ridge with the town below us. Beyond, on the other mountain, stretched the chain of lights where the mine stood, and the track out to the end of the dump.

The moon was high, and the mining town lay in the cupped hand of the hills like a cluster of black seeds. To the left and near us lay the sprawling, California-style ranch house where Blacky Caronna lived and made his headquarters. Beyond that, across a ravine and a half-mile further along the hill, lay the gallows frame and gathered buildings of the Bitner Gold Mine, and beyond it, the mill.

On our right, also above and a little away from the town, loomed the black bulk of the mesa. There were few lights anywhere, but with the moon they weren't needed. For a few minutes we stood quiet, our thoughts caught up and carried away by the quiet and the beauty, a quiet broken only by the steady pound of the mine's compressor.

Then, from the shadows behind the buildings along the town's one business street, a dark figure moved. Whether I saw it first, or whether Karen saw it first, I don't know. Her hand caught my wrist suddenly, and we stood there, staring down into the darkness.

It struck me as strange that we should have been excited by that movement. There were many people in the town, most of them still awake, and any one of them might be out and around. Or was there something surreptitious about this figure that gave us an instinctive warning?

I glanced at my watch. By the luminous dial I could see that it was ten minutes after ten. At once, as though standing beside her in the darkness, I knew who was walking down there, and I had a hunch where she was going.

The figure vanished into deep shadows, and I turned to Karen. "You'd better go back to the hotel," I told her. "I know this is a lousy way to treat a girl, but I've some business coming up."

She looked at me thoughtfully. "You mean . . . about the murder?"

"Uh-huh. I think our Cleopatra of the café is about to make a call, and the purpose of that call and what is going to be said interest me. You go back to the hotel, and I'll see you in the morning."

"I will not. I'm coming with you."

Whatever was done now would have to be done fast, and did you ever try to argue with a woman and settle any point in a hurry? So she came along.

We had to hurry, for we had further to go than our waitress, and a ravine to enter and climb out of, and much as I disliked the idea of a woman coming with me into such a situation, I had to hand it to Karen Bitner. She kept right up with me and didn't do any worrying about torn hose or what she might look like when it was over.

This Caronna was no dope. Stopped flat-footed by the hedge around his place, I found myself respecting him even more. This was one hedge no man would go through, or climb over, either. For the hedge was of giant suguaro cactus, and between the suguaro trunks were clumps of ocotillo, making a barrier that not even a rattlesnake would attempt. Yet even as we reached it, we heard footsteps on the path from town, and then the jangle of a bell as the front gate opened.

That would be the girl from the café. It also meant that no entry could be gained by the front gate. Avoiding it, I walked around to the rear. There was a gate there, too, but I had no desire to try it, being sure it would be wired like the front gate.

Then we got a break. There was a window open in the garage. Crawling in, I lifted Karen in after me, and then we walked out the open door and moved like a couple of shadows to the wall of the house. I didn't need to be told that both of us were right behind the eightball, if caught.

Blacky Caronna wouldn't appeal to the law if he caught us. Knowing the man, I was sure he would have his own way of dealing with the situation.

UNTIL MIDNIGHT

Caronna was seated in a huge armchair in a large living room hung with choice Navajo rugs. With his legs crossed, his great shoulders covering the back of the chair, he looked unbelievably huge. He was glaring up at the girl.

Taking a chance, I tried lifting the window. Everything here seemed in excellent shape, so I hoped it would make no sound. I was lucky. Caronna's voice came clearly. "Haven't I told you not to come up here unless I send for you? That damn cowtown sheriff is too smart, Toni. You've got to stay away."

"But I had to come, Blacky. I had to! It was that detective, the one you hired. I saw him looking at my copy of *Billboard*."

"You had that where he could see it?" Caronna lunged to his feet, his face a mask of fury. "What kind of brains you got, anyway?" he snarled, thrusting his face at her. "Even that dope of a dick will get an idea if you throw it at him. Here we stand a chance to clean up a million bucks, and you pull a stunt like that! If he ever gets wise, we're through!"

"But they've nothing on you, Blacky," she protested. "Nothing at all."

"Not yet, they ain't, but if you think I'm letting anybody stand in my way on account of that sort of dough, you're wrong, see? This stuff I've been pickin' up is penny-ante stuff. A million bucks, an' I'm set for life. What do you think I brought you up here for? To make a mess of the whole works?

"The way it stands, nobody knows a thing but me. Loftus don't know what the score is, an' neither does this dick, an' they ain't got a chance of finding out unless you throw it in their faces. Let this thing quiet down, an' that dough go where it's gonna go, an' we're set."

"You'd better watch your step," Toni protested. "You know what Leader said about him."

"Leader's a pantywaist. All he can do is handle that pen, but he can do that, I'll give him that much. I'll handle this deal, an' if that baby ever wants to play rough, I'll give him a chance."

"You shouldn't have hired that detective," Toni said worriedly. "He bothers me."

"He don't bother me any." Caronna's voice was flat. "Who would think the guy would pull this truth-and-honor stuff on me? It looked like a good play. It would cover me an' at the same time cinch the job on that dame, which was the right way to have it. Then he won't go for a payoff. It don't make no difference, though. He's dumb. He ain't smart enough to find his way out of a one-way street."

There was a subdued snicker behind me, and I turned my head and put a hand over her mouth. It struck me afterward that it was a silly thing to do. If a man wants a girl to stop laughing or talking, it is always better to kiss her. Which, I thought, was not a bad idea under any circumstances.

"Now, listen." Caronna stopped in front of her with his finger pointed at her. "You go back downtown an' stay there until I send for you. Keep your ears open. That café is the best listening post in town. You tell me what you hear an' all you hear, just like you have been. Keep an eye on Loftus, and on that dick. Also, you listen for any rumble from Johnny Holben."

"That old guy? You really are getting scary, Blacky."

"Scary nothing!" he snapped. "You listen to me, babe, an' you won't stub any toes. That old blister is smart. He's been nosin' around some, an' he worries me more than the sheriff. If he should get an idea we had anything to do with that, he might start shootin'. It's all right to be big and rough, but Holben is no bargain for anybody. He'll shoot first and talk after!"

She turned to the door, and he walked with her, a hand on her elbow. At the door they stopped, and from the nearness of their shadows I deduced the business session was over. This looked purely social. It was time for us to leave.

Surprisingly, we got out without any excitement. It

all looked pretty and sweet. We had heard something, enough to prove that my first guess was probably right, and it didn't seem there was any chance of Caronna ever knowing we had visited him.

That was a wrong guess, a very wrong guess, but we didn't know at the time.

We didn't know that Karen's shoe left a distinct print in the grease spilled on the tool bench inside that garage window. We didn't know that she left two tracks on the garden walk, or that some of the grease rubbed off on a stone under Blacky Caronna's window.

In the morning I sat over my coffee for a long time. No matter how I sized up the case, it all came back to the same thing. Caronna hadn't killed Old Man Bitner, but he knew who had. And despite the fact that he wasn't the killer, he was in this up to his ears and definitely to be reckoned with.

That copy of *Billboard* was the tipoff. And it meant that I had to get out of here and locate the Greater American Shows, so I could have a look at Dick Castro. Richard Henry Castro, showman and importer of animals.

Caronna came into the café and he walked right over and sat down at the table. I looked up at him. "I can clear you," I said. "I know who the killer was, and you're definitely in the clear. All I need to know now is how he did it."

He dismissed my information with a wave of the hand. His eyes were flat and black. "Here." He peeled off five century notes. "Go on home. You're through."

"What?"

His eyes were like a rattlesnake's. "Get out of town," he snarled. "You been workin' for that babe more than for me. You've been paid—now beat it."

That got me. "Supposing I decide to stay and work on my own?"

"You've got no right unless you're retained," he said. "Anyway, your company won't let you stay without dough. Who's going to pay off in this town? And," he said coldly, "I wouldn't like it."

"That would be tough," I said. "I'm staying."

The smile left his lips. It had never been in his eyes. "I'm giving you until midnight to get out of town," he snarled. Then he shoved back his chair and got up. There was a big miner sitting at the counter, a guy I'd noticed around. When I stopped to think about it, I'd never seen him working.

Caronna stopped alongside of him. "Look," he said, "If you see that dick around here after midnight, beat his ears off. If you need help, get it!"

The miner turned. He had flat cheekbones and ears back against his skull. He looked at me coldly. "I won't need help," he said.

It was warm in the sunlight, and I stood there a minute. Somehow, the sudden change didn't fit. What had brought about the difference in his feelings between the time he had talked with Toni and now? Shrugging that one off, I turned down the street toward the jail.

Loftus had his heels on the rolltop desk. He smiled at me. "Got anything?" he asked.

"Yeah," I said. "Trouble."

"I don't mind admittin'," Loftus said, "this case has got me stopped. Johnny Holben knows somethin', but he won't talk. That Caronna knows somethin', too. He's been buyin' highgrade, most of it from the Bitner Mine. That was probably what their fuss was about, but that ain't the end of it."

"You're right, it isn't." Briefly, I explained about being fired, and then added, "I don't want to leave this case, Loftus. I think I can break it within forty-eight hours. I think I have all the answers figured out. Whether I do it or not is up to you."

"To me?"

"Yes. I want you to make me a deputy sheriff for the duration of this job."

"Workin' right for me?"

"That's right."

He took his feet off the desk. "Hold up your right hand," he said.

When I was leaving, I turned suddenly to Loftus. "Oh, yes. I'm going out of town for a while. Over to Ogden on the trail of the Greater American Shows."

"There's a car here you can use," he said. "When are you leav.in'?"

"About ten minutes after midnight," I said.

Then I explained, and he nodded. "That's Nick Ries, and he's a bad number. You watch your step."

At eleven-thirty I walked to the jail and picked up the keys to the car. Then I drove it out of the garage and parked it in front of the café. It was Saturday night, and the café was open until twelve.

Karen's eyes brightened up when I walked into the café. Toni came over to wait on us. Giving her plenty of time to get close enough to hear, I said to Karen, "Got my walking papers today. Caronna fired me."

"He did?" She looked surprised and puzzled. "Why?"

"He thinks I've been spending too much time with you. He also gave me until midnight to get out of town or that"—I pointed at Nick Ries at the counter—"gives me a going-over."

She glanced at her watch, then at Ries. "Are—are you going?"

"No," I said loud enough for Ries to hear. "Right now I'm waiting for one minute after twelve. I want to see what the bear-that-walks-like-a-man can do besides look tough."

Ries glanced over at me and turned another page of his newspaper.

We talked softly then, and somehow the things we found to talk about had nothing to do with murder or crime or Caronna; they were the things we might have talked about had we met in Los Angeles or Peoria or Louisville.

She was getting under my skin, and somehow I did not mind in the least.

Suddenly, a shadow loomed over our table. Instinctively, my eyes dropped to my wristwatch. It was one minute past twelve.

Nick Ries was there beside the table, and all I had to do was make a move to get up and he would swing.

It was a four-chair table, and Karen sat across from

me. Nick was standing by the chair on my right. I turned a little in my chair and looked up at Nick.

"Here's where you get it," he said.

My left foot had swung over when I turned a little toward him and I put it against the rung of the chair in front of Nick and shoved, hard.

It was just enough to throw him off balance. He staggered back a step, and then I was on my feet. He got set and lunged at me, but that was something I liked. My left forearm went up to catch his right, and then I lifted a right uppercut from my belt that dipped him on the chin. His head jerked back and both feet flew up and he hit the floor in a lump.

Shaking his head, he gave a grunt, then came up and toward me in a diving run. I slapped his head with an open left palm to set him off balance and to measure him, and then broke his nose with another right uppercut.

The punch straightened him up, and I walked in, throwing them with both hands. Left and right to the body, then left and right to the head. He hit the counter with a crash, and I followed him in with another right uppercut that lifted him over the counter. He dropped behind it and hit the floor hard.

Reaching over, I got a lemon pie with my right hand and plastered it in his face, rubbing it well in. Then I straightened up and wiped my hands on a napkin.

Toni stood there staring at me as if I had suddenly pulled a tiger out of my shirt, and when I turned, Jerry Loftus was standing in the door, chuckling.

TROUBLE STOP

Finding Castro's show was no trouble. It was the biggest thing on the midway at the fair, and when I got inside I had to admit the guy had something.

There were animals you didn't see in any zoo, and rarely even in a circus. Of course, he had some of the usual creatures, but he specialized in the strange and unusual. Even before I started looking around for Castro himself, I looked over his show.

A somewhat ungainly looking animal, blackish in color with a few spots of white on his chest and sides, took my interest first. It was a Tasmanian Devil, a carnivorous animal with powerful jaws noted for the destruction of small animals and young sheep. There was also a Malay Civet, an Arctic Fox, a short-tailed mongoose, a Clouded Leopard, a Pangolin or scaly anteater, a Linsang, a Tamarau, a couple of pygmy buffalo, a babirusa, a duckbilled platypus, a half-dozen bandicoots, a dragon lizard from Komodo, all of ten feet long and weighing three hundred pounds, and last, several monitor lizards, less than half the size of the giants from Komodo, India.

I glanced up when a man in a white silk shirt, white riding breeches, and black, highly polished boots came striding along the runway beside the pits in which the animals were kept. On a hunch I put out a hand. "Are you Dick Castro?"

He looked me up and down. "I am, yes. What can I do for you?"

"Have you been informed about your uncle, Jack Bitner?"

His handsome face seemed to tighten a little, and his eyes sharpened as he studied me. Something inside me warned: This man is dangerous. Even as I thought it, I realized that he was a big, perfectly trained man, who could handle himself in any situation. He was also utterly ruthless.

"Yes, I received a forwarded message yesterday. However, I had already had my attention called to it in the papers. What have you to do with it?"

"Deputy sheriff. I'd like to ask you a few questions."

He turned abruptly. "Bill! Take over here, will you? I'll be back later." He motioned to me. "Come along."

With a snappy, military stride, he led me to the end of the runway and through a flap in a tent to a smaller tent adjoining. He waved me to a canvas chair, then looked over his shoulder. "Drink?"

"Sure. Bourbon if you've got it."

He mixed a drink for each of us, then seated himself opposite me. "All right, you've got the ball. Start pitching."

"Where were you last Sunday night?"

"On the road with the show."

"Traveling where?"

"Coming here. We drove all night."

"How often do you have rest stops on such a drive as that?"

"Once every hour for a ten-minute rest stop and to check tires, cages, and equipment." He didn't like the direction my questions were taking, but he was smart enough not to make it obvious. "I read in the papers that you had three likely suspects."

"Yes, we have. Your cousin, Johnny Holben, and—" deliberately I hesitated a little—"Blacky Caronna."

He looked at me over his glass, direct and hard. "I hope you catch the killer. Do you think you will?"

"There isn't a doubt of it." I threw that one right to him. "We'll have him within a few hours."

"You say *him*?"

"It's a manner of speaking." I smiled. "You didn't think we suspected you, did you?"

He shrugged. "Everybody in a case like that can be a suspect. Although I'm in no position to gain by it. The old man hated me and wouldn't leave me the dirtiest shirt he had. He hated my father before me. Although," he added, "even if I could have gained by it, there wouldn't have been any opportunity. I don't dare leave the show and my animals. Some of them require special care."

"That Komodo lizard interested me. They eat meat, don't they?"

He looked up under his eyebrows. "Yes. On Flores and Komodo they are said to catch and kill horses for food. Men, too, I expect, if the man was helpless. They might even get him if he wasn't. They are surprisingly quick, run like a streak for a short distance, and there are native stories of them killing men. Most such stories are considered fantastic and the stories of their ferocity exaggerated. But me, I think them one of the most dangerous of all living creatures." He looked at me again. "I'd hate to fall into that pit with one of them when nobody was around to get me out."

The way he looked at me when he said that sent goose-flesh up my spine.

"Any more questions?"

"Yes. When did you last hear from Blacky Caronna?"

He shifted his seat a little, and I could almost see his mind working behind that suave, handsome face. "What ever gave you the idea I might hear from him? I don't know the man. Wouldn't know him if I saw him."

"Nor Toni, either?"

If his eyes had been cold before, they were ice now. Ice with a flicker of something else in them. "I don't think I know anyone named Toni."

"You should," I said grimly. "She knows you. So does Caronna. And just for your future information, I'd be very, very careful of Caronna. He's a big boy, and he plays mighty rough. Also, unless I'm much mistaken, he served his apprenticeship in a school worse than any of your jungles—the Chicago underworld of the late Capone era."

That was news to him. I had a hunch he had heard from Caronna but that he imagined him to be some small-time, small-town crook.

"You see," I added, "I know a few things. I know that you're set to inherit that dough, and I know that Blacky Caronna knows something that gives him a finger in the pie."

"You know plenty, don't you?" His eyes were ugly

and sneering. "This is too tough a game for any small-town copper, so stay out, get me?"

I laughed. "You wrong me, friend. I'm not a small-time cop. I'm a private dick from L.A. whom Caronna brought over to investigate this murder. I learned a good deal and he fired me, and then the sheriff swore me in as a deputy."

He absorbed that and he didn't like it. Actually, I was bluffing. I didn't have one particle of evidence that there was a tie-up between Castro and Caronna, nor did I know that Castro was to inherit. It was all theory, even if fairly substantial theory. However, the hint of my previous connection with Caronna worried him, for it could mean that I knew much more about Caronna's business than I should know.

This was the time to go, and I took it. My drive over had taken some time, and there had been delays. It was already growing late. I got up. "I'll be running along now. I just wanted to see you and learn a few things."

He got up, too. "Well," he said, "I enjoyed the visit. You must come again sometime—when you have some evidence."

"Why sure!" I smiled at him. "You can expect me in a few days." I turned away from him, then glanced back. "You see, when you were in this alone, it looked good, but that Caronna angle is going to do you up. Caronna and Toni. They'd like to cut themselves in on this million or so you'll inherit."

He shrugged, and I turned away. It was not until I had taken two full steps into the deserted and darkened tent that I realized we were alone. While we were talking the last of the crowd had dwindled away, and the show was over.

My footsteps sounded loud on the runway under my feet, but there was a cold chill running up my spine. Castro was behind me, and I could hear the sound of his boots on the boards. Only a few steps further was the pit in which the huge dragon lizard lay.

The dank, fetid odor that arose from the pit was strong in the close air of the darkened tent with all the flaps down. With every sense in me keyed to the highest pitch, I walked on by the pit and turned down the runway to the exit. He drew alongside me then, and there was a queer look in his eyes. He must have been tempted, all right.

"You think I killed Bitner," he said. He had his feet wide apart and he was staring at me.

Why I said it, I'll never know, but I did. "Yes," I said, "I think you killed him."

There was a sneer in his eyes. "Why, you fool!" he said. "You damned fool! If I had, you couldn't prove it. You'd only make a fool of yourself."

That, of course, was the crux of the problem. I had to have evidence, and I had so little. I knew now how the crime had been done. This day had provided that information, but I needed proof, and my best bet was to push him into some foolish action, into taking some step that would give me further evidence. He was, as all criminals are, overly egotistical and overly optimistic, so with the right words I might light a fuse that would start something.

We had turned away from each other, but I could not resist the chance, for what it was worth. *"Ati, ati,"* I said, *"sobat bikin salah!"*

His spine went rigid, and he stopped so suddenly that one foot was almost in the air. He started to turn, but I was walking on, and walking fast. I had told him, "Be careful, you have made a mistake!" in Malayan . . . for the solution to this crime lay in the Far East.

At the edge of the grounds I stopped to light a cigarette. He was nowhere in sight, but I noticed a canvasman I had seen nearby and the man walked up. "How's for a light, mister?"

"Sure," I said. "Wasn't this show in Las Vegas a few days ago?"

"Yeah," he said. "You from there?"

"Been around there a good bit. Have a hard drive over?"

"Not so bad. We stop ever' so often for a rest."

"Who starts you again—Castro? I mean, after a rest stop?"

"Yeah, an' he usually gives us a break once in a while. I mean, sometimes when we're movin' at night he lets us rest a while. Got to, or we'd run off the road."

"Stop many times out of Las Vegas? That desert country must have been quiet enough to sleep."

"We stopped three, maybe four times. Got a good rest out in the desert. Twice he stopped quite a while. Maybe an hour once, maybe thirty minutes again. Boy, we needed it!"

Leaving him at a corner, I walked over to my car and got in. There were several cars parked along the street and in one of them I saw a cigarette glow. Lovers, I thought. And that took my mind back to Karen Bitner. A lot of my thinking had been centered around her these last few hours, and little of it had to do with crime.

The car started easily and I swung out on the highway and headed west. It was a long road I had to drive, across a lonely stretch of desert and mountain road with few towns. When I had been driving for about an hour, a car passed me that looked familiar, but there was a girl and man in it. I grinned. Probably the two I'd seen back in town, I thought.

Wheeling the car around a climbing turn, I made the crest and leveled off on a long drive across some rough, broken country. Rounding a curve among some boulders, I saw a car ahead of me and a man bending over a rear wheel. A jack and some tire tools lay on the pavement, and a girl, her coat collar turned up against the cool wind, waved at me to flag me down.

Swinging to the opposite side of the road, I thrust my head out. "Anything I can do?" I asked.

The girl lifted her hand and she held a gun. "Yes," she said, "you can get out."

It was Toni. If the motor had been running, I'd have taken a chance, but I'd killed it when I stopped, believing they needed help. The man was coming toward us now, and with him was still another man who had unloaded from the car. The first was Nick Ries, Caronna's man, but the other I had never seen before. "Yeah," Nick said, "you can get out."

I got out.

My gun was in my hand, and I could have taken a chance on a gun battle, but it was three to one, and they had a flashlight on my face. I'd have been cold turkey in a matter of seconds. With a flit of my right hand I shoved my gun off my lap and behind the cushion, covering the movement by opening the door with my left. I got out and stood there with my hands up while they frisked me.

"No rod," the new man told Nick. "He's clean."

"Okay, get him off the road. We've got work to do."

They pushed me around behind some rocks off the road. I could have been no more than fifty yards from the road when we stopped, but I might as well have been as many miles. Nick stared at me, his eyes hard with enjoyment.

"Looks like it's my turn now. Tough guy, huh? All right, you tell us what we want to know, or we'll give you a chance to show us how tough you are." He waved the gun at me. "Did you see Castro? What did you tell him?"

"Sure I saw him. I told him he was the guy who murdered Bitner. I asked him what Caronna wanted from him, and when Caronna got in touch with him last. It struck me," I added, and this was for Toni's benefit, "that he was a pretty smart joe. I think you guys are backing the wrong horse. Anyway," I continued, "I'm riding with him."

"You?" Toni snapped. "What do you mean?"

"Hell," I said, offhand, "figure it out for yourself. I was ready to do business with Blacky, but he wouldn't offer enough dough. Castro's a gentleman. He'll play ball with you. That's what you guys should be doing, getting on his side!"

"Shut up!" Nick snapped. Then he sneered, "You know what happens to guys that double-cross Blacky Caronna? I do. An' I don't want any part of it."

"That's if he's alive," I said. "You guys do what I tell you. You go to Castro."

The line I was using wasn't doing me any good with Nick, I could tell, but I wasn't aiming it at him. I was pretty sure that Toni had her own little game, and that she was playing both ends against the middle. If I could convince her I was playing ball with Castro there was a chance she would lend a hand. A mighty slim chance, but I was in no mood or position to bargain with any kind of a chance.

Of one thing I was sure. When they stopped that car they had no idea of ever letting me get away from this place alive. I had to talk fast. "I never expected," I said, flashing a look at Toni, "to find you out here. If we're going to get anything done, it will have to be done in Ranagat."

"Shut up!" Nick snarled.

"Hold it up a minute, Nick," Toni said. "Let the guy talk. Maybe we'll learn something."

"What I was going to say was this. I'm in this for the dough, like you are. Caronna fires me, so I tie on with Loftus, figuring if I stay where the big dough is, I'll latch onto some of it. So what do I find out? That Loftus and some others have a beautiful case built against Blacky. He's got a bad rep, and the owners are figuring on getting rid of him over this highgrade deal. So they have all gone in together—the mine owners, Loftus, Holben, an' all the rest. They are going to swear Caronna right into the death penalty. By the time that case goes to trial Caronna will be framed so tight he can't wiggle a toe.

"Why do you suppose he wanted me up here? Because he knows they're out to get him. Because he's hotter than a firecracker right now and he can't afford to go on trial.

"What I'm getting at is, why tie yourself to a sinking ship? Caronna's through. You guys can go down with him, or you can swing over to Castro and make more money than you ever will from Caronna."

"But," Ries objected, "the will Castro has leaves the money to him. Why should he give us a split?"

"He's leery of Caronna. Also," I said, grinning, "I've got my own angle, but I'll need help. I know how Castro killed the old man."

"How?" Ries said shrewdly.

I chuckled. In the last few minutes I'd been lying faster than I ever had in my life, but this I really knew. "Don't ask me how. You guys play ball with me, and I'll play ball with you."

"No," Nick said. "We got orders to bump you, and that's what we do."

"Wait, Nick." Toni waved a hand at him. "I've got an idea. Suppose we take this lug back to town. We can cache him in the basement at the café, and nobody'll know. Then we can study this thing over a little. After all, why should Blacky get all the gravy?"

"How do we know this guy is leveling with us?" Nick said. "He gives us a fast line of chatter, an'—"

"Wait!" Toni turned to me. "If you know Castro, and if you're working that close to him, you know about the will. Tell us."

Cold sweat broke out all over me. Here it was, and if I gave the wrong answer they'd never listen to me again. Hell. I wouldn't have time to talk! I'd be too dead.

Still, I had an idea, if no more. "Hell," I said carelessly, "I don't know what anybody else knows, but I know that Johnny Leader wrote that will, and I know that Castro stashed it away when he killed Bitner."

"That's what Caronna figured," Toni said. "This guy is right!"

They didn't see me gulp and swallow. It was lucky I had seen that sign over the small concession on the midway, a sign that said, JOHNNY LEADER, WORLD'S GREATEST PENMAN. And I remembered the comments Caronna had made to Toni about Leader. When I'd glimpsed that sign, it had all come back to me.

At last they let me put my hands down, and we started back to the cars. I wasn't out of the woods by a long way, but I had a prayer now. "Toni," Nick said, "you come with me in this mug's car. Peppy can drive ours. We'll head for Ranagat."

It couldn't have worked out better unless Ries had let Toni and me drive in alone. Nick had Toni get behind the wheel and he put me in alongside of her, then he got in behind. That guy wouldn't trust his grandmother. Still, it couldn't have been much better. My .45 was tucked into the crack behind the seat cushion right where I sat.

As we drove, I tried to figure my next play. One thing

I knew, I wasn't taking any chance on being tied up in that basement, even if it meant a shoot-out in the streets of Ranagat. Then I heard something that cinched it.

"Blacky's figurin' on an out," Nick said to Toni. "He don't know about this frame they're springin' on him. He's all set to bump the babe and make it look like suicide, with a note for her to leave behind, confessin' she killed Bitner."

A match struck behind me as Nick lit a cigarette. "He's got the babe, too. We put the snatch on her tonight after he found them tracks she left."

"Tracks?" I tried to keep my voice casual. My right hand had worked behind me as I half turned away from Toni toward Nick, and I had the gun in my hand, under the skirt of my coat.

"Yeah," Nick chuckled. "She got into his place through the garage window an' stepped in some grease on a tool bench. She left tracks."

Toni glared sidewise at me. "Weren't you kind of sweet on her?"

"Me?" I shrugged, and glanced at her with a lot of promissory notes in my eyes. "I like a smart dame!"

She took it big. I'm no Clark Gable or anything, but alongside of Caronna I'd look like Galahad beside a gorilla.

THE FIGHT

We rolled into the streets of Ranagat at about daybreak, and then I saw the sight that thrilled me more than any I could have seen unless it was Karen herself. It was Jerry Loftus. He was standing in the door of his office, and he saw us roll into town. This was a sheriff's office car, and he would know I wouldn't be letting anyone else drive for fun, not with Nick Ries in the back seat, whom he had seen me bash the night before.

Something made me glance around then, and I saw two things. I saw a gray convertible, the one I had seen standing back of Castro's tent, turning into Caronna's drive, and I saw Nick Ries leaning over on his right elbow, fishing in his left-hand pants pocket for matches.

My own right hand held the gun, and when I saw Ries way over on his elbow, I shoved down with my elbow on the door handle. The door swung open, and at the same instant I grabbed at the wheel with my left.

The car swung and smashed into the curb and then over it. We weren't rolling fast, but I hit the pavement gun in hand and backing up, and saw Loftus coming toward us as Peppy rolled down the hill in the following car. "Get that guy!" I yelled.

Nick was screaming mad. "It's a double cross! It's a—" His gun swung up, and I let him have it right through the chest, squeezing the two shots off as fast as I could pull the trigger of my gun.

Nick screamed again and his mouth dropped open, and then he spilled out of the car and landed on his face in the dust and dirt of the gutter.

Another shot boomed behind the car, and I knew it was Loftus cutting loose with his six-shooter. He only shot once.

For once Toni had been caught flat-footed. My twist

of the wheel and leap from the car had caught her unawares, and now she stared, for one fatal instant, as though struck dumb. Then her face twisted into a grimace of hate and female fury, and she grabbed at her purse. Knowing where her gun was, I went into action a split second sooner and knocked it from her hand. She sprang at me, screaming and clawing, but Loftus and a couple of passing miners pulled her off me.

"Hold her," I said. "She's in it, too."

"Karen Bitner's disappeared," Loftus told me. "Have you seen her?"

"Caronna's got her."

Diving around the sheriff's car, I sprang for the seat of Peppy's convertible, which had been stopped alongside the street. I kicked her wide open and went up the winding road to Caronna's house with all the stops out. Skidding to a halt in front of the gate, I hit the ground on both feet, and this time I wasn't caring if there was a warning signal on the gate or not. I jerked it open, heard the bell clang somewhere in the interior, and then I was inside the gate and running for the steps.

As I went through the gate I heard something crash, and then a scream as of an animal in pain—a hoarse, gasping cry that died away in a sobbing gasp. I took the steps in a bound and went through the door.

Caronna, his eyes blazing, his shirt ripped half off, was standing in the middle of the room, his powerful, trunk-like legs wide spread, his big hands knotted into fists.

In the corner of the room Castro was lying, and I needed only a glance to see that Richard Henry Castro had tackled a different kind of jungle beast, and had come out on the short end. I could surmise what had happened. Castro must have jumped him, and Caronna had torn the man loose and hurled him into that corner and then jumped right in the middle of him with both feet. If Castro wasn't ready for the hospital I never saw a man who was, and unless I was mistaken, he was a candidate for the morgue.

One chair was knocked over, and the broken body of Castro lay on the floor, blood trickling from a corner of his mouth, blood staining the front of his white shirt and slowly turning it to a wide crimson blotch. Yet his eyes were alive as they had never been, and they blazed up to us like those of a trapped and desperate animal brought to its last moment and backing away from the trapper with bared teeth.

Caronna was the thing that centered on my mind and gripped every sense in my being. Somehow, from the first I had known I would fight that man. Perhaps it began when Shanks had told me I wasn't man enough for him. That had rankled.

I stood there looking at Blacky Caronna, a solid block of bone and muscle mounted on a couple of powerful and thick legs, a massive chest and shoulders, and a bull neck that held his blunt, short-haired head thrust forward. He saw me and lunged.

Did I shoot him? Hell, what man who fights with his hands can think of a gun at such a moment? I dropped mine as Caronna lunged for me, and as I dropped it I hooked short and hard with both hands.

My feet were firmly anchored. I was set just right and

he was coming in. My left smashed a bit high, slicing a deep cut in his cheekbone, and then my right smacked on his chin. I might as well have hit a wall. He grabbed at my coat, thinking perhaps to jerk it down over my shoulders, but I whipped up a right uppercut that clipped him on the chin, and as all my weight was driving toward him, I jerked my chin down on my chest and butted him in the face, blocking his arms with my elbows.

He grabbed my forearms and hurled me away from him so hard that I hit a chair and it splintered under me. He came in with a rush, ready to give me the boots as he had Castro, but that was an old story for me from lumber camps and waterfronts, and just as he started to jump, I hurled my body at his legs. He tottered and fell over me, kicking out blindly for my face, and one boot grazed my head, but then I rolled over and came up. He was up with me, and we rushed together like a couple of berserk cavemen.

It was wicked, brutal battling. Through a kind of smoky haze in my mind, caused by crashing punches to my head and chin, I drove into him, swinging with both hands, and he met me halfway. It was fist and thumb, gouging, biting, kneeing. Using elbows and shoulders, butting and kicking. It was barroom, backroom, waterfront style, where anything goes and the man who goes down and doesn't get up fast enough is through . . . and he rarely gets up.

Somebody had said that Caronna had once been a puddler in a steel mill, and he had lost none of his strength. A rocklike fist smashed against my chin, bursting a million lights in my brain. A thumb stabbed at my eye in a clinch, and I butted and gouged my way out of it and then clipped him with a right to the chin as he came in. I struck at his throat with my elbow in close, and then grabbing him by the belt, heaved him from the floor and hurled him back on a table. He kicked me in the chest as I came in, and knocked me into the wall.

Castro was staring at us from the floor, and as well as if it had been my own mind, I knew what went on in his. He had seen no jungle beasts fighting as we fought then, for no jungle beast has ever achieved the refinements of cruelty that man has learned to inject into his fighting. A beast fights to win, and men fight and hate while they fight.

My coat and shirt were gone. Blood streaked my body. I could feel a stiffness in the side of my face, and I knew my eye was swelling shut. There was no time to rest, no rounds, no stopping. I stepped in on the balls of my feet and hooked hard to his chin. He blinked and slammed a right at me that I ducked but I caught a sweeping left that rocked me. Weaving to escape his bludgeoning fists, I got in close and whipped both hands to the body, and then a hard right. I forced him back against the desk and jamming my left forearm against his throat, I slammed three right hands into his body before he threw me off and charged at me like a mad bull. I stabbed a left at his face and he took it coming in as though I'd hit him with a feather duster. My right missed and he hit me in the belly with one that knocked every bit of wind out of me.

He hurled me to the floor and jumped for me with both feet, but I jerked up my knees and kicked out hard with both feet. They caught him midway of his jump and put him off balance, and he fell beside me. I rolled over, grabbing at his throat, but he threw a right from where he lay that clipped me, and then I ground the side of his face into the floor by crushing my elbow against his cheek.

We broke free and lunged to our feet, but he caught me with a looping right that staggered me. I backed up, working away from him, fighting to get my breath. My mouth hung open and I was breathing in great gasps, and he came around the wreck of the table, coming for me.

The cut on his cheekbone was wider now and blood trickled from it, staining the whole side of his face and shoulder. His lips were puffed and bloody, and his nose looked out of line.

He came into me then, but I had my wind and I was set. I jabbed with a left and moved away. He pushed on in, bobbing his head to make my left miss, so I shortened it to a hook and stepped in with both hands. They caught him solidly, and he stopped dead in his tracks. I pulled the trigger on my hard one, and his knees crumpled. But he didn't go down. He shook his head and started for me, his eyes glazed. My left hook came over with everything I had on it, and his cheek looked as if somebody had hit it with an axe.

He came on in, and I let go with my Sunday punch. Sunday punch, hell. He took it coming in and scarcely blinked, hurt as he was. For the first time in my life I was scared. I had hit this guy with everything but the desk and he was still coming. He was slower, but he was coming, and his wide face looked as if somebody had worked on it with a meat axe and a curry comb.

My knees were shaky and I knew that no matter how badly he was hurt, I was on my last legs. He came on in, and I threw a right into his stomach. He gasped and his face looked sick, but he came on. He struck at me, but the power was gone from his punches. I set myself and started to throw them. I threw them as if I was punching the heavy bag and the timekeeper had given me the ten-second signal. I must have thrown both hands into the air after he started to fall, but as he came down, with great presence of mind, I jerked my knee into his chin.

Jerry Loftus came into the room as I staggered back, staring down at Caronna. "I could have stopped it," he said, "but I—"

"Why the hell didn't you?" I gasped.

"What? Am I supposed to be off my trail?" He glared at me, but his eyes twinkled at the corners. "Best scrap I ever saw, an' you ask me why I didn't stop it!"

"You'd better get cuffs on that guy," I said, disgusted. "If he gets up again I'm going right out that window!"

We found Karen in another room, tied up in a neat bundle, which, incidentally, she is at any time. When I turned her loose, she kissed me, and while I'd been looking forward to that, for the first time in my life I failed to appreciate a kiss from a pretty woman. Both my lips were split and swollen. She looked at my face with a kind of horror that I could appreciate, having seen Caronna.

Hours later, seated in the café over coffee, Johnny Holben and Loftus came in to join us. Holben stared at me.

Even with my face washed and patched up, I looked like something found dead in the water.

"All right," Loftus said doubtfully, "this is your show. We've got Caronna no matter how this goes, due to an old killing back east. That's what he was so worried about. Somebody started an investigation of an income-tax evasion and everybody started to talk, and before it was over, three old murders had been accounted for, and one of them was Caronna's.

"However, while we don't know now whether Castro will live or not with that rib through his lung, you say he was the one who killed Bitner."

"That's right," I said. "He did kill him."

"He never came up that trail past my place," Holben said.

"But there isn't any other way up, is there?" Karen asked.

"No, not a one," Loftus said. "In the thirty years since I came west with a herd of cattle to settle in this country, I've been all over that mesa, every inch of it, and there's no trail but the one past Holben's cabin."

"Your word is good enough for me," I said, "but the fact is, Castro did not come by any trail when he murdered Old Jack Bitner. How it was done I had no idea until I visited Castro's show. You must remember that he specializes in odd animals, in the strange and the unusual.

"Crime and criminal practices have been a hobby with me for years. In all the reading and traveling I've done, I've collected lots of odd facts about the ways of criminals in our own and a lot of other countries. Usually, methods are very much in pattern. The average criminal, no matter how he may think of himself, is a first-class dope.

"If he had imagination, he wouldn't be a criminal in the first place. When one does encounter the exception, it is usually in the field of murder. Castro was an exception.

"He was a man who spent money and who liked to spend money, and he was getting old enough so that the jungles held no more lure. He wanted money, and he wanted it fast. There was some old family trouble, of no importance to us, that left a decided dislike between Castro and his uncle. He knew he could never inherit in any legitimate way.

"He got his method from India, a place where he had traveled a good deal. When I saw his animals, something clicked into place in my mind, and then something else. I knew then he had scaled the wall under Bitner's window."

"That's a sheer cliff," Loftus protested.

"Sure, and nothing human could climb it without help, but Richard Henry Castro went up that cliff, and he had help."

"You mean, there was somebody in it with him?"

"Nothing human. When I saw his show, I tied it in with a track I saw on the ledge outside Bitner's window. The trouble was that while I knew how it was done, and that his show had been stopped on the highway opposite the mesa, I had no proof. If Castro sat tight, even though I knew how it was done, it was going to be hard to prove.

"One of the great advantages the law has over the criminal is the criminal's mind. He is always afraid of being caught. He can never be sure he hasn't slipped up; he never knows how much you know. My problem was to get Castro worried, and his method was one so foreign to this country that he never dreamed anyone would guess. I had to worry him, so in leaving I made a remark to him in Malayan, telling him that he had made a mistake.

"Once he knew I had been in the Far East, he would be worried. Also, he knew that Caronna had seen him."

"Caronna saw him?" Loftus demanded.

"Yes, that had to be it. That was the wedge he was using to cut himself in on Castro's inheritance."

"How could Castro inherit?"

"There's a man in his show named Johnny Leader, a master penman with a half-dozen convictions for forgery on his record. He was traveling with that show writing visiting cards for people, scrolls, etc. He drew up a will for Castro, and it was substituted at the time of the killing."

"Get to the point," Holben said irritably. "How did he get up that cliff?"

"This will be hard to believe," I said, "but he had the rope taken up by a lizard!"

"By a *what*?" Holben demanded.

I grinned. "Look," I said, "over in India there are certain thieves and second-story workers who enter houses and high buildings in just that way.

"Castro has two types of monitor lizards over there in his show. The dragon lizards from Komodo are too big and tough for anyone to handle, and nobody wants to. However, the smaller monitor lizards from India, running four to five feet in length, are another story. It is those lizards that the thieves use to gain access to locked houses.

"A rope is tied around the lizard's body, and he climbs the wall, steered by jerks on the rope from below. When he gets over a parapet, in a crevice, or over a window sill, the thief jerks hard on the rope and the lizard braces himself to prevent being pulled over, and they are very strong in the legs. Then the thief goes up the wall, hand over hand, walking right up with his feet against the wall."

"Well, I'll be damned!" Loftus said. "Who would ever think of that?"

"The day you took me up there," I told him, "I noticed a track that reminded me of the track of a gila monster, but much bigger. The idea of what it meant did not occur to me until I saw those monitor lizards of Castro's.

"Now that we know what to look for, we'll probably find scratches on the cliff and tracks at the base."

Karen was looking at me, wide-eyed with respect. "Why, I never realized you knew things like that!"

"In my business," I said, "you have to know a little of everything."

"I'll stick to bank robbers an' rustlers," Loftus said. "Or highgraders."

"You old false alarm!" Holben snorted. "You never arrested a highgrader in your life!"

We were walking out of the door, and somehow we

just naturally started up the hill. Dusk was drawing a blanket of darkness over the burnt red ridges, and the western horizon was blushing before the oncoming shadows.

When we were on top of the hill again, looking back over the town, Karen looked up at me. "Are your lips still painful?"

"Not that painful," I said.

AUTHOR'S NOTE

UNGUARDED MOMENT

The lead character of UNGUARDED MOMENT is neither a professional criminal nor detective. Arthur Fordyce is very much an "average" man who in an "unguarded moment" is confronted with some terrible acts of crime and violence.

I have always been aware of the fact that all of us walk a very thin line. When you step out of a doorway whether you turn right or left may change the whole course of your life. We all have "unguarded moments," maybe not exactly like Fordyce in my story, but there are times when we do things that we hadn't planned on doing. Suddenly we make a move this way or that, or say something inadvertently that we hadn't even thought about saying, and it can change the whole course of events.

It's very easy for a person to get himself in lots of

unplanned trouble. For example, you have lots of time on your hands and you sit at a bar having a drink. A girl sits alongside you and is having one too, and all of a sudden her boyfriend or husband comes in and thinks you're trying to pick her up and he gets sore at you and you wind up in a fight when you were an entirely innocent bystander. Maybe you never even spoke to the girl, but the trouble can happen.

UNGUARDED MOMENT

Arthur Fordyce had never done a criminal thing in his life, nor had the idea of doing anything unlawful ever seriously occurred to him.

The wallet that lay beside his chair was not only full; it was literally stuffed. It lay on the floor near his feet where it had fallen.

His action was as purely automatic as an action can be. He let his *Racing Form* slip from his lap and cover the billfold. Then he sat very still, his heart pounding. The fat man who had dropped the wallet was talking to a friend on the far side of the box. As far as Fordyce could see, his own action had gone unobserved.

It had been a foolish thing to do. Fordyce did not need the money. He had been paid a week's salary only a short time before and had won forty dollars on the last race.

With his heart pounding heavily, his mouth dry, he

made every effort to be casual as he picked up his *Form* and the wallet beneath. Trying to appear as natural as possible, he opened the billfold under cover of the *Form*, extracted the money, and shifted the bills to his pocket.

The horses were rounding into the home stretch, and when the crowd sprang to its feet, he got up, too. As he straightened, he shied the wallet, with an underhand flip, under the feet of the crowd off to his left.

His heart was still pounding. Blindly he stared out at the track. He was a thief . . . he had stolen money . . . he had appropriated it . . . how much?

Panic touched him suddenly. Suppose he had been seen? If someone had seen him, the person might wait to see if he returned the wallet. If he did not, the person might come down and accuse him. What if, even now, there was an officer waiting for him? Perhaps he should leave, get away from there as quickly as possible.

Cool sanity pervaded him. No, that would never do. He must remain where he was, go through the motions of watching the races. If he were accused, he could say he had won the money on the races. He had won money—forty dollars. The man at the window might remember his face but not the amount he had given him.

Fordyce was in the box that belonged to his boss, Ed Charlton, and no friend of Charlton's would ever be thought a thief. He sat still, watching the races, relaxing as much as he could. Surprisingly, the fat man who had dropped the wallet did not miss it. He did not even put a hand to his pocket.

After the sixth race, several people got up to leave, and Fordyce followed suit. It was not until he was unlocking his car that he realized there was a man at his elbow.

He was a tall, dark-eyed handsome young man, too smoothly dressed, too—slick. And there was something sharply feral about his eyes. He was smiling unpleasantly.

"Nice work!" he said. "Very nice! Now, how about a split?"

Arthur Fordyce kept his head. Inside, he seemed to feel all his bodily organs contract as if with chill. "I am afraid I don't understand you. What was it you wanted?"

The brightly feral eyes hardened just a little, and although the smile remained, it was a little forced. "A split, that's what I want. I saw you get that billfold. Now let's bust it open and see what we've got."

"Billfold?" Fordyce stared at him coldly, although he was quivering inside with fear. He *had* been seen! What if he should be arrested? What if Alice heard? Or Ed Charlton? Why, that fat man might be a friend of Ed's!

"Don't give me that," the tall young man was saying. "I saw the whole thing. You dropped that *Racing Form* over the billfold and picked it up. I'm getting a split or I'll holler bull. I'll go to the cops. You aren't out of the grounds yet, and even if you were, I could soon find out who used Ed Charlton's box today."

Fordyce stood stock-still. This could not be happening to him. It—it was preposterous! What ever had possessed him? Yet, what explanation could he give now? He had thrown away the wallet itself, a sure indication that he intended to keep the money.

"Come on, Bud"—the smile was sneering now—

"you might as well hand it over. There was plenty there. I'd had my eye on Linton all afternoon, just watching for a chance. He always carries plenty of dough."

Linton—George Linton. How many times had Ed Charlton spoken of him. They were golfing companions. They hunted and fished together. They had been friends at college. Even if the money were returned, Fordyce was sure he would lose his job, his friends—Alice. He would be finished, completely finished.

"I never intended to do it," he protested. "It—it was an accident."

"Yeah"—the eyes were contemptuous—"I could see that. I couldn't have done it more accidentally myself. Now, hand it over."

There was fourteen hundred dollars in fifties and twenties. With fumbling fingers, Fordyce divided it. The young man took his bills and folded them with the hands of a lover. He grinned suddenly.

"Nice work! With my brains and your in we'd make a team!" He pocketed the bills, anxious to be gone. "Be seeing you!"

Arthur Fordyce did not reply. Cold and shaken, he stared after the fellow.

Days fled swiftly past. Fordyce avoided the track, worked harder than ever. Once he took Alice to the theater and twice to dinner. Then at a party the Charltons gave, he came face to face with George Linton.

The fat man was jovial. "How are you, Fordyce? Ed tells me you're his right hand at the office. Good to know you."

"Thanks." He spoke without volition. "Didn't I see you at the track a couple of weeks ago? I was in Charlton's box."

"Oh, yes! I remember you now. I thought your face seemed familiar." He shook his head wryly. "I'll not soon forget that day. My pocket was picked for nearly two thousand dollars."

Seeing that Alice was waiting, Fordyce excused himself and joined her. Together they walked to the terrace and stood there in the moonlight. How lovely she was! And to think he had risked all this, risked it on the impulse of a moment, and for what? She was looking up at him, and he spoke suddenly, filled with the sudden panic born of the thought of losing her.

"Alice!" He gripped her arms, "Alice! Will you marry me?"

"Why, Arthur!" she protested, laughing in her astonishment. "How rough you are! Do you always grab a girl so desperately when you ask her to marry you?"

He released her arms, embarrassed. "I—I guess I was violent," he said, "but I just—well, I couldn't stand to lose you, Alice."

Her eyes were wide and wonderfully soft. "You aren't going to, Arthur," she said quietly. "I'm going to stay with you."

"Then—you mean—"

"Yes, Arthur."

Driving home that night his heart was bounding. She would marry him! How lovely she was! How beautiful her eyes had been as she looked up at him!

He drove into the garage, snapped out the lights and got his keys. It was not until he came out to close the doors that he saw the glow of a suddenly inhaled cigarette in the shadow cast by the shrubbery almost beside him.

"Hello, Fordyce. How's tricks?" It was the man from the track. "My name's Chafey, Bill Chafey."

"What are you doing here? What do you want?"

"That's a beautiful babe you've got. I've seen her picture on the society pages."

"I'm sorry. I don't intend to discuss my fiancée with you. It's very late and I must be getting to bed. Good night."

"Abrupt, aren't you?" Chafey was adopting a George Raft manner. "Not going to invite an old friend inside for a drink? An old friend from out of town—who wants to meet your friends?"

Arthur Fordyce saw it clearly, then, saw it as clearly as he would ever see anything. He knew what this slick young man was thinking—that he would use his hold over Fordyce for introductions and for better chances to steal. Probably he had other ideas, too. Girls—and their money.

"Look, Chafey," he said harshly, "whatever was between us is finished. Now beat it! And don't come back!"

Chafey had seen a lot of movies. He knew what came next. He snapped his cigarette into the grass and took a quick step forward.

"Why, you cheap thief! You think you can brush me off like that? Listen, I've got you where I want you, and before I'm through, I'll have everything you've got!"

Chafey's voice was rising with some inner emotion of triumph or hatred. "You think you're so much! Figure you can brush me off, do you?"

He stepped close. "What if I got to that fancy babe of yours and told her what I know? What if I go to Linton and tell him? Why, you're a thief, Fordyce! A damned thief! You and that fancy babe of yours! Why—"

Fordyce hit him. The action was automatic and it was unexpected. In the movies it was always the tough guy who handed out the beatings. His fist flew up and caught Chafey on the jaw. Chafey's feet flew up, and he went down, the back of his neck hitting the bumper with a sickening crack. Then his body slipped slowly to the ground.

Arthur Fordyce stood very still, staring down at the crumpled form. His breath was coming in great gasps, and his fist was still clenched hard. Some instinct told him the man was dead.

"Mr. Fordyce?" It was his neighbor, Joe Neal, calling. "Is something wrong?"

Fordyce dropped to one knee and touched the man's head. It lolled loosely, too loosely. He felt for the heart. Nothing. He bent over the man's face, but felt no breath, nothing.

Neal was coming out on the lawn, pulling his belt tight. "Fordyce? Is anything wrong?"

He got to his feet slowly. "Yes, Joe. I wish you'd come down here. I've been held up and I think—I think I've killed him."

Joe Neal hurried up, flashlight in hand. He threw the

light on the fallen man. "Good heavens!" he gasped. "What did you hit him with? What happened?"

"He was waiting there by the tree. He stepped out with his hand in his pocket—you know, like he had a gun. I hit him before I realized."

That was the story, and he made it stick. For several days it was the talk of all his friends. Fordyce had killed a holdup man. That took nerve. And a punch, too. Didn't know he had it in him. Of course, it was the bumper that actually broke his neck. Still—had there been any doubts—and there were none—a check of Chafey's record would have removed them.

He had done time and was on parole at the moment. He had gone up for armed robbery and had been arrested a score of times for investigation. He was suspected of rolling drunks and of various acts of petty pilfering and slugging. A week passed, and a second week. Arthur Fordyce threw himself into his work, never talking about what had happened.

Others forgot it, too, except Joe Neal. Once, commenting on it to his wife, he looked puzzled and said, "You know, I'd have sworn I heard voices that night. I'd have sworn it."

"You might have. They might have argued. I imagine that a man might say a lot when excited and not remember it." That was what his wife said, and it was reasonable enough. Nevertheless, Joe Neal was faintly disturbed by it all. He avoided Fordyce. Not that they had ever been friends.

Arthur Fordyce had been lucky. No getting away from that. He had been very lucky, and sometimes when he thought about it, he felt a cold chill come over him. But it was finished now.

Only it wasn't.

It was Monday night, two weeks after the inquest, the first night he had been home since it had happened. He was sitting in his armchair listening to the radio when the telephone rang. Idly, he lifted it from the cradle.

"Mr. Fordyce?" The voice was feminine and strange. "Is this Arthur Fordyce?"

"Speaking."

There was an instant of silence. Then, "This is Bill Chafey's girlfriend, Mr. Fordyce. I thought I would call and congratulate you. You seem to be very, very lucky!"

The cold was there again in the pit of his stomach. "I—I beg your pardon? I'm afraid I don't know what you mean."

"He told me all about it, Mr. Fordyce. All about that day at the track. All about what he was going to do. Bill had big ideas, Mr. Fordyce, and he thought you were his big chance. Only he thought you were scared. He got too close to you, didn't he, Mr. Fordyce?"

"I'm sure," he kept his voice composed, "that you are seriously in error. I—"

She interrupted with a soft laugh, a laugh that did not cover an underlying cruelty. "I'm not going to be as dumb as Bill was, Mr. Fordyce. I'm not going to come anywhere within your reach. Two murders are no worse than one, so I'll stay away. But you're going to pay off, Mr. Fordyce. You're going to pay off like a slot machine. You're going to pay off with a thousand dollars now and five hundred a month from now on."

"I don't know what you're talking about, but you are probably insane," he said quietly. "What you assume is ridiculous. If you are a friend of Chafey's, then you know he was a criminal. I am sorry for you, but there is nothing I can do."

"One thousand dollars by Friday, Mr. Fordyce, and five hundred a month from now on. I don't think you were scared when Bill went to you, but how about the gas chamber, Mr. Fordyce? How about that?"

"What you assume is impossible." He fought to keep his voice controlled. "And you are absurd to think I have that kind of money."

She laughed again. "But you can get it, Buster! You can get it when it means the difference between life as you live it and the gas chamber."

Her voice grew brusque. "Small bills, understand? Nothing bigger than a twenty. And send it to Gertrude Ellis, Box X78, here in town. Send me that thousand dollars by Friday and send the five hundred on the fifth of every month. If you miss by as much as ten days, the whole story goes to your girl friend, to your boss, and to the police." The phone clicked, the line buzzed emptily. Slowly, Fordyce replaced the phone.

So there it was. Now he had not only disgrace and prison before him, but the gas chamber.

A single mistake—an instant when his reason was in abeyance—and here he was—trapped.

He could call her bluff. He could refuse. The woman was obviously unprincipled and she had sounded vindictive. She would certainly follow through as she had threatened.

For hours, he paced the floor, racking his brain for some way out, some avenue of escape. He could go to Charlton, confess everything, and ask for help. Charlton would give it to him, for he was that kind of man, but when it was over, he would drop Fordyce quickly and quietly.

Alice—his future—everything depended on finding some other way. Some alternative.

If something should happen to this woman— It might. People were killed every day. There were accidents. He shied away from the idea that lay behind this, but slowly it forced its way into his consciousness. He was considering murder.

No. Never that. He would not—he could not. He had killed Chafey, but that had been different. It had not been murder, although if all the facts were known, it might be considered so. It had been an accident. All he had done was strike out. If he killed now, deliberately and with intent, it would be different.

He ran his fingers through his hair and stared blindly at the floor. Accidentally, he caught a glimpse of his face in a mirror. He looked haggard, beaten. But he was not beaten. There was a way out. There had to be.

Morning found him on the job, working swiftly and silently. He handled the few clients who came in, talked with them and straightened out their problems. He was aware that Charlton was watching him. Finally, at noon, the boss came over.

"Fordyce," he said, "this thing has worried you. You're doing a fine job this morning, so it looks as though you're getting it whipped, but nevertheless, I think a few days' rest would put you right up to snuff. You just go home now, and don't come in until Monday. Go out of town, see a lot of Alice, just anything. But relax."

"Thanks." A flood of relief went over Fordyce as he got up, and genuine gratitude must have showed in his eyes, for Charlton expanded. "I do need a rest."

"Sure!" Ed put a hand on his shoulder. "You go call Alice. Take her for a drive. Wonderful girl that. You're lucky. Good connections, too," he added, almost as an afterthought.

The sun was bright in the street, and he stood there thinking. He would call Alice, make a date if possible. He had to do that much, for Ed would be sure to comment later. Then—then he must find this woman, this Gertrude Ellis.

He got through the afternoon without a hitch. He and Alice drove out along the ocean drive, parked by the sea, and then stopped for dinner. It was shortly after ten when he finally dropped her at her home.

He remembered what the police had said about Bill Chafey. They had known about him and they had mentioned that he had been one of several known criminals who frequented a place called Eddie's Bar. If Chafey had gone there, it was possible his girl did, too.

It was a shadowy place with one bartender and a row of leather-covered stools and a half-dozen booths. He picked out a stool and ordered a drink. He was halfway down his second bourbon and soda before the first lead came to him.

A tall Latin-looking young man was talking to the bartender. "Gracie been around? I haven't seen her but once since Chafey got it in the neck."

"You figuring on moving in there?"

"Are you crazy? That broad gives me the shivers. She's stacked, all right, but she'd cut your heart out for a buck."

"Bill handled her."

"You mean she handled him. She was the brains of that setup."

"Leave it to Bill to try to pick up a fast buck."

"Yeah, and look at him now."

There was silence, and Fordyce sipped his drink unconcernedly, waiting. After a while it started again.

"She's probably working that bar on Sixth Street."

"Maybe. She said the other day she was going to quit. That she was expecting a legacy."

"I'll bet. She's got a take lined up."

A few moments later, Fordyce finished his drink and left the place. He went to Sixth Street, studied the bars as he drove along. It might be any one of them. He tried a couple but without luck.

The next morning he slept late. While he was shaving, he studied his face in the mirror. He told himself he did not look like a murderer. But then, what did murderers look like? They were just people.

His face was long, his cheekbones high, and he had a quick, easy smile. His hair was straight and brown, his eyes a light blue. He was nearing thirty and had the assured manner of any young professional man. Despite the fact that he had always held good jobs, he had saved no money to speak of, had always looked ahead for a better position and better chances at money.

He dressed carefully, thinking as he dressed. To get the money, Gertrude Ellis would have to go to the box. She would not expect him to be watching, since she would probably believe he would be at work. Even so, he would have to be careful, for she would be careful herself. She might walk by and merely glance in at first. He would have to get her to open the box. He considered that, then had a hunch.

Shuffling through his own mail, he found what he wanted. It was an advertisement of the type mailed to Boxholder or Occupant. He withdrew the advertising matter to make sure his own name was not on it. Then he carefully removed the address with ink eradicator and substituted the number she had given him.

Her true name would probably be not unlike Gertrude Ellis, which was obviously assumed. The first name was Gracie, and it was a fairly safe bet the last would begin with an E. Unless, as sometimes happened, she used the name of a husband or some friend.

Considering the situation, he had another idea. Eddie's Bar and Sixth Street were not far apart. Hence, she must live somewhere in that vicinity.

He returned to Eddie's that night, and the bartender greeted him briefly. They exchanged a few comments, and then Fordyce asked, "Many babes come in here?"

"Yeah, now and again. Most of 'em are bags. Once in a while, something good shows up."

He went away to attend to the wants of another customer, and Arthur Fordyce waited, stalling over his drink, listening. He heard nothing.

It was much later, when he had finished his third drink, and was turning to look around, that he bumped into someone. She was about to sit down, and he collided with her outstretched arm.

"Oh, I'm sorry! Pardon me."

"That's all right." She was a straight-haired brunette with rather thin lips and cool eyes. But she was pretty, damned pretty. Her clothes were not like those Alice wore, but she did have a style of her own.

She ordered a drink, and he ignored her. After a minute, she got up and went to the ladies' room. The bartender strolled over. "Speaking of babes," he said, "there's a cute one. Should be about ready, too. She's fresh out of boyfriends."

"Her? How come? She's really built."

The bartender shrugged. "Runs with some fast company sometimes. Her boyfriend tried to make a quick buck with a gun and got killed. Chafey. Maybe you read about it."

"Chafey?" Fordyce looked puzzled, although inside he was jumping. "Don't recall the name." He hesitated. "Introduce me?"

"You don't need it. Just buy her a drink." Then the bartender grinned. "But if you go home with her, take your own bottle and pour the drinks yourself. And don't pass out."

"You mean she'd roll me?"

"I didn't say that, chum. I didn't say anything. But you look like a good guy. Just take care of yourself. After all," he added, "a guy can have a good time without making a sucker of himself."

The girl returned then and sat down on her stool. He waited out her drink, and as she was finishing it, he turned. "How about having one with me? I feel I owe it to you after bumping you like that."

She smiled quickly. "Oh, that's all right! Yes, I'll drink with you."

Her name was Gracie Turk. She had been divorced several years ago. They talked about dance bands, movies, swimming. She liked to drink, she admitted, but usually did her drinking at home.

"I'd like that," he said. "Why don't we pick up a bottle and go there?"

She hesitated, then smiled. "All right, let's go."

Fordyce glanced back as he went out. The bartender grinned and made a circle of his thumb and forefinger.

Not tonight, Fordyce told himself. Whatever happens, not tonight. He will remember this. They got the bottle and went to her apartment. It was small, cheaply furnished with pretensions toward elegance. Bored, he still managed to seem interested and mixed the drinks himself. He let her see that he had money on him and suddenly, recalled that he was expecting a business call at night.

"From back East, you know," he said by way of explanation.

He left, but with a date for the following evening. An

hour later, he called back and canceled the date. His call had come, he said, and he would be out of town.

He made his plans with utmost care. He drove out of town and deliberately wound along dusty roads for several hours, letting his car gather dust. In town, at the same time, he carefully chose a spot at which to dispose of the body.

At eight, he drove around and parked his car near the entrance to the alley behind the girl's apartment. There was a light in the window, so he went into the front entrance, hoping desperately that he would meet no one. Luck was with him, and he reached her door safely. It was around a corner in a corridor off the main hall. At the end was a door to the back stairs.

He tapped lightly and then heard the sound of heels. The door was opened, and Gracie Turk stepped back in surprise.

"Al!" That was the name he had given her. "I thought you were out of town?"

"Missed my train, and I just had a wild idea you might not have gone out."

"Come in!" She stepped back. "I was just fixing something to eat. Want a sandwich? Or a drink?"

He closed the door behind him and looked at her shoulders and the back of her head. That coldness was in the pit of his stomach again. His mouth felt dry, and the palms of his hands were wet. He kept wiping them off, as if they were already— He shook himself and accepted the drink she had fixed for him.

She smiled quickly, but her eyes seemed cold. "Well, drink up! There's more where that came from! I'll go get things ready, and then we'll eat. We'll just stay home tonight."

She had good legs, and the seams in her stockings were straight. He was cold. Maybe the drink would fix him up. He drank half of it at a gulp. It was lousy whisky, lousy—The words of the bartender at Eddie's came back to him. "Take your own bottle," he had said, "and pour your own drinks." He stared at the glass, put it down suddenly.

Suppose it was doped? He had had only half of it. What would that much do to him? He might not pass out, but would he be able to carry out his plans if—

He sat down abruptly. She would be coming in soon. He glanced hastily around, then took the drink and reaching back under the divan, poured it, little by little, over the thick carpet. When she came back into the room, he was sitting there holding his empty glass. "Lousy whisky," he commented. "Let me get some for you."

She smiled, but her eyes were still cold and calculating. She seemed to be measuring him as she took the glass from his hand. "I'll just fill this up again. Why don't you lie down?"

"All right," he said, and suddenly made up his mind. He would not wait. It would be now. She might—

If he passed out, she would open his billfold, and in his billfold was his identification! He started to get up, but the room seemed to spin. He sat down, suddenly filled with panic. He was going; he—He got his hand into his pocket, fumbled for the identification card. He got it out of the window in the billfold and shoved it down in another pocket. The money wasn't much, only—

He had been hearing voices, a girl's and a man's for some time. The girl was speaking now. "I don't care where you drop him. Just take him out of here. The fool didn't have half the money he had the other night! Not half! All this trouble for a lousy forty bucks! Why, I'd bet he had—What's the matter?"

"Hey!" The man's voice was hoarse. "Do you know who this is?"

"Who it is? What does it matter?"

Fordyce lay very still. Slowly but surely he was recovering his senses. He could hear the man move back.

"I don't want this, Gracie. Take back your sawbuck. This is *hot!* I want no part of him! None at all!"

"What's the matter?" She was coming forward. "What have you got there?"

"Don't kid me!" His voice was hoarse with anger. "I'm getting out of here! Just you try to ring me in on your dirty work!"

"Johnny, have you gone nuts? What's the matter?" Her voice was strident.

"You mean you don't know who this is? This is Fordyce, the guy who knocked off Bill Chafey."

There was dead silence while she absorbed that. Fordyce heard a crackle of paper. That letter—it had been in his pocket. It must have fallen out.

"Fordyce." She sounded stunned. "He must have found out where I was! How the—" Her voice died away.

"I'm getting out of here. I want no part of killing a guy."

"Don't be a fool!" She was angry. "I didn't know who the sap was. I met him at Eddie's. He flashed a roll, and I just figured it was an easy take. How did he locate me?"

"What gives, Gracie?" The man's voice was prying. "What's behind this?"

"Ah, I just was going to take the sap for plenty, that's all. Now what happens?" She stopped talking, then started again. "Bill saw him grab a wallet some guy dropped. This guy didn't return it, so Bill shook him for half of it. He figured on more, and this guy wouldn't stand for it."

"So you moved in?"

"Why not? He didn't know who I was or where I was. What I can't figure is how he found out. The guy must be psychic."

Arthur Fordyce kept his eyes closed and listened. While he listened, his mind was working. He was a fool. An insane fool. How could he ever have conceived the idea of murder? He knew now he could never have done it, never. It wasn't in him to kill or even to plan so cold-bloodedly. He would have backed down at the last moment. He would have called it off. Suddenly, all he wanted was to get out, to get away without trouble. Should he lie still and wait to find out what would happen? Or should he get up and try to bluff it out?

"What are you going to do now?"

Gracie Turk did not reply. Minutes ticked by, and then the man turned toward the door. "I'm getting out of here," he said. "I don't want any part of this. I'd go for dumping the guy if he was just drunk, but I want no part of murder."

"Who's talking about murder?" Gracie's voice was shrill. "Get out if you're yellow."

Fordyce opened one eye a crack. Gracie was facing the other way, not looking directly at him. He put his hands on the floor, rolled over, and got to his feet. The man sprang back, falling over a chair, and Gracie turned quickly, her face drawn and vicious.

Fordyce felt his head spin, but he stood there, looking at them. Gracie Turk stared, swore viciously.

"Give him his ten," Fordyce told her, "out of the money you took from me."

"I will like—"

"Give it to him. He won't go for a killing, and you don't dare start anything now because he'd be a witness. For that matter, he would be a witness against me, too."

"That's right," the man said hastily. It was the same Latin-looking man he had seen in Eddie's. "Give me the sawbuck and I'll get out of here—but fast."

Gracie's eyes flared, her lips curled. "What do you think you're pulling, anyway? How'd you find me? Who told you?"

Fordyce forced himself to smile. "What's difficult about finding you? You're not very clever, Gracie." Suddenly, he saw his way clear and said with more emphasis, "Not at all clever."

The idea was so simple that it might work. He was no murderer, nor was he a thief. He had only been a fool. Now if he could assume the nerve and the indifference it would take, he could get safely out of this.

"Look, Gracie," he said quietly, "like Chafey, you walked into this by accident. He misunderstood what he saw and passed it on to you, and neither of you had any idea but making a fast buck.

"Bill"—and he knew it sounded improbable "—stepped into a trap baited for another guy. You know as well as I do that Bill was never very smart. He was neither as smart nor as lucky as you. You're going to get out of this without tripping."

"What are you talking about?" Gracie was both angry and puzzled. Something had gone wrong from the start. That was Bill for you. And now the easy money was glimmering. This guy hinted that Bill had blundered into something, which was just like him.

"The wallet I picked up"—Fordyce made his voice sound impatient "—was dropped by agreement. We were trying to convince a man who was watching that I was taking a payoff." The story was flimsy, but Gracie would accept a story of double-dealing quicker than any other. "Bill saw it, and I paid off to keep him from crabbing a big deal."

"I don't believe it!" Her voice was defiant, yet there was uncertainty in her eyes. "Was murdering Bill part of the game?"

He shrugged it off. "Look Gracie. You knew Bill. He was a big, good-looking guy who couldn't see anything but the way he was going. He thought he had me where the hair was short when he stopped me outside my garage. Once away from that track, I was clean, so he had no hold over me at all. My deal had gone through. We had words, and when he started for me, I hit him. He fell, and his neck hit the bumper. He was a victim of his own foolishness and greed."

"That's what you say."

"Why kill him? He could be annoying, but he could prove nothing, and nobody would have believed him. Nor," he added, "would they believe you."

He picked up his hat. "Give this man the ten spot for his trouble. You keep the rest and charge it up to experience. That's what I'll do."

The night air was cool on his face when he reached the street. He hesitated, breathing deep, and then walked to his car.

At the Charlton party, one week later, he was filling Alice's glass at the punch bowl when George Linton clapped him on the shoulder. "Hey, Art!" It was the first time, he thought suddenly, that anybody had called him Art. "I got my money back! Remember the money I lost at the track? Fourteen hundred dollars! It came back in the mail, no note, nothing. What do you think of that?"

"You were lucky." Fordyce grinned at him. "We're all lucky at times."

"Believe me," Linton confided, "if I'd found that fourteen hundred bucks, I'd never have returned it! I'd just have shoved it in my pocket and forgotten about it."

"That," Art Fordyce said sincerely, "is what you think!"

AUTHOR'S NOTE

DEAD MAN'S TRAIL

DEAD MAN'S TRAIL involves the first case of a private detective character I featured in a number of stories (of which three are represented in this collection)—a character I enjoyed creating very much.

Kip Morgan is an ex-prizefighter struggling to make a new career for himself as a private operator. He's had a lot of contacts with the types generally referred to as the "underworld" throughout his boxing days. He knew how to cope with such people, and so the transition to private detective work was a relatively natural one for him. He also had experience working on waterfronts and on circus roughnecking gangs.

I fought professionally myself for a while and although the part of boxing I was associated with was usually on the level, there was no shortage of disreputable characters congregating around the fight game.

There were a lot of them around who were involved in gambling. Some came around selling all kinds of odd merchandise they picked up or had stolen to sell to others who were always eager to strike a bargain. Also, since many of the gymnasiums in the towns, like the Main Street Gym in Los Angeles, were in rather rundown sections, you came into contact with your share of such people. You knew them. They kind of took it for granted that you were one of them, even though you weren't. You would find that sometimes they talked freely about their activities. I knew quite a few of these less than honorable citizens at one time or another.

DEAD MAN'S TRAIL

Kip Morgan sat unhappily over a bourbon and soda in a bar on Sixth Street. How did you find a man who did not want to be found when all you knew about him was that he was thirty-six years old and played a saxophone?

Especially when some charred remains, tagged with this man's name, had been buried in New Jersey? All you had to go on was a woman's hunch.

Not quite all. The lady with the hunch was willing to back her belief with fifty dollars a day for expenses and five thousand if the man was found.

Kipling Morgan had set himself up as a private detective and this was his first case. Five thousand dollars would buy a lot of ham and eggs, and at the moment, the expense money was important.

"No use to be sentimental about this," he told himself. "This babe has the dough, and she wants you to look. So all right, you're looking. What is there to fuss about?"

He was conscientious; that was his trouble. He did not want to spend her money without giving something in return. Moreover, he was ambitious. He wanted very much to succeed with his first case, particularly such a case as this. He could use some headlines.

Kip Morgan ordered another drink and thought about it. He took his battered black hat off his head and ran his fingers through his dark hair. He stared at the glass and swore. He picked up the glass, sipped the drink, and muttered to himself.

Five days before, sitting in the cubbyhole he called an office, the door opened, and a mink coat walked in with a blonde inside. She was in her late twenties, had a model's walk, and a figure made to wear clothes, but one that would look pretty good without them.

"You are Kip Morgan?"

He pulled his feet off the desk and stood up. He was a lean, hard-muscled six feet and over who had been until that moment debating as to whether he should skip lunch and enjoy a good dinner or just save the money.

"Yes," he said, "what can I do for you?"

"Do you have any cases you are working on now?" Her eyes were gray, direct, sincere. They were also beautiful.

"Well, ah—" He hesitated, and his face flushed, and that made him angry with himself. What could he tell her? That he was broke and she was the first client to walk into his office? It would scarcely inspire confidence.

"As a matter of fact," she said, the shadow of a smile on her lips, "I am quite aware you have no other cases. I made inquiries and was told you were the youngest, newest, and least occupied private detective in town."

He chuckled in spite of himself. "That's not very good advertising, is it?"

"It is to me. I want an investigator with ambition. I want a fresh viewpoint. I want someone who can devote all his time to the job."

"That's my number you're calling." He gestured to a chair. "It looks like we might do business. Will you sit down?"

She sat down and showed a lot of expensive hosiery and beautifully shaped legs. "My name is Mrs. Roger Whitson. I am a widow with one child, a boy.

"Four years ago, in New Jersey, my husband, who was a payroll messenger, left the bank acting as a guard for a teller named Henry Willard and a fifty-thousand-dollar payroll.

"They were headed for the plant of what was then called Adco Products. They never arrived. Several days later, hunters found the badly charred body of a man lying beside an overturned and burned car in a gully off a lonely road. The body was identified as that of Henry Willard.

"The police decided my husband had murdered him and stolen the fifty thousand dollars. They never found him or any clue to his whereabouts."

"What do you need me for?" Kip asked. "It sounds like a police matter. If they can't find him with all their angles, I doubt if I can."

"They can't find him because they are looking for the wrong man," Helen Whitson declared. "Mr. Morgan, you may not have much faith in women's intuition. I haven't much myself, but there's one thing of which I am sure. That charred body they found was my husband!"

"They can identify a body by fingerprints, by dental records."

"I know all that, but it so happened that the dead man's fingertips were badly burned. Their argument was that he burned them trying to force open the car door. It looked to me like somebody deliberately burned those fingertips!

"They found a capped tooth in the dead man's mouth. Henry Willard had a capped tooth, but so did my husband. There were no dental records on either man, and the police disregarded my statement.

"They discovered fragments of clothing, a key ring, pocketknife, and such things that were positively identified as belonging to Henry Willard. The police were convinced. They would not listen to me because they thought I was covering for my husband.

"Mr. Morgan, I have a son growing up. He will be asking about his father. I will not have him believing his father a criminal when I know he is not!

"My husband was murdered by Henry Willard. The reason he has not been found is because his body lies in that grave. I know Henry Willard is alive today and is safe because they have never even looked for him."

"But," he objected, "you apparently have money. Why should your husband steal, or why should they believe he stole, when you are well-off?"

"When my husband was alive, we had nothing. We lived on his salary, and I kept house like any young wife. After he was killed, I went to New York and worked. I was doing well, and then my uncle died and left me a wealthy woman. I am prepared to retain you for a year, if it takes that long, or longer. I want to find that man!"

The information she could give him was very little. Henry Willard would now be thirty-six years old. He played a saxophone with almost professional skill. He neither gambled nor drank. He seemed to have little association with women. He had been two inches over six feet and weighed one seventy.

He had, in her presence, expressed an interest in California, but that had been over a year before the crime.

They sat for hours, and Kip questioned her. He started her talking about her life with her husband, about the parties they had, the picnics. Several times, Henry Willard had been along. She had seen him many times at the bank. For over a year, he had, at the request of the company, carried the payroll of Adco Products.

He had never played golf or tennis. He expressed a dislike for horses, and Helen recalled during that long session that he disliked dogs, also.

"He must be a crook"—Kip Morgan smiled—"if he didn't like dogs!"

"I know he was!" Helen stated. She described his preferences for food, the way he walked, and suddenly she recalled, "There's something! He read *Variety*! I've seen him with it several times!"

Kip Morgan noted it and went on. The man had

black hair. Birthmarks? Yes, seen when swimming at the club. A sort of mole, the size of a quarter, on his right shoulder blade.

The question was—how to find a man thirty-six years old who played the saxophone, even if he did have a birthmark? The only real clue was the link between *Variety* and the saxophone. He played with "almost" professional skill. Who added that "almost," and why not just professional skill?

"How about a picture? There must have been one in the papers at the time?"

"No, there wasn't. They couldn't find any pictures of him at the time. Not even in his belongings. But I do have a snapshot. He's one of a group at the club. As I recall, he did not want to be in the picture, but one of the girls pulled him into it."

Kip studied the picture. The man was well muscled, very well muscled. He looked fit as could be, and that did not fit with a bank job or with a man who played neither tennis nor golf. One who apparently went in for no sports but occasional swimming.

"How about his belongings? Were they called for?"

She shook her head. "No, he had no relatives."

"Leave any money? In the bank, I mean?"

"Only about a thousand dollars. When I think of it, that's funny, too, because he was quite a good businessman and never spent very much. He lived very simply and rarely went out."

Through a friend in the musician's union, Kip tried to trace him down and he came to a dead end. Kip haunted nightclubs and theaters, listened to gossip, worried at the problem like a dog over a bone.

"You know what I think?" he told Helen Whitson the next time he saw her. "I've a hunch this Willard was a smart cookie. No relatives showed up, and that's unusual. No pictures in his stuff. No clues to his past. Aside from an occasional reference to Los Angeles, he never mentioned any place he had been or where he came from.

"I think he planned this from the start. I think he did a very smart thing. I think he stepped out of his own personality for the five years you knew him, or knew of him. I think he deliberately worked into that job at the bank, waited for the right moment, then killed your husband and returned to his former life with the fifty thousand dollars!"

He turned that over in his mind in the bar on Sixth Street. The more he considered it, the better he liked it, but if such was the case, he was bucking a stacked deck. He would be well covered. He was not a drinking man, but he was almost finished with his second drink when the idea came to him. He went to the telephone and called Helen Whitson.

A half hour later, they sat across the table from each other. "I've had a hunch. You have hunches, and so can I.

"Listen to this." He leaned across the table. "This guy Willard is covered, see? He's covered like a blanket. He's had four years and fifty thousand dollars to work with. He's supposed to be dead. If my guess is right, all that personality at the bank was assumed. He stepped out of himself and his natural surroundings long enough to steal fifty grand; then he stepped right back into his old life. He will be harder to locate than a field mouse in five hundred acres of cornfield. We've got just one chance. His mind."

"I don't understand."

"It's like this. He's covered, see? The perfect crime. But no man who has committed a crime, a major crime, is ever sure he's safe. There is always a little doubt, a little fear. He may have overlooked something; somebody might recognize him.

"That's where he's vulnerable. In his mind. We can't find him, so we'll make him come to us!"

She shook her head doubtfully. "How can we possibly do that?"

"How?" He grinned and sat back in his chair. "We'll advertise!"

"Advertise? Are you insane?"

Kip was smiling. "We'll run ads in the *Times* and the *Examiner.* If he's in Los Angeles, he'll see them. Take my word for it, it'll scare the blazes out of him. We'll run an ad inviting him to come to a certain hotel to learn something of interest.

"He will be shocked. He's been thinking he is safe. Still, under that confidence is a little haunting fear. This ad will bring all that fear to the surface. With the fifty thousand he had to start with, he's probably become an important man. He could be big stuff now.

"All right, suppose he sees that ad? He will know somebody knows Willard is alive. Don't you see? That was his biggest protection, the fact that everybody believed Henry Willard to be dead. He'll be frightened; he will also be curious. Who can it be? What do they know? Are the police closing in? Or is this blackmail?"

Helen was excited. "It's crazy! Absolutely crazy! But I believe it will work!"

"He won't dare stay away. He will be shocked to the roots of his being. His own anxiety will be our biggest help. He'll try, discreetly, to find out who ran that advertisement. He'll try to find out who has that particular room in the hotel. Finally, he will send someone, on some pretext, to find out who or what awaits him. In any event, we'll have jarred him loose. He'll be scared, and he'll be forced by his own worry to do something. Once he begins, we can locate him. He won't have the iron will it would take to sit tight and sweat it out."

She nodded slowly. "Yes, it may work." She looked at him doubtfully. "But what if—what do you think he will do?"

Morgan shrugged. He had thought about that a lot. "Who knows? He will try to find out who it is that knows something. He will want to know how many know. If he discovers it is just we two, he will probably try another murder."

"Are you afraid?"

Kip shrugged. "Not yet, but I will be. Scared as a man can be, but that won't stop me."

"And that goes for me, too!" she said.

The ad appeared first in the morning paper. It was brief and to the point, and it appeared in the middle of the real estate ads. (Everybody reads real estate advertisements in Los Angeles.) The type was heavy. It read:

HENRY WILLARD
Who was in Newark in 1943? Come to Room 1340 Hayworthy Hotel and learn something of interest.

Kip Morgan sat in the room and waited. Beside him were several paperback detective novels and a few magazines. His coat was off and lying on the table at his right. Under the coat was his shoulder holster and the butt of his gun, where he could drop a hand on it.

Down the hall, in a room with its door open a crack, waited three newsboys. They were members of a club where Kip Morgan taught boxing. Outside, the newsboy on the corner was keeping his eyes open, and three other boys loitered together, talking.

Noon slipped past, and it was almost three o'clock when the phone rang. It was the switchboard operator.

"Mr. Morgan? This is the operator. You asked us to report if anyone inquired as to who was stopping in that room? We have just had a call, a man's voice. We replied as suggested that it was John Smith but he was receiving no calls."

"Fine!" Kip hung up and walked to the window.

It was working. The call might have come from some curious person or some crank, but he didn't think so.

He rang for a bottle of beer and was tipped back in a chair with a magazine half in front of his face when the door opened. It was a bellman.

Alert, Kip noticed how the bellman stared at him, then around the room. The instant the door closed after him, Kip was on his feet. He went to the door and gave his signal. The bellman had scarcely reached the elevator before a nice-looking youngster of fourteen in a blue serge suit was at his elbow, also waiting.

A few minutes later, the boy was at Kip's door. His eyes were bright and eager.

"Mr. Morgan! The bellman went to the street, looked up and down, then walked to a Chevrolet sedan and spoke to the man sitting in the car. The man gave him some money.

"I talked to Tom, down on the corner, and he said the car had been there about a half hour. It just drove up and stopped. Nobody got out." He reached in his pocket. "Here's the license number."

"Thanks." Kip picked up the phone and called, then sat down.

A few minutes later, the call was returned. The car was a rental. And, he reflected, certainly rented under an assumed name.

The day passed slowly. At dusk, he paid the boys off and started them home, to return the next day. Then he went down to the coffee shop and ate slowly and thoughtfully. After paying his check, he walked outside.

He must not go anywhere near Helen Whitson. He would take a walk around the block and return to the hotel room. It had been stuffy, and his head ached. He turned left and started walking. He had gone less than half a block when he heard a quick step behind him.

Startled by the quickening steps, he whirled. Dark shadows moved at him, and before he could get his hands up, he was slugged over the head. Even as he fell to the walk, he remembered there had been a flash from a green stone on his attacker's hand, a stone that caught some vagrant light ray.

He hit the walk hard and started to get up. The man struck again, and then again. Kip's knees gave way, and he slipped into a widening pool of darkness, fighting to hold his consciousness. Darkness and pain, a sense of moving. Slowly, he fought his way to awareness.

"Hey, Bill." The tone was casual. "He's comin' out of it. Shall I slug him again?"

"No, I want to talk to the guy."

Bill's footsteps came nearer, and Kip Morgan opened his eyes and sat up.

Bill was a big man with shoulders like a pro football player and a broken nose. His cheeks were lean, his eyes cold and unpleasant. The other man was shorter, softer, with a round, fat face and small eyes.

"Hi!" Kip said. "Who you boys workin' for?"

Bill chuckled. "Wakes right up, doesn't he? Starts askin' questions right away." He studied Morgan thoughtfully, searching his mind for recognition. "What we want to know is who you're workin' for. Talk and you can blow out of here."

"Yes? Don't kid me, chum! The guy who hired you yeggs hasn't any idea of lettin' me get away. I'm not workin' for anybody. I work for myself."

"You goin' to talk or take a beatin'?"

His attitude said plainly that he was highly indifferent to the reply. Sooner or later, this guy was going to crack, and if they had to give him a beating first, why, that was part of the day's work.

"We know there's a babe in this. You was seen with her."

"Her?" Kip laughed. "You boys are way off the track. She's just a babe I was on the make for, but I didn't score. Private dicks are too poor.

"This case was handed to me by an agency in Newark, an agency that does a lot of work for banks."

He glanced up at Bill. "Why let yourself in for trouble? Don't you know what this is? It's a murder rap."

"Not mine!" Bill said. The fat man glanced at him, worried.

"Ever hear of an accessory? That's where you guys come in."

"Who was the babe?" Bill insisted.

Kip was getting irritated. "None of your damn business!" he snapped, and came off the cot with a lunge.

Bill took a quick step back, but Kip was coming too fast, and he clipped the big man with a right that knocked him back into the wall.

The fat man came off his chair, clawing at his hip, and Kip backhanded him across the nose with the edge of his hand. He felt the bone break and saw the gush of blood that followed. The fat man whimpered like a baby, and Kip ducked a left from Bill and slammed a fist into the big man's midsection. Bill took it with a grunt and threw a left that Kip slipped, countering with a right cross that split Bill's eye.

"A boxer, huh?"

He caught Kip with a glancing left, then closed. The big man's arms went around him, and his chin dug into

Kip's shoulder as the larger man began pressing him back.

Morgan got one hand free and hooked to Bill's ear, then chopped a blow to the man's kidney with the edge of his hand. He jerked, trying to worm to one side, then kicked up his feet and fell.

The move caught the bigger man by surprise and sent him sprawling, clawing air for support. Kip was on his feet and coming up when the fat man hit him. He felt blood stream into his eyes, but he caught the fat man by the belt, jerked him forward, then shot him back with all the force of his arm.

The fat man hit the table and fell just as Kip turned to see Bill swinging a chair at him. He dropped to one knee, and the force of Bill's rush carried him over Kip's back to the floor.

Kip got up then, pawing blood from his eyes. This was his dish. Several years on the waterfronts and working with circus roughneck gangs had prepared him for it. He got the blood out of his eyes, and as the fat man started to rise, he kicked him in the neck. If they wanted trouble, they could have it.

Bill was on his feet, and when Kip looked around, he was looking into Bill's gun. Kip never stopped moving. When the gun went off, he felt the sting of powder on his face, and the roar filled his ears; but the bullet missed, and then Kip swung a right, low down, for Bill's stomach. He was coming in with the punch, and it sank to the wrist bone.

The gun flew into the air, and Bill started to fall. Kip grabbed him, thrust him against the wall with his left, and hit him three times in the stomach with all the power he could muster. Then he stepped back and hit him in the face with both hands.

Bill slumped to a sitting position, bloody and battered. Kip glanced quickly at the fat man. He was lying on the floor, groaning. Morgan grabbed Bill and hoisted him into a chair.

"All right, talk!" Morgan's breath was coming in gasps. "Talk or I start punching!"

Bill's head rolled back, but he lifted a hand. "Don't! I'll talk! The money . . . it was in an envelope. The bartender at the Casino gave it to me. There was a note. Said to get you, make you tell who you worked for, and we'd get another five hundred."

"If you're lyin'," Kip said, "I'll come lookin' for you!"

"If you do, you'd better pack a heater! I'll have one!"

Kip took up his battered hat and put it on his head, then retrieved his gun as he was going out and thrust it into his shoulder holster.

He stepped outside and looked around. He had been in a shanty in the country. Where town was he did not know. Where—

The shot sounded an instant after he heard the angry whip of a bullet past his ear. As he dropped, he heard the roar of a motor. Instantly, he was on his feet, gun in hand, running to the road. He was just in time to see a car whip around a corner and vanish up the highway. Without a glance back, he started after it, walking over the rutted country road.

On the highway, he shoved the gun back in its holster

and straightened his clothing. Pulling his tie around, he drew the knot back into place and stuffed his shirt back into his pants. Gingerly, he felt of his face. One eye was swollen, and there was blood on his face from a cut on his scalp. Wiping it away with his handkerchief, he started up the road. He had gone but a short distance when a car swung alongside him.

"Want a lift?" a cheery voice sang out.

He got in gratefully, and the driver stared at him. He was a big, sandy-haired man with a jovial face.

"What happened to you? Accident?"

"Not really. It was done on purpose."

"Lucky I happened along. You're in no shape to walk. Better get into town and file a report." He drove on a little way. "What happened? Holdup?"

"Not exactly. I'm a private detective."

"Oh? On a case, huh? I don't think I'd care for that kind of work."

The car picked up speed. Kip laid his head back. Suddenly, he was very tired. He nodded a little, felt the car begin to climb.

The man at the wheel continued to talk, his voice droning along, talking of crimes and murders and movies about them. Kip, half asleep, replied in monosyllables. Through the drone of talk, the question slipped into his consciousness even as he answered, and for a startled moment, his head still hanging on his chest, the question and answer came back to him.

"Who are you working for?" the driver had asked.

And mumbling, only half awake, he had said, "Helen Whitson."

As realization hit him, his head came up with a jerk, and he stared into the malevolent blue eyes of the big man at the wheel. He saw the gun coming up. With a yell, he struck it aside with his left hand, and his right almost automatically pushed down on the door handle. The next instant, he was sprawling in the road.

He staggered to his feet, grabbing for his own gun. The holster was empty. His gun must have fallen out when he spilled into the road. A gun bellowed, and he staggered and went over the bank just as the man fired again.

How far he fell, he did not know, but it was all of thirty feet of rolling, bumping, and falling. He brought up with a jolt, hearing a trickle of gravel and falling rock. Then he saw the shadow of the big man on the edge of the road. In a minute, he would be coming down. The shape disappeared, and he heard the man fumbling in his glove compartment.

A flashlight! He was getting a flashlight!

Kip staggered to his feet, slipping between two clumps of brush just as the light stabbed the darkness. Catlike, he moved away. Every step was agony, for he seemed to have hurt one ankle in the fall. His skull was throbbing with waves of pain. He forced himself to move, to keep going.

Now he heard the trickle of gravel as the man came down the steep bank. Stepping lightly, favoring the wounded ankle, he eased away through the brush, careful to make no sound. Somewhere he could hear water falling, and there was a loom of cliffs. The big man was not using the flashlight now but was stalking him as a hunter stalks game.

Kip crouched, listening, like a wounded animal. Then he felt a loose tree limb at his feet. Gently, he placed it in the crotch of a low bush so it stuck out across the way the hunter was coming. Feeling around, he found a rock the size of his fist.

Footsteps drew nearer, cautious steps and heavy breathing. Listening, Kip gained confidence. The man was no woodsman. Pain wracked his head, and his tongue felt clumsily at his split and swollen lips.

Carefully, soundlessly, Kip moved back. The other man did what he hoped. He walked forward, blundered into the limb, and tripped, losing his balance. Kip swung the rock, and it hit, but not on the man's head. The gun fired, the shot missing, and Kip hobbled away.

He reached the creek and followed it down. Ahead of him, a house loomed. He heard someone speaking from the porch. "That sounded like a shot. Right up the canyon!"

He waited; then, after a long time, a car's motor started up. Kip started for the house in a staggering run. He stumbled up to the porch and banged on the door.

A tall, fine-looking man with gray hair opened it. "Got to get into town and quick! There's going to be a murder if I don't!"

Giving the man's wife Helen Whitson's number to call, he got into the car.

All the way into town he knotted his hands together, staring at the road. He had been back up one of the canyons. Which one or how far, he did not know. He needed several minutes to show the man identification and to get him to drive him into town. It had taken more effort to get the man to lend him a gun.

However, the older man could drive, and did. Whining and wheeling around curves and down the streets, he finally leveled out on the street where Helen Whitson lived. As they turned the corner, Kip saw the car parked in front of the house. The house was dark.

"Let me out here and go for the police!"

Moving like a ghost despite the injured ankle, Kip crossed the lawn and moved up to the house. The front door was closed. He slipped around to the side where he found a door standing open. He got inside, and as he eased up three steps, he heard a gasp and saw a glimmer of light.

"Hello, Helen!" a man's voice said.

"*You,* Henry!"

"Yes, Helen, it has been a long time. Too bad you could not let well enough alone. If your husband hadn't been such an honest fool, I could not have tricked him as I did. And this detective of yours is a blunderer!"

"Where is Morgan? What have you done to him?"

"I've killed him, I believe. Anyway, with you dead, I'll feel safer. I was afraid this might happen so I have plans to disappear again, if necessary. But first I must kill you."

Kip Morgan had reached the door, turning into it gradually. Helen's eyes found him, but she permitted no flicker of expression to warn Willard. Then a board creaked, and Willard turned. Before he could fire, Kip knocked the gun from his hand, then handed his own to Helen.

"I want you," Morgan said, "for the chair!"

The big man lunged for him, but Kip hit him left and right in the face. The man squealed like a stuck pig and stumbled back, his face bloody. Morgan walked in and hit him three times. Desperately, the big man pawed to get him off, and Kip jerked him away from the bed and hit him again.

A siren cut the night with a slash of sound, and almost in the instant they heard it, the car was slithering to a stop outside.

Helen pulled her robe around her, her face pale. Kip Morgan picked up Willard and shoved him against the wall. Hatred blazed in his eyes, but what strength there had been four years before had been sapped by easy living. The door opened, and two plainclothes detectives entered, followed by some uniformed officers.

The first one stopped abruptly. "What's going on here?" he demanded.

"Lieutenant Brady, isn't it?" Kip said. "This man is Henry Willard, and there is a murder rap hanging over him from New Jersey. Also, a fifty-thousand-dollar payroll robbery!"

"Willard? This man is James Howard Kendall. He owns the Mario Dine & Dance spot and about a dozen other things around town. Known him since he was a kid. I was just a couple of years older than he was."

"He went back East, took the name Willard, and—"

"Brady," Willard interrupted, "this is a case of mistaken identity. You know me perfectly well. Take this man in. I want to prefer charges of assault and battery. I'll be in first thing in the morning."

"You'll leave over my dead body!" Kip declared. He turned to Brady. "He told Mrs. Whitson that he had already made plans to disappear again if need be."

"Morgan, I've known Mr. Kendall for years, now—"

"Ask him what he is doing in this house. Ask him how he came to drive up here in the night and enter a dark house."

Kendall hesitated only a moment. "Brady, I met this girl only tonight, made a date with her. This is an attempt at a badger game."

"Mighty strange," the gray-haired man who had driven Kip to town interrupted. "Might strange way to run a badger game. This man"—he indicated Kip—"staggered onto my porch half beaten to death and asked me to rush him to town to prevent a murder. It was he who sent me for the police. This house was dark when he started for it."

"All you will need are his fingerprints," Kip said. "This man murdered a payroll guard, changed clothes with the murdered man. Then he took the money and came back here and went into business with the proceeds from the robbery."

"Ah? Maybe you've got something, Morgan. We always wondered how he came into that money."

Kendall wheeled and leaped for the window, hurling himself through it, shattering it on impact. He had made but two jumps when Morgan swept up the gun and fired. The man fell, sprawling.

"You've killed him!" Brady said.

"No, just a broken leg. He's all yours."

As the police left, Kip turned to Helen Whitson. "You did it! I knew you could! And you've earned that five thousand dollars!"

"It's a nice sum." He looked at her again. "When are you leaving?"

"I've got to go back to New York for Bobby."

"Don't go yet." He took her by the shoulders. "In a couple of days, my lips won't be so swollen. They aren't right for kissing a girl now, but—"

"But I'll bet you could," she suggested, "if you tried!"

AUTHOR'S NOTE

WITH DEATH IN HIS CORNER

Kip Morgan's mother took a fancy to the writing of Rudyard Kipling and named her son after that great author of adventure tales. Kip is always a direct-action man who likes to bull right into the middle of things. Nobody puts the arm on him and gets away with it.

Following his debut in DEAD MAN'S TRAIL, Kip builds his reputation for being a young and hungry professional operator, but WITH DEATH IN HIS CORNER is an example of the way Kip got many of his cases: by helping out a friend. During his boxing days he had a knack for getting his fellow fighters out of trouble, and it was only natural that many of those same gentlemen called on Kip when they continued to get into difficulties long after their days in the ring. Kip always heeded their call, even though the results were frequently far more punishing than any of them ever faced as prizefighters.

WITH DEATH IN HIS CORNER

The ghost of a mustache haunted his upper lip, and soft blond hair rolled back from a high white brow in a delicately artificial wave. He walked toward me with a quick, pleased smile. "A table, sir? Right this way."

There was a small half-circle bar at one end of the place and a square of dance floor about the size of two army blankets.

On a dais about two feet above the dance floor a lackadaisical orchestra played desultory music. Three women and two men sat at the bar and several of the tables were occupied. From the way the three women turned their heads to look, I knew all were hoping for a pickup. I wasn't.

A popeyed waiter in a too-tight tux bustled over, polishing a small tray suggestively. Ordering a bourbon and soda, I asked, "Where's Rocky Garzo?"

The question stopped him as if he'd been slugged in the wind, and he turned his head as if he were afraid of what he would see.

"I don't know him," he said too hastily. "I never heard of the guy."

He was gone toward the bar before I could ask anything further, but come what may, I knew I'd started the ball rolling. Not only did the waiter know Garzo, but he knew something was wrong. One look at his face had been enough. The man was scared.

He must have tipped a sign to the tall headwaiter, because when he returned with my drink, the blond guy was with him.

"You were asking for someone?" There was a slight edge to his voice, and the welcome sign was gone from his eyes. "What was the name again?"

"Garzo," I said, "Rocky Garzo. He used to be a fighter."

"I don't believe I know him," he replied. "I don't meet many fighters."

"Possibly not, but it is odd you haven't met him. He used to work here."

"Here?" His voice shrilled a little, then steadied down. He was worried; that was obvious. Whatever trouble Garzo was in it must be serious. "You're mistaken, I believe. He did not work here."

"Apparently, you and Social Security don't agree," I commented. "They assured me he worked here, at least until a day or so ago."

He did not like that, and he did not like me. "Well"—

his tone showed his impatience—"I can't keep up with all the help. I hope you find him."

"Oh, don't worry! I will! I will!"

He could not get away fast enough, seeming to wish as much distance between us as possible. All Rocky's letter had said was that he was in trouble and needed help, and Rocky was not one to ask for help unless he needed it desperately.

It began to look as if my hunch was right. Also, I did not like the way they were refusing to admit Garzo had even been around. I am not one to be irritated by small things, but I was beginning not to like what was happening. All I wanted was to know where Rocky was and what was wrong, if anything.

Rocky Garzo was a boy who had been around. A quiet Italian from the wrong side of the tracks, but a simple-hearted, friendly sort who could really fight. He wanted no trouble with anyone and, except as a youngster, never had a fight in his life he didn't get paid for. I've heard men call him everything they could think of, and he would just walk away. But when the chips were down, Rocky could really throw them. Back in the days when—Well, he fought the best of them.

The fleshpots got him. He was a kid who never had anything until he got into big money in the fight game, and he liked the good food, flashy women, and clothes. His money just sort of dribbled away, and the easy life softened him up. Then the boys began to tag him with the hard ones. It was Jimmy Hartman who wound him up with the flashiest right hand on the Coast.

He quit then. He went to waiting on tables. He was a

fast-moving, deft-handed man with an easy smile. He quit drinking, and the result was he was doing all right until something went wrong here at the Crystal Palace.

There was a pretty girl sitting at the table next to mine. She was with a bald-headed guy who was well along in his cups. She was young and shaped to be annoyed, if you get what I mean. The new look didn't keep the boys from giving her the old looks. Not with the set of fixtures she had.

All of a sudden, she is talking to me. She is talking without turning her head. "You'd better take it out of here," she said. "These boys play rough, even for you, Kip Morgan!"

"What's the catch?" I didn't turn my head, either. "Can't a guy even ask for his friends?"

"Not that one. He's hotter than a firecracker, and I don't mean with the law. Meet me at the Silver Plate in a half hour or so and I'll ditch this dope and tell you about it."

This place was not getting me anywhere. The waiter was pointedly ignoring my empty glass, and in such places as this they usually take it out of your hand before you can put it down. I took a gander at Algy or whatever his name was and saw him talking with a hefty lad at the door. This character had bouncer written all over him and looked like a moment of fun. I hadn't bounced a bouncer in some time.

As I passed them, I grinned at Algy. "I'll be back," I said. "I like to ask questions."

This was the cue the bouncer needed. He walked over, menace in his every move. "You've been here too long an' too much." He made his voice ugly. "We don't want you here no more! Get out an' stay out!"

"Well, I'll be swiped by a truck!" I said. "Pete Farber!"

"Huh?" He blinked at me. "Who are you, huh?"

"Why, Pete! You mean you don't remember? Of course, our acquaintance was brief, and you couldn't see very well through all that blood. I had just hung that eyebrow down over your right eye and had you set for the payoff. Naturally, you didn't see me later because I was home in bed before they brought you out of it."

"Huh?" Then awareness came, and his eyes hardened but grew wary also. He did have a memory, after all. "Kip Morgan!" he said. "Sure, it's Kip Morgan."

"Right, and if you'll recall, Rocky Garzo and I teamed up in the old days. He was going down, but I was coming up, but we were pals. Well, I am a man who remembers his friends, and I am getting curious about this stalling I am getting."

"Play it smart," Farber said, "and get out while you're all in one piece. This is too big for you. Also"—he moved closer—"I got no reason to like you. I'd as soon bust you as not."

That made me smile. "Pete, what makes you think you could do something now you couldn't do six years ago? You're fatter now, Pete, and slower. If you want a repeat on that job at the Olympic, just start something."

Pete Farber's next remark stopped me cold.

"You beat me," he said, "but you dropped a duke to Ben Altman. Well, you just forget Garzo, because Altman's still a winner."

When I got outside that one puzzled me. What was the connection between Ben Altman, formerly a top-ranking light heavyweight, and Garzo?

Then I began to remember a few things I'd forgotten. There had been some shakeups in the mobs, and Altman, a boy from the old Alberta section of Portland, had suddenly emerged on top. He was now a big wheel.

So Rocky didn't work here anymore. I climbed into a cab and gave the cabbie the address of Rocky's rooming house. He turned his head for a second look. "Chum," he said. "I'd not go down there dressed like you are. That's a rough neighborhood."

"You're telling me? Let her roll, Ajax. Anybody who shakes me down is entitled to what he gets."

He was disgusted. "Big talk won't get you no place. All men are equal at the point of a gun."

"Not quite. When somebody tries to make it with a gun, he has already admitted he hasn't the guts to make it the honest way. Whether he realizes it or not, life has already whipped him. From there on, it's all downhill."

"Sometimes I figure it would beat hackin', but I don't know."

"A while back, somebody took an average of all the boys in for larceny. The average sentence served was four years, the average take was twenty-one bucks."

"I'll stick to hackin'."

The rooming house was a decrepit frame building of two rickety stories. The number showed above a doorway that opened on a dark, dank-looking stairway. The place smelled of ancient meals, sweaty clothing, and the dampness of age. Hesitating a moment, I struck a match to see the steps, then felt my way up to the second floor of this termite heaven.

At the top of the stairs, a door stood partly open, and I had the feeling of somebody watching.

"I'm looking for Rocky Garzo," I said.

"Don't know him." It was a woman's husky voice. I could picture the woman.

"Used to be a fighter," I explained. "A flat nose and a tin ear."

"Oh, him. End of the hall. He came in about an hour ago."

My second match had flickered out, so I struck another and went down the hall, my footsteps echoing in the emptiness. The walls were discolored by dampness and ancient stains, no doubt left by the first settler.

A door at the end of the hall stared blankly back at me. My fist lifted, and my knuckles rapped softly. Suddenly, I had that strange and lonely feeling of one who raps on the door of an empty house. My hand dropped to the knob, and the door protested faintly as I pushed it open. A slight grayness from a dusty, long-unwashed window showed a figure on the bed.

"Rocky?" I spoke softly, but when there was no reply, I reached for the light switch. The light flashed on, and I blinked. I needed no second look to know that Rocky Garzo had heard his last bell, and from the look of the room he had gone out fighting.

He was lying on his right cheek and stomach and there was a knife in his back, buried to the hilt. It was low down on the left side and seemed to have an upward inclination.

The bedding was mussed, and a chair was tipped on its side. A broken cup lay on the floor. Stepping over the cup, I picked up his hand. It wasn't warm, but it wasn't cold, either.

His knuckles were skinned.

"Anything wrong, mister?" It was the woman from down the hall. She was behind me in the light of the door, a faded blonde who had lost the battle with graying hair. Her face was puffed from too much drinking, and only her eyes held the memory of what her beauty must have been.

She was sober now, and she clutched a faded negligee about her.

"Yeah," I said, and something of my feelings must have been in my voice, for quick sympathy showed in her eyes. "The Rock's dead. He's been murdered."

She neither gasped nor cried out. She was beyond that. Murder was not new to her, nor death of any kind. "It's too bad," she spoke softly. "He was a good guy when he had it. In fact, he was always a good guy."

My eyes swept the room, and I could feel that old hard anger coming up inside me. Rock had been a good guy, one of the best. There had to have been two men. No man fighting with the Rock ever got behind him. He must have been slugging one when the other stepped in from the hall with the shiv.

"You'd better leave, mister. No use to get mixed up in this."

"No, I'm not getting out. This boy was a beat-up ex-fighter and he's been murdered. Maybe he wasn't in the chips. Maybe he wasn't strictly class, but he was my friend."

She was uneasy. "You'd better go. This is too big for you."

"You know something about this?"

"I don't know anything. I never know anything."

"Look"—I kept my voice gentle—"this man was my friend. You're regular. I saw it in your eyes; you're the McCoy." I waved a hand at Rock. "He was one of the good ones. It isn't right for him to go out this way."

She shook her head. "I'm not talking."

"All right. You call the cops. I'll look around."

She went away, and I heard her dialing the phone. I looked at Rock. He was a good Italian boy, that one. He came from the wrong side of the tracks, but he never let it start him down the wrong streets. He could throw a wicked right hand, that one. And he liked his spaghetti.

"Pal," I said quietly, "I'm still in your corner."

Without touching anything, I looked around, taking in the scene. One hood must have circled to get Rock's back to the door where the other one was waiting.

When you knew about fights, in and out of the ring, and when you knew about killings, it wasn't hard to picture. Rock had come in, taken off his shirt, and the door opened. He turned, and the guy circled away from him. The Rock had moved in, slugging. Then the shiv in the back.

But those knuckles.

"You put your mark on him, Rock. I'll be looking for a hood with a busted face. The left side for sure, maybe the right, too."

The woman came back to the room and stood in the door. "I've been trying to place you. You used to work out at the old Main Street Gym, and Rock talked about you. He figured Kip Morgan was the greatest guy on earth."

She looked down, twisting her fingers. Her hands once had been beautiful.

"Listen," she pleaded. "I've had so much trouble. I just can't take any more. I'm scared now, scared to death. Don't tell anybody, not even the police, but there were two of them. Both were well dressed. One was tall with broad shoulders; the other was heavy, much heavier than you."

The siren sounded, then whined away and died at the foot of the steps. Detective Lieutenant Mooney was the first one up the steps. "Hi," he said, then looked again. "You, is it? Who's dead?"

"Rocky Garzo. He was a fighter."

"I know he was a fighter. I go out nights myself. Who did it? You?"

"He was my friend. I came out from New York to see him."

They started to give the room the business, and they knew their job, so I just stepped into the hall and kept out of the way. What little I had I gave to Mooney while they were shaking the place down.

"If you want me," I said, "I'll be at the Plaza."

"Go ahead, but don't leave town."

A glance at my watch told me it was only forty minutes since I'd left the Crystal Palace, and I was ten minutes late for my date. The cab took ten more getting me there, but the babe was patient. She was sitting over coffee and three cigarette stubs.

"They called them coffin nails when I was a kid," I told her.

She had a pretty smile. "I thought you had decided not to come. That man I was with was harder to shake than the seven-year itch."

"If you can help me," I said, "it would mean a lot. Garzo was my pal."

"Sure, I know. I'm Mildred Casey, remember? I lived down the block from Rock's old man. You two used to fix my bike."

That made me look again. Blue eyes, the ghosts of freckles over the bridge of her nose, and shabby clothes. An effort to be lively with nothing much to be lively or happy about, but great courage. She still had that, with a fine sort of pride. There was hurt in her eyes where her heart showed, eyes that had kept looking at men wondering if this was the right one.

"I remember," I said. She had been a knobby-kneed kid with stars for eyes. "How could I forget? It was your glamour that got me."

She laughed, and it was a pretty sound. "Don't be silly, Kip. My knees were always skinned, and my bike was always busted."

Her eyes went from my face to the clothes I was wearing. "You've done well, and I'm glad." If I do say so, they were good. I'd always liked good clothes, liked the nice things that money could buy. Often they hadn't been easy to have because I also liked being on the level.

Two of the boys I'd grown up with had ended in the chair, and another was doing time for a payroll job.

"Kid"—I leaned toward her—"tell me about Rock. You've got to think of everything, and after you've told me, forget about it unless you talk to the police."

Her face went dead white then, and her eyes grew larger. She took it standing, but I knew she understood. In the world where we'd grown up, you didn't have to draw the pictures.

"Rock worked at the Crystal Palace only three weeks. He was a good waiter, but after his first week, something was bothering him. He talked to me sometimes, and I could see he had something on his mind. Then, one night, he quit and never even came back for his money."

"What happened that night?"

"Nothing, really. After a rather quiet evening, some people came in and sat at one of Rock's tables. Horace, he's the blond boy, made quite a fuss over them, but nothing happened that I could see. Then, all of a sudden, Rock went by me, stripping off his apron. He must have gone out the back way."

"Do you know who they were?"

Milly hesitated, concentrating. "There were four in the party, two men and two women. All were well dressed, and the men were flashing big rolls of bills. One of the men was larger than you. He wore a dark suit. A blond girl was with him, very beautiful."

"The big guy? Was he blond, too? With a broken nose?"

She nodded, remembering his eyes. "Yes, yes! He looked like he might have been a fighter once."

For a moment, I considered that. "Have you ever heard of Benny Altman?"

Her face changed as if somebody had slapped her. "So that was Ben Altman!" She sat very quiet, her coffee growing cold in front of her. "He knew a friend of mine once, a girl named Cory Ryan." She thought for a minute, then added, "The other man was shorter and darker."

She reverted to the former topic. "If you want to know anything about Ben Altman, ask Cory Ryan. He treated her terribly."

"Where is she now?"

"She went to San Francisco about two—maybe it was three weeks ago. I had a wire from her from there."

"Thanks. I'm leaving now, Milly, and the less you're seen with me the better. I'm in this up to my ears."

"Be careful, Kip. He was always bragging to Cory about what he could do and how much he could get away with."

We parted after exchanging phone numbers, and then I caught a cab and returned to the Plaza. Some of my friends were around, but I wasn't listening to the usual talk. The story would break the next day about Garzo's murder, but in the meantime I had much to do.

The one thing I had to begin with was Rock himself. He had always been strictly on the level. I knew that from years of knowing him, but the police would not have that advantage. At the Crystal Palace, he must have stumbled into something that was very much out of line. The arrival of Ben Altman must have proved something he only suspected. I might be wrong about that, but Altman had certainly triggered something in Garzo's thinking.

During the war and the years that followed, I had seen little of my old friends on the Coast, so I knew little about the activities of Garzo, Altman or any of the others.

"What are you so quiet about?" Harry asked. Harry was the bartender, and he had been behind bars in that part of town for nearly forty years. There was very little he didn't know, but very little he would talk about unless he knew you well, and that meant no more than four or five people in town.

"Remember Rocky Garzo? He was killed tonight. I used to work out with the guy."

"Isn't he the brother of that kid that was shot about a year ago?" Harry asked. "You know? Danny Garzo? He was shot by the police in some sort of a mix-up. Somebody said he was on the weed."

On the weed . . . the reefer racket . . . Ben Altman . . . things were beginning to fall into place. I left my drink on the bar. I wasn't much of a drinker, anyway, and I had some calls to make.

Bill would be on the job at the *News* office. As expected, it was on the tip of his tongue. "Danny Garzo? Eighteen years old, supposedly hopped up on weed and knifed some guy in a bar and then tried to shoot it out with the police. He was Garzo's brother."

"What do you know about Ben Altman? I hear he's a big man in the rackets now?"

"Brother"—I could fairly see the seriousness in his

face—"if you want to live to be an old man, forget it. That's hot! Very, very hot!"

"Then keep your eyes and ears open, because I am going to walk right down the middle of it. Incidentally, if your boys haven't got it already, Rocky Garzo was murdered. They just found the body."

Rocky's brother, high on marijuana, got himself killed when, according to the report, he had gone off his head and started cutting people. Marijuana was tricky stuff. The strength could vary from area to area, and nobody knew what they were really getting until it was used.

Rock Garzo had loved his brother. I remembered the kid only as somebody who played ball in the streets, a dark-eyed, good-looking youngster. Evidently, Rock had started out looking for the source of the weed. His looking took him to the Crystal Palace, and then Altman comes in, recognizes Garzo, and has a hunch why he's there. Maybe more than a hunch. Maybe he had come there to check on something, a tip, maybe, that Garzo was asking questions or showing too much interest. Garzo leaves at once, and a short time later he is dead.

Maybe that was right and maybe wrong. If I could tie it to Altman, I'd have something. If I had the right hunch, I had another hunch that Mooney wouldn't be far behind me. It was a job for the law, and I believe in letting the law handle such things. However, if I could come up with some leads because of the people I knew—well, it might help.

For two days I sat tight and nothing happened; then I

ran into Mooney. He was drinking coffee in a little spot where I occasionally dropped in.

"What happened to the Garzo case?" I asked him.

His expression wasn't kind. "I'm on another case."

"You've dropped it?"

"We never drop them."

"I think Rock had something on Ben Altman. I believe Rock was playing detective because of what happened to Danny."

"Who are you? Sherlock Holmes? We thought of that. It was obvious, but Altman has an alibi, and so have his boys. The worst of it is, they are good alibis, and he has good lawyers. Before you arrest a man like that, you've got to have a case, not just suspicion. It looks like Altman; it could have been Altman. We would like it if it was Altman, but we're stuck."

"Foolproof, is it?"

Mooney studied me over his coffee cup. "Look, Kip. I know you, see? I know you from that Harley case. You have a way of barging into things that could get you killed. I like you, so don't mess with this one. And don't worry about Ben Altman. We'll keep after him."

They would keep after him, and eventually they would get him. Crooks sometimes win battles, but they never win the war. However, I had to be back in New York, and I did not have the time to waste, and the old Rock had been a friend. I like to finish them quick, like Pete Farber.

How about Pete Farber? Did he have an alibi? Or what about Candy Pants, the blond headwaiter?

Then I remembered Corabelle Ryan, Milly's friend, who had known Altman. How much did she know?

One of the greatest instruments in the world is the telephone. It may cause a lot of gray hairs in the hands of an elderly lady with nothing else to do; still, it can save a lot of legwork.

A few minutes on the telephone netted me this. Cory was still, apparently, in San Francisco. Milly had not heard from her again. No, she had no address except that Milly had said she would be at the Fairmont for a few days.

The Fairmont had no such party registered. Nor had anybody by that name been registered there. The mail desk did have a letter for her, but it had been picked up. The man picking it up had a note of authorization. She remembered him well—a short, dark man.

"Cory," I muttered as I came out of the booth, "I am afraid you did know something. I am afraid you knew too much."

When it was dark, I changed into a navy blue gabardine suit and a blue and gray striped tie; then I took a cab to the Crystal Palace. I knew exactly what I was getting into, and it was trouble, nothing but trouble.

Horace was nowhere in sight when I went in, nor was Pete Farber. I got a seat in a prominent position, ordered a bourbon and soda, and began to study the terrain. If all went as expected before the evening was over, they would try to bounce me out of there.

The door from the office opened, and Horace emerged, talking to Farber. They both saw me at the same moment. As they saw me, the door opened, and two men walked in. Between them was Milly.

That did not strike me at first, but the next thing did. They did not stop at the hatcheck counter.

Now no nightclub, respectable or otherwise, is going to let two men and a woman go back without checking something without at least an attempt. The girl just looked at them and said nothing. That meant they were employees of the place or somebody close to the management. That last was the order I bought.

Particularly when I took a second look at Milly's face. If ever I saw a girl who was scared to death, it was Milly Casey. They started past me, headed for the office, and I knew Milly was in trouble.

Behind me, I heard a grunt of realization and knew Pete Farber was coming for me. The moment needed some fast work. Just as the two men came abreast of my table, I got up quickly.

"Why, hello! Don't I know you?" I smiled at her. "You're the girl I met at the Derby. Why don't you all sit down and let me buy drinks?"

"We're busy! This is a private matter. We've no time for a drink, bud, so roll your hoop."

Pete's arm slid around my neck from behind, which I had been expecting. Pete was never very smart that way. With my left hand, I reached up and grabbed his hand, my fingers in his palm, my thumb on the back, and with my right hand I reached back and grabbed Pete's elbow. It was a rapid, much-rehearsed move, and as I got my grip, I dropped quickly to one knee and whipped Pete over my shoulder.

He had been coming in, and I used his impetus. He went over flying and hit the table in front of me with a crash; the table collapsed like a sick accordion and with about the same sound. Being on my knees, I grabbed the legs of the nearest man with Milly and jerked hard. His head hit the table when he fell, and I was up fast to see Milly break away and the other man clawing at his hip.

It was a bad move, leaving him as open as a Memphis crap game, and I threw my right down the groove with everything on it but my shoelaces. When a man grabs suddenly at his hip, his face automatically comes forward. His did, and brother, it was beautiful!

His face came forward as if it had a date with my fist, and it was a date they kept. You could have heard the smack of that fist clear into the street, and his feet went from under him as if they'd been jerked from behind. He went down to all fours. Naturally, I didn't kick him. In police reports that might not look good, so when I sort of bent over him, my knee sort of banged into his temple. It was what might have been termed a fortuitous accident.

Garzo had gone out the back door, so there must have been one. Grabbing Milly, I started for it. Blond Horace was somewhere behind me, and he was screaming. My last glimpse of the room was one I'd not soon forget. It was the face of a big Irishman, built like a lumberjack, who was staring down at those three hoodlums with such an expression of admiration at the havoc I'd wrought that it was the finest compliment a fighting man could receive.

The kitchen clattered and banged behind us, then the door.

We raced down the alley. We reached the street, slowing down, but just as we reached it, a car swung in and stopped us cold.

It was a shock to them and to us, but I'll hand it to Ben Altman. He thought fast, and there was no arguing with the gun in his mitt. "Get in," he said. "You're leaving too soon."

"Thanks," I told him. "Do you mind if we skip this one? We've got a date, and we're late."

"I do mind," he said. He was taking it big, like in the movies. "We can't have our guests leaving so early. Especially when I came clear across town to see the lady."

Milly had a grip on my fingers, and that grip tightened spasmodically when he spoke. She had heard about him from Cory, but that gun was steady. Had it been aimed at me, I'd have taken a chance.

A bullet has to hit a bone or go right through the heart or head to stop you, and well, I'd have gambled.

"Suppose you take us along?" I said. "The cops will be riding your tail within an hour."

Ben Altman smiled. "I'll have an alibi."

Footsteps came up the alley behind me, and then a gun was jammed into my back so hard it peeled hide. "Get moving!" It was Pete Farber.

Milly was beside me as they walked us back to the club. She was tense and scared, but game. Just why they wanted her, I did not know. Maybe they believed she knew something, being a friend of Corabelle's.

Back in the office at the Crystal Palace, the two hoods

I'd worked over came in. Rather, one walked in, the other was half carried.

So there we were: Ben Altman, his three stooges, Milly and myself.

Now Benny was a lad who could scrap a little himself, and with Benny, I had an old score to settle. He got a decision over me in the ring once although I'd had him on the floor three times in the first four rounds. He had a wicked left, and I think on any other night I could have beaten him. On the night that counted, I did not do well enough after that fast start, and it always griped me because Ben Altman was a fighter I had never liked.

"Looks like you banged the boys around a little," Ben said. "But they'll have their innings before this night is over."

"What's the matter, Ben? Do you have to hire your fighting done now?"

He did not like that, and he walked over to me, staring at me out of those white blue eyes. "I could take you any day in the week and twice on Sunday, so why bother now?"

"With the right referee you could," I agreed, "but there isn't any referee now."

He ignored me and walked over to Milly. "Where's the diary?" he demanded. When he asked that question, a great light broke over me. Why had I not thought of that? Cory had kept a diary!

"I don't know anything about it." Milly held her head up and faced him boldly, proudly. I never saw anybody more poised. "If Cory kept a diary, she certainly never showed it to me. Why don't you ask her?"

Altman's face was ugly. "You'll tell me," he said, "or I'll break every bone in your body!"

"He can't ask Cory," I said, "because he murdered her."

Milly's face paled, and her eyes widened a little. Altman turned on me. "Shut up, damn you!" he shouted.

"Had help, I'll bet." I was trying to distract his attention from Milly. "Ben never saw the day he could whip a full-grown woman."

He wheeled on me, his face a mask of fury, and he lashed out with a wicked left. He wasn't thinking or reasoning, he just peeled that punch off the top of the deck and threw it at me, and I rolled my head, slipping the punch and letting it go past my ear.

"Missed," I said. "Your timing is off, Ben."

With a kind of whining yelp, he wheeled and grabbed a gun from a drawer and brought it up, his face white to the lips. In that instant, my life wasn't worth the flip of a coin, but Pete grabbed him.

"Not here, Ben! These walls are almost soundproof, but they could hear a gun. Let's get him out of here."

Ben must have caught the expression on Milly's face from the corners of his eyes, because he turned on her.

"Why, no, Pete," Altman was himself again. "We'll keep him here. I think he'll be the way to make this babe talk. She might get very conversational when we start burning Morgan's toes."

Milly Casey, cute as she could be usually, looked sick and scared. "Now tell us where the diary is and we'll let you both go."

"Don't tell him a thing, Milly. That diary is our ace in the hole."

Farber gave me a disgusted look. "Shut up! Don't you realize when you're well off?"

"Sure, and I'd like it if Ben blew his top again and started shooting. We'd have the law all over the place in minutes, quicker than you could trip a blind man."

Altman was mad, but he was cold mad now, and he was thinking. He had a temper, but he had more than an ounce of brains.

As for me, I was sure I had guessed right. Corabelle had been murdered, but was her murder as well covered as that of Garzo? If it had happened out of town, as seemed likely, it might not have gone off so smoothly. It was an idea. Also, two men had done the job on Garzo—which two?

As if in reply to my question, the short, dark man who had been with Altman came into the room, and I saw the side of his face. He had been one of them. Who used the knife?

Altman? That did not seem logical, as Altman was too smart to do his own work. He was a fist and gun man, not apt to use a knife. Yet the man had been tall with broad shoulders and who else fitted that but Ben?

"Let's get them out of here," Altman said changing his mind suddenly. "Well take them where we can do as we like. If they don't talk, we'll just get rid of them and hunt for the diary. After all, how many hiding places can there be?"

"It must be in the place where this babe lived," Pete suggested.

"Now," Ben Altman said.

"Okay, boss, with pleasure!" The blackjack sapped me behind the ear, and I went down hard. I faded and must have gone limp as a wet necktie, but I wasn't quite out because I remember hearing them complaining about my weight.

Next I knew, I was on the floor of a car. They had their feet resting on me, and we were driving. I'd passed out again, because we were already climbing, and I thought I could smell pines. This time, they were really taking us out into the country. All that was happening was like a foggy dream through which a few rays of intelligence found their way.

When I became conscious again, I could hear a faint sound as of someone not far from me, but I kept my eyes closed. I was lying on a floor with my cheek against it.

"Leave him with the babe," Farber was saying. "Let's rustle some chow."

"Is he still out cold? I haven't looked at him."

"He's cold," Pete said. "I clipped him good, and I'd been wanting to do just that."

They went out and closed the door, and I opened my eyes to slits. They were scarcely open when hands touched me, and I let them close again, liking the hands. Very gently, I was turned over, and praise be, I'd had the sense to keep my eyes closed, for in the next minute, my head was lifted, and Milly was kissing me and calling me a poor, dear fool.

Now in one sense, the term is unflattering, but when a good-looking girl holds your head and kisses you, who is to complain? I stayed right in there, taking it very gamely, until, inspired by what was happening, I decided it was time to do something about it and responded.

Milly let out a gasp and pulled away. "Oh, you—!"

"Ssh!" I whispered. "They'll hear you."

"Oh, you devil! You were awake all the time!"

"Yes, thank the Lord, but Milly, if I was dead and you started fussing over me like that, I'd climb right out of the coffin!"

She was blushing, so to ease her embarrassment, I asked, "How many of them are there?"

"Two. Pete Farber and the one called Joe. They're waiting for Ben Altman to come back. Kip, what are we going to do?"

"I wish I knew." I sat up, and my head swam. "If we could get away from here and lay hands on that diary, Mooney could do the rest. Do you know where we are?"

A quick look around the room had indicated there was nothing there to be used as a weapon. Carefully, I got to my feet, leaning against the wall as the room seemed to spin.

We had no time. Once Altman returned, and I had no doubt he was searching Milly's apartment for the diary, we simply would have no chance.

"Open the door and walk out there. I'll wait by the door. You go out and turn on the charm. Tell them you're hungry, too, and then keep out of the way."

She went without a second's hesitation, and as she stepped through the door, I heard her say, "What's the matter? Do I have to starve, too? Why don't you give a girl a break?"

"Eat!" Farber's voice was hearty. "Sure! Come on

out, babe! It may be hours before the boss gets back, and maybe we could make a deal, you an' me." I could imagine the smirk on his face. "I don't think the boss is goin' about this in the right way."

"You'd better have a look," Joe warned, "and see if the chump is still bye-bye."

"You have a look," Farber said. "When I hit 'em, they stay hit."

Joe's footsteps sounded, and the door opened. Joe stuck his head in, and that was all I needed. The blow I landed just below and slightly behind his ear, and he started to fall. I grabbed him before he could hit the floor and threw a punch to the wind.

"How's about it, babe?" Farber was saying. "Ben's a tough cookie, but why should you get knocked off? You give me all the right answers and maybe we can figure out something. An' let me tell you, kid. I'm the only chance you've got."

With Joe's necktie I bound his hands behind him and then tied his ankles with his belt. Milly was keeping Joe busy with conversation and hesitations. I stuffed a handkerchief into Joe's mouth, and started for the door with his gun.

"Hey, Joe!" Farber yelled. "This dame's okay! Come on out!"

Joe's gun was on my hip, but I wasn't thinking of using it yet. Milly was sitting on Pete's lap and was keeping his head turned away from the door.

Something warned him, probably the extended silence. He turned his head and opened his mouth to yell.

Milly was off his lap like a shot, as he lunged to his feet to meet a left hook to the teeth.

Farber was in no shape to either take it or dish it out, but he tried. He didn't reach for a gun; he just came in throwing punches. I stabbed a left to the mouth and threw a bolo punch into his belly, and he went to his knees, but as he fell, his mouth open and gasping, I hooked again to his jaw. For an instant, I waited for him to get up, but his jaw was broken, and he was moaning. Taking the gun out of his pocket, I shucked the cartridges, and as we headed for the road, I threw the gun into the brush.

There was no car. There was a road toward the highway, but we didn't take it. We ran into the woods at right angles to the highway, and I took the lead, running until Milly's face was white and she was gasping.

We slowed to a walk and headed downhill in the right direction. Almost before we realized it, we reached a highway. We were lucky, the first car stopped, and one look at Milly seemed to satisfy him that we needed help.

Once in town, I put Milly in a cab to headquarters. "Tell Mooney all about it."

"Where are you going?"

"To your place, after that diary. Do you have any idea where it might be?"

"No . . . I honestly did not know she kept one, although she did sit up late writing sometimes." She paused a moment. "One thing that might help. Did you ever read Poe's 'The Purloined Letter'? It was one of her favorite stories. At least she spoke about it a good deal."

First I checked the .38 Colt automatic I had taken

from Joe. The clip was fully loaded. I jacked a cartridge into the chamber. After paying off the cab, I went into the apartment house. Having Milly's key, I went right in. Nobody was there; nobody seemed to have been there. Maybe "The Purloined Letter" was a clue; the chances were that it was not. Yet I had some ideas of my own.

Corabelle Ryan had not gone to San Francisco by accident. She was hoping to get away from Altman. She did not get away, but the diary was not with her. Result: It must be where she had lived with Milly.

Wherever it was, I had very little time. From then on, things were going to move fast. Much would depend on how soon Ben found I was on the loose once again and that Milly was. Altman could not know what was in the diary, but he was afraid of what it might be. She might have threatened him with it for her own protection.

It was a two-bedroom apartment, with a living room, kitchenette, and bath. I recognized Milly's room at once from some clothes I'd seen her wear and the fact that it was obviously in use. The other room did not appear to have been occupied for several days.

The bureau offered nothing a quick search could reveal. The pockets of the clothes hanging in the closet took but a minute, boxes on the shelf, under the carpet, behind pictures, the bed itself. I checked her makeup kit, obviously a spare, and one of those small black cases that for a time every showgirl or model seemed to have. Nothing there.

For thirty minutes, I worked, going over that apartment like a custom's agent over a smuggler, and then I heard the faintest click from the lock. When I looked around, a hand was coming inside the door, and then he stepped into the room, a tall man with broad shoulders.

It was Horace, Candy Pants himself, and he held a knife low down in his right hand, cutting edge up. There was no love light in his eyes as he moved toward me.

It was like a French poodle baring his teeth to reveal fangs four inches long. From some, I might have expected it, but not from him. He did not say a word, just started across the room toward me, intent and deadly. He was unlike anyone I had ever seen before, but suddenly I got it. He was all hopped up on weed.

With his eyes fixed on mine, he closed in. It was like me that I did not think of the gun I carried. The weed made him dangerous. Hopped up as he was, he could still handle a shiv, and I moved around, very cautious, studying how I'd better handle him. It was not in me to kill a man if I didn't have to, and quite often there are other ways. His eyes were on my stomach, and that was his target. If you're afraid of getting cut, you shouldn't try to handle a man with a knife, just as you should lay off a fist fighter if you can't take a punch.

Feinting, I tried to get that right hand out away from his body, but he held it close, offering me nothing. He took a step nearer, and the blade came like a striking snake; I felt the point touch my thigh. Jerking back, I swung a left that caught him alongside the head, and he almost went down.

He was catlike in his movements, and he turned to face me. His eyes had noted the blood on my leg, and he liked the sight of it. He moved closer. During a conversation, one time, a cop told me that the best place to hit a weed head was in the stomach. Make 'em sick. Whether it was true or not, I didn't know.

He was coming for me now, and grabbing a pillow, I snapped it at his face. He ducked and lunged, and it was the chance I wanted.

Slapping his knife wrist out of line with my body, I dropped my right hand on his wrist and jerked him forward, throwing my left leg across in front of him. He spilled over it to the floor, and he hit hard. The knife slithered from his hand and slid under the bed. He struggled to get up, one of his arms hanging awkwardly—broken, I was sure.

He came up, staggering, and I threw a left into his belly. He fell near the bed, the knife almost under his hand. As I jumped to grab it, my shoulder hit Corabelle's makeup kit. It crashed to the floor, scattering powder, lipstick and—

My eyes fastened on the mirror, and on a hunch, drawn by the apparent looseness of it, I ripped the mirror from its place, and there, behind it, were several sheets of paper covered with writing, possibly torn from a diary. I grabbed them and backed off.

"All right, I'll take that!"

"You will like—!" It dawned on me that it was not Candy Pants speaking but Ben Altman, and he had a gun. The makeup kit was in my left hand, and I threw it, underhanded, at Ben; then I went for him.

The gun barked, and it would have had me for sure if I had not tripped over Candy Pants, who was trying to get up. Ben kicked at my head, but I threw myself against his anchoring leg, and he went down. We came up together and he swung the gun toward me as I came up, jamming the papers into my pocket.

By that time, I was mad. I went into him fast, the gun blasted again, and something seared the side of my neck like a red-hot iron. My left hooked for his wind, and my right hacked down at his wrist. The gun fell, and I clobbered him good with a right.

Suddenly, the apartment, the knifes, guns, and Horace on the floor were forgotten. It was as if we were back in the ring again. He slipped a jab, and the right he smashed into my ribs showed me he could still hit. I belted him in the wind, hooked for the chin, and landed a right uppercut while taking a left and right. I threw a right as he ducked to come in and filled his mouth full of teeth and blood. I finished what teeth he had with a wild left hook that had everything and a prayer on it.

Crook he might be, but he was game, and he could still punch. He came at me swinging with both hands, and I nailed him with a left, hearing the distant sounds of sirens. I was hoping I could whip him before the cops got there.

As for Benny, I doubt if he even heard the siren. We walked into each other punching like crazy men, and I dropped him with a right and started for a neutral corner before I realized there weren't any corners and this was no ring.

His left found my face again and again. Then I caught his left hook with my right forearm and chopped down to his cheek and laid open a cut you could have laid your finger in.

He tried another left, and I hit him with a right cross,

and his knees buckled. He went down hard and got up too quickly, and I nailed him with a left hook. When Mooney and the cops came in you could have counted a hundred and fifty over him. He was cold enough to keep for years.

Mooney looked at me, awed. "What buzz saw ran into you?"

I glanced in the mirror, then looked away quickly. Altman always had a wicked left.

Handing Mooney the pages from the diary, I said, "That should help. Unless my wires are crossed, it was Candy Pants here who put the knife into Garzo."

Milly came through the open door as I was touching my face with a wet towel, trying to make myself look human. "Come," she said, "we'll go to my place. There's something to work with there, and I'll make coffee."

Rocky Garzo could rest better now, and so could his brother. I could almost hear the Rock saying, as he had said to me after so many fights, "I knew you could do it, kid. You fought a nice fight."

"Thanks, pal," I said aloud. "Thanks for everything."

"What are you talking about?" Milly asked. "Are you punchy or something?"

"Just remembering Garzo. He was a good boy."

"I know." Milly was suddenly serious. "You know what he used to say to me? He'd say 'You just wait until Kip gets back, things will be all right!' "

Well, I was back.

AUTHOR'S NOTE

THE STREET OF LOST CORPSES

In a story like THE STREET OF LOST CORPSES Kip Morgan shows that even though he can handle the knives and guns preferred by his criminal adversaries he is most comfortable defending himself with his fists.

This makes perfect sense for Morgan. A fighter has to be very fast on his feet; Kip could move like a big cat. In his day the fighters were very quick, most were also very athletic. Boxing in those days was much more skillful than it is now. Boxing was a matter of making someone miss punches by a fraction of an inch and landing your punches by just about that margin, too.

Kip Morgan, at about 175 pounds would have been classified as a light heavyweight. His fight career was successful up to a point, but like many fighters of his time he decided to go on to other pursuits. He may have given up the canvas but he did not give up his professional edge.

THE STREET OF LOST CORPSES

In a shabby room in a dingy hotel on a street of pawnshops, cheap nightclubs, and sour-smelling bars, a man sat on a hard chair and stared at a collection of odds and ends scattered on the bed before him. There was no sound in the room but the low mutter of a small electric fan throwing an impotent stream of air against his chest and shoulders.

He was a big man, powerfully built, yet lean in the hips and waist. His shoes were off, and his shirt hung over the foot of the bed. It was hot in the room despite the open windows, and from time to time, he mopped his face with a towel.

The bed was ancient, the washbasin rust-stained, the bedspread ragged. Here and there, the wallpaper had begun to peel, and the door fit badly. For the forty-ninth time, the man ran his fingers through a shock of dark, unruly hair.

Kip Morgan swore softly. Before him lay the puzzle of the odd pieces. Four news clippings, a torn bit of paper on which was written all or part of a number, and a crumpled pawn ticket. He stared gloomily at the assortment and muttered at the heat. It was hot—hotter than it had a right to be in Los Angeles.

Occupied though he was, he did not fail to hear the click of heels in the hall outside or the soft tap on his door. He slid from his chair, swift and soundless as a big cat, and in his hand there was a flat, ugly .38 automatic.

Again, the tap sounded. Turning the key in the lock to open the door, he stepped back and said, "Who is it?"

"It's me." The voice was low, husky, feminine. "May I come in?"

He drew back, shoving the gun into his waistband. "Sure, sure. Come on in."

She was neat, neat as a new dime, and nothing about the way she was dressed left anything to the imagination. Her blouse was cheap and the skirt cheaper. She wore too much mascara, too much rouge, and too much lipstick. Her hose were very sheer, her heels too high.

He waved her into a chair. There was irritation in his eyes. "At least you had sense enough to look the part. Didn't I tell you to stay away from me?" His voice was purposely low, for the walls were thin. "I had to come!" Marilyn Marcy stepped closer, and despite the heat and the cheapness of her makeup he felt the shock of her nearness and drew back. "I've been worried and frightened! You must know how worried I am! Have you learned anything?"

"Shut up!" His tone was ugly. Her coming into that part of town worried him, and dressed like that? She was asking for it. "Now you listen to me! I took the job of finding your brother, and if he's alive, I'll find him. If he's dead, I'll find out how and why. In the meantime, stay away from me and leave me alone! Remember what happened to that other dick."

"But you've no reason to believe they killed him because of this investigation!" she protested. "Why should they? You told me yourself he had enemies."

"Sure Richards had enemies. He was a fast operator and a shrewd one. Nevertheless, Richards had been around a long time and had stayed alive.

"As to why they should kill him for looking into this case, I have no idea. All I know is that anything can happen down here, and everything has happened at one time or another. I don't know what happened to your brother or why a detective should get a knife stuck into him for trying to find out. Until I do know I am being careful."

"It's been over a week. I just had to know something! Tell me what you've found out, and I'll go."

"You'll stay right here," he said, "until I tell you to go. You came of your own accord, now you'll leave when I tell you. You'll stay for at least an hour, long enough to make anybody believe you're my girl. You look the part. Now act it!"

"Just what do you expect?" she demanded icily.

"Listen, I'm just talking about the looks of the thing.

I'm working, not playing. You've put me on the spot by coming here, as I'm not supposed to know anybody in town. Now sit down, and if you hear any movement in the hall, make with the soft talk. Get me?"

She shrugged. "All right." She shook out a cigarette, offering him one. He shook his head impatiently, and she glared at him. "I wonder if you're as tough as you act?"

"You better hope I am," Kip replied, "or you'll have another stiff on your hands."

He stared grimly at the collection on the bed, and Marilyn Marcy stared at him. Some, she reflected, would call him handsome, and men would turn to look because of his shoulders and a certain toughness that made him seem as if he carried a permanent chip on his shoulder. Women would look, then turn to look again. She had seen them do it.

"Let's look at the facts," he said. "Your brother was an alcoholic. He was on the skids and on them bad. Even if we find him, he may not be alive."

"I realize that, but I must know. I loved my brother despite his faults, and he took care of me when I was on my way up, and I will not forget him now. Aside from George, he was all I had in the world.

"We loved each other and we understood each other. Either of us would do anything to help the other. He was always weak, and both of us knew it, yet when he went into the army, he was a fairly normal human being. He simply wasn't up to it, and when he received word his wife had left him, it broke him up.

"However, there is this I know. If my brother is dead,

it was not suicide. It would have to be accident or murder. If it was the former, I want to know how and why; if the latter, I want the murderer brought to trial."

Kip's eyes searched her face as he listened. Having seen her without makeup, he knew she was a beautiful girl, and even before she hired him, he had seen her on the stage a dozen times. "You seem ready to accept the idea of murder. Why would anybody want to kill him?"

"I've heard they kill for very little down here."

"That they do. In a flophouse up the street, there was a man killed for thirty-five cents not long ago. Value, you know, is a matter of comparison. A dollar may seem little, but if you don't have one and want it badly, it can mean as much as a million."

"I've seen the time." Drawing her purse nearer, she counted out ten fives and then ten tens. "You will need expense money. If you need more, let me know."

His attention was on the collection on the bed. "Did Tom ever say anything about quitting the bottle? Or show any desire to?"

"Not that I know of. I've told you how he was fixed. Each month he received a certain sum of money from me. We always met in a cheap restaurant on a street where neither of us was known. Tom wanted to keep everyone from knowing I had a brother who was a drunk. He believed he'd disgrace me. I sent him enough to live as he wished. He could have had more but refused it."

Morgan nodded, then glanced at her. "What would you say if I told you that for three weeks prior to his disappearance he hadn't touched a drop?"

Marilyn shook her head. "How could you be sure? That doesn't sound like Tom. Whatever would make him change?"

"If I knew the answer to that I'd have the answer to a lot of things, and finding him would be much easier. Tom Marcy changed suddenly, almost overnight. He cleaned up, had his clothes pressed and his shoes shined. He took out his laundry and then began doing a lot of unexpected running around."

Obviously, she was puzzled, but a sudden glance at her watch and she was on her feet. "I must go. I've a date with George and that means I must go home and change. If he ever guessed I had come down here looking like this, he would—"

Kip stood up. "Sure, you can go." Before she could protest he caught her wrist, spun her into his arms, and kissed her soundly and thoroughly. Pulling away, she tried to slap him, but he blocked it with an elbow. "Don't be silly!" he said. "I'm not playing games, but this hotel is a joint. When you leave here, you're going to look like you should, and your lipstick will be smeared, but good!"

He caught her again and kissed her long and thoroughly. She began to struggle, but he held her, and she quieted down. After a moment he let go of her and stepped back. She stared at him, her eyes clouded and her breast heaving. "Did you have to be so—thorough about it?"

"Never do anything by halves," he said, dropping back into the chair. He looked up at her. "On second thought, I—"

"I'm leaving!" she said hastily, and slipped quickly out of the door.

He grinned after her and wiped the lipstick from his mouth, then stared at the red smear on his handkerchief, his face sobering. He swore softly and dropped back into the chair. Despite his efforts, he could not concentrate.

He walked to the washbasin and wiped away the last of the lipstick.

What did he know, after all? Tom Marcy was an alcoholic with few friends, and only one or two who knew him at all well. Slim Russell was a wino he occasionally treated, and another had been Happy Day. Marcy minded his own affairs, drank heavily, and was occasionally in jail for it. Occasionally, too, he was found drunk in a doorway on skid row. The cops knew him, knew he had a room, and from time to time, rather than take him to jail, they'd take him to his room and dump him on his bed.

Then something happened to change him suddenly. A woman? It was unlikely, for he did not get around much where he might have met a woman. Yet suddenly he had straightened up and had become very busy. About what?

The pawn ticket might prove something. The ticket was for Tom Marcy's watch. Obviously, he had reached the limit of his funds when some sudden occasion for money arose, and rather than ask his sister for it, he had pawned his watch.

When he failed to appear at the restaurant, something that had not happened before, Marilyn was worried.

She returned to the restaurant several times, but Tom Marcy had not showed up. When the following month came around, she went again, and again he had not appeared. In the meantime, she had watched the newspapers for news of deaths and accidents. Then she hired a detective.

Vin Richards was a shrewd operative with connections throughout what has been called the underworld. A week after taking the case, he was found dead in an alley not far from the hotel in which Kip Morgan sat. Vin Richards had taken a knife in the back and another under the fifth rib. He was very dead when discovered.

Morgan began with a check of the morgue and a talk to the coroner's assistants. He had checked hospitals and accident reports, then the jails and the police.

The officers who worked the street in that area agreed that Tom Marcy never bothered anybody. Whenever he could, he got back to his room, and even when very drunk, he was always polite. It was the police who said he had straightened up.

"Something about it was wrong," one officer commented. "Usually when they get off the bottle they can't leave the street fast enough, but not him. He stayed around, but he wouldn't take a drink."

Seven weeks and he had vanished completely; seven weeks with no news. "We figured he finally left, went back home or wherever. To tell you the truth, we miss him.

"The last time I saw him, he was cold sober. Talked

with me a minute, asking about some old bum friend of his. He hesitated there just before we drove away, and I had an idea he wanted to tell me something, maybe to say good-by. That was the last time I saw him."

He had disappeared, but so had Vin Richards. Only they found Vin.

"Odd," the same officer had commented. "I would never expect Vin to wind up down here. He used to be on the force, you know, and a good man, too, but he wanted to work uptown. Hollywood, Beverly Hills, that crowd."

The pawn ticket answered one question but posed another. Tom Marcy needed money, so he hocked his watch, something he had not done before. Why did he need money? If he did need it, why hadn't he asked Marilyn?

The news clippings now—two of them were his own idea, one he found in Tom's room. And there was a clue, a hint. His clipping and one of Tom's were identical.

It was a tiny item from the paper having to do with the disappearance of one Happy Day, a booze hound and clown. Long known along East Fifth Street and even as far as Pershing Square, he had been one of Marcy's friends.

Marcy's second clipping was about a fire in a town sixty miles upstate in which the owner had lost his life. There was little more except that the building was a total loss.

The last clipping, one Kip Morgan had found for himself, was a duplicate of one Tom Marcy left behind in the hockshop. The owner, thinking it might be important, had put it away with Tom's watch and mentioned it to Kip Morgan. At Kip's request, the pawnbroker had shown him the clipping. In a newspaper of the same date as the hocking of the watch, Morgan found the same item. It was a simple advertisement for a man to do odd jobs.

That Marcy had it in his hand when he went to hock his watch might indicate a connection. The pawning of the watch could have been an alternative to answering the ad. Yet Marcy had straightened up immediately and had begun his unexplained running around.

Could the advertisement tie in with the disappearance of Happy Day? A hunch sent Morgan checking back through the papers. Such an ad appeared in the papers just before the disappearance of Happy Day! Once Kip had a connection, he had followed through. Had there been other disappearances? There had.

Slim Russell, Marcy's other friend, had vanished in the interval between the disappearance of Happy Day and that of Tom Marcy himself. Apparently, it had been these disappearances that brought about the change in Tom Marcy.

Why?

Checking the approximate date of Slim Russell's disappearance, for which he had only the doubtful memories of various winos, he found another such ad in the newspaper.

The newspaper's advertising department was a blind alley. On each occasion, the ad came by mail, and cash was enclosed, no check.

Morgan paced the floor, thinking. Not a breeze

stirred, and the day was hot. He could be out on the beach now instead of there, sweating out his problem in a cheap hotel, yet he could not escape feeling he was close to something. Also, and it could be his imagination, he had the feeling he was being watched.

Richards, cold and cunning as a prairie wolf, an operator with many connections and many angles, had been trapped and murdered. Before that, three men had disappeared and were probably dead.

Clearing away the Marcy collection, Morgan packed it up, then shifting the gun to a spot beneath his coat, which lay along one side of the bed, he stretched out and fell into an uncomfortable state of half awake, half asleep.

Hours later, his mind fogged by sleep, he felt rather than heard a faint stirring at the door. His consciousness struggled, then asserted itself. He lay very still, every sense alert, listening.

Someone was at the door fumbling with the lock. Slowly, the knob turned.

Morgan lay still. The slightest creak of the springs would be audible. Perspiration dried on his face and he tried to keep his breathing even and natural. Now the darkness seemed thicker where the door had opened. A soft click of the lock as the door closed.

His throat felt tight, his mouth dry. A man with a knife? Gathering himself, every muscle poised, he waited.

A floorboard creaked ever so slightly, a dark figure loomed over his bed, and a hand very gently touched his chest as if to locate the spot. Against the window's vague light, he saw a hand lift, the glint of a knife. Traffic rumbled in the street, and somewhere a light went on, and the figure beside the bed was starkly outlined.

With a lunge, he threw himself against the standing man's legs. Caught without warning, the man's body came crashing down and the knife clattered on the floor. Kip was up on his feet as the man grasped his fallen knife and turned like a cat. Blocking the knife arm, Kip whipped a wicked right into the man's midsection. He heard the *whoosh* of the man's breath, and he swung again. The second blow landed on the man's face, but he jerked away and plunged for the door.

Going after him, Kip tangled himself in a chair, fell, broke free, and rushed for the door in time to see his attacker go into a door across the hall.

Doors opened along the hall and there were angry complaints. He whipped open the door into which the attacker had vanished, a light went on, and a man was sitting up in bed. A window stood open, but his attacker was gone.

"Who was that guy?" the man in bed protested. "What's goin' on?"

"Did you see him?" The man in bed showed no signs of excitement, nor was he breathing hard.

"See him? Sure, I saw him! He came bustin' in here and I flipped the switch, and he dove out that window!"

The alley was dark and the fire escape empty. Whoever he had been, he was safely away now. Kip Morgan walked back to his room. They had killed Richards when he got too close for comfort, and now they were after him.

When the hotel quieted down, he pulled on his shoes and shirt. It was not as late as he had believed, for he had fallen asleep early. He went downstairs into the dingy street; a man was slumped against a building nearby, breathing heavily, an empty wine bottle lying beside him. Another man, obviously steeped in alcohol, lurched against a building staring blearily at Morgan, wondering whether his chance of a touch was worth recrossing the street.

It was early, as it had been still light when he stretched out on the bed. It was too early for the attacker to have expected Morgan to be in bed unless he already knew he was there. That implied the attacker either lived in the hotel or had a spy watching him.

Weaving his way down the street through the human driftwood, Morgan considered the problem. The killer of Richards used a knife, and so had his attacker. It was imperative he take every step with caution, for a killer might await him around any corner. Whatever Tom Marcy had stumbled upon, it had led to murder.

Back to the beginning, then. Marcy had straightened up and quit drinking after the disappearance of Slim Russell. He had known enough to arouse his suspicions and obviously connected it to the disappearance of Happy Day.

It was not coincidence that the two men who vanished had been known to him, for the winos along the streets nearly all knew each other, at least by sight. Many times, they had shared bottles or sleeping quarters, and Marcy might have known sixty or seventy of them slightly.

What aroused Marcy's suspicions? Obviously, he had begun an investigation of his own. But why? Because of fear? Of loyalty to the other derelicts? Or for some deeper, unguessed reason?

Another question bothered Morgan. How had the mysterious attacker identified him so quickly? How had he known about Richards? Richards, of course, had been a private operator for several years, but he, Kip Morgan, had never operated in that area and would be unknown to the underworld except by name from his old prizefighting days.

Something had shocked Tom Marcy so profoundly that he stopped drinking. The idea that was seeping into Morgan's consciousness was one he avoided. To face it meant suspicion of Marilyn Marcy, but how else could the attacker have known of him? Yet why should she hire men, pay them good money, and then have them killed?

If not Marilyn then somebody near her, but that made no sense, either. The distance from East Fifth to Brentwood was enormous, and those who bridged it were going down, not up. It was a one-way street lined with empty bottles.

Instead of returning to his room, Morgan went to the quiet room where Tom Marcy had lived when not drinking heavily. It was a curious side of the man that during his drinking spells, he slept in flophouses or in the hideouts of other winos. In the intervals, he returned to the quiet, cheap little room where he read, slept, and seemed to have been happy.

At daybreak Morgan was up and made a close, careful search of the room. It yielded exactly nothing.

Three men missing and one murdered; at least two of the missing men had answered ads. What of Marcy? Had he done the same?

The idea gave Morgan a starting point, and he went down into the street. The crowding, pushing, often irritable crowd had not yet reached the downtown streets. The buses that fed their streams of humanity into the downtown areas were still gathering their quotas in the outskirts, miles away.

The warehouse at the address in the advertisement was closed and still. He walked along the street on the opposite side, then crossed and came hack down. Several places were opening for business, a feedstore, a filling station, and a small lunch counter across the way.

The warehouse itself was a three-story building, large and old. There was a wooden door, badly in need of paint, a blank, curtained window, and alongside the door a large vehicle entrance closed by a metal door that slid down from above.

Kip crossed the street and entered the café. The place was empty but for one bleary-eyed bum farther down the counter. The waitress, surprisingly, was neat and attractive.

Kip smiled, and his smile usually drew a response from women. "How's about a couple of sinkers? And a cup of Java?"

She brought the order, hesitating before him. "It's slow this morning."

"Do you do much business? With all these warehouses, I should imagine you'd do quite well."

"Sometimes, when they are busy, our breakfast and

lunch business can be good. As for the late trade, there's just enough to keep us open. We get some truck and cab drivers in here at all hours, and there's always a few playing the pinball machines."

Kip indicated the warehouse across the street. "Don't they hire men once in a while? I saw an ad a few days ago for a handyman."

"That place?" She shrugged. "It wouldn't be your sort of work. Occasionally, they hire a wino or street bum, and not many of those. I imagine it's just for cleaning up, or something, and they want cheap labor.

"There was a fellow who came in here a few times. I think he went to work over there. At least he waited around for a few days waiting for somebody to show up."

"Did he actually get a job?"

"I believe so. He waited, but when they actually did show up he did not go over. Not for the longest time. He was like all of them, I guess, and really didn't want work all that bad. He did finally go over there, I think."

"He hasn't been in since?"

"I haven't seen him. But they haven't been working over there, either. If they've been around at all, it was at night."

"They work at night?"

"I don't know about that, but one day I saw the shade was almost to the bottom, and the next day it was a little higher. Again, it was drawn to the bottom."

Kip smiled and asked for a refill. A smart, observant girl.

"I'd make a bet the guy you speak of was the one I

talked to. We were looking over the ads together." Kip squinted his eyes as if trying to remember. "About forty? Forty-five, maybe? Medium height? Hair turning gray? Thin face?"

"That's the one. He was very pleasant, but I think he'd been sick or something. He was very nice, but jittery, on edge, like. He was wearing a pin-striped suit, neatly pressed, and you don't see that down here."

So Marcy had been there, too? Kip sipped his coffee while she worked at the back bar doing some of her side work.

"What kind of business are they in?" He turned his side to the counter so he could look across the street. "I could use some work myself, although I'm not hurting."

"You've got me. I have no idea what they do, although I see a light delivery truck, one of those panel jobs, once in a while. One of their men, too, comes in once in a while, but he doesn't talk much. He's a blond, stocky, Swedish type."

Morgan glanced down the counter at the somnolent bum whose head was bowed over his coffee cup.

Through another cup of coffee and a piece of apple pie, they talked. Twice, truck drivers came in, had their coffee and departed, but Kip lingered, and the waitress seemed glad of the company.

They talked of movies, dancing, the latest songs, and a couple of news items.

The warehouse across the street was rarely busy, but occasionally they moved bulky boxes or rolls of carpet from the place in the evening or early morning. Some building firm, she guessed.

The bum got slowly to his feet and shuffled to the door. In the doorway, he paused, and his head turned slowly on his thin neck. For a moment, his eyes met Morgan's. They were clear, sharp, and intelligent. Only a fleeting glimpse and then the man was outside. Kip got to his feet. How much had the man heard? Too much, that was sure. And he was no stewbum, no wino.

Kip walked to the door and stood looking after the bum, if such he was. The man was shuffling away, but he turned his head once and looked back. Kip was well inside the door and out of view. Obviously the man had paused in the door to get a good look at Morgan. He would remember him again.

The idea disturbed him. Of course, it might be only casual interest. Nevertheless there was a haunting familiarity about the man, a sort of half recognition that would not quite take shape.

There was no time to waste. The next step was obvious. He must find out what went on inside that warehouse, who the two men were who had been seen around and what was in the boxes or rolls of carpet they carried out. The last carried unpleasant connotations to Kip Morgan. More than ever, he was sure that Tom Marcy had been murdered.

Except for the narrow rectangle of light where the lunch counter was, all the buildings were blank and shadowed when Kip Morgan returned. Nor was there movement along the street, only the desolation and emptiness that comes to such streets after closing hours.

Like another of the derelicts adrift along neighboring streets, sleeping in doorways or alleys, Morgan slouched along the street, and at the corner above the warehouse, he turned and went along the back street to the alley. No one was in sight, so he stepped quickly into the alley and stopped still behind a telephone post.

He waited for the space of two minutes, and nobody appeared. Staying in the deeper shadows near the building Morgan went along to the loading dock at the back of the warehouse.

A street lamp threw a triangle of light into the far end of the alley, but otherwise it was in darkness. A rat scurried across the alley, its feet rustling on a piece of torn wrapping paper. Kip moved along the back of the building, listening. There was no sound from within. He tried the door and it was locked.

There was a platform and a large loading door, but the door was immovable. There were no windows on the lower floors, but when he reached the inner corner of the building he glanced up into the narrow space between the warehouse and the adjoining building and saw a second-story window that seemed to be open. The light was indistinct, but he decided to chance it.

Both walls were of brick and without ornamentation but to an experienced rock climber they offered no obstacle.

Putting his back against the warehouse and his feet against the opposite building he began to work his way up. It needed but two or three minutes before he was seated on the sill of the warehouse window.

It was open but a few inches, propped there by an old putty knife. Hearing no sound he eased the window higher, stepped in, and returned the window to its former position. Crouching in the darkness, he listened.

Gradually, his ears sorted the sounds—the creaks and groans normal to an old building, the scurrying of rats—and his nostrils sorted the smell. There was a smell of tarpaper and of new lumber. Cautiously, he tried his pencil flash, keeping it away from windows.

He was in a barnlike room empty except for some new lumber, a couple of new packing cases, both open, and tools lying about.

Tiptoeing, he found the head of the stairs and went down. In the front office was an old-fashioned safe, a rolltop desk, and a couple of chairs. The room was dusty and showed no signs of recent use.

It was in the back office where he made his discovery, and it was little enough at first, for the lower floor aside from the front office was unfurnished and empty. And then he glimpsed a door standing open to a partitioned off room in a corner.

Inside was an old iron cot, a table, washstand, and chair. There was a stale smell of sweaty clothing and whisky. The bedding was rumpled. On the floor were several bottles.

Here someone had slept off a drunk, awakening to what? Or had he ever awakened? Or forfeited one kind of sleep for another? The heavy sleep of drunkenness, perhaps, for the silence of death?

Morgan shook his head irritably. What reason had he to believe these men dead? Was he not assuming too much?

He moved around. Kicking a rumpled pile of sacks, he disclosed *a blue, pin-striped suit!*

Tom Marcy had worn such a suit when last seen! Dropping to his knees, Kip made a hasty search of the pockets, but they yielded nothing. He was straightening up when he heard movement from the alley entrance and a mutter of voices.

Dropping the clothing, he took one hasty glance around and darted for the stairway. He went up on his toes, swiftly and silently, then flattened against the wall, listening.

"Hey? Did you hear something?" The voice was low but distinct.

"I heard rats. This old place is full of them! Come on, let's get that pile of junk out and burn it. If the boss found we'd left anything around, he'd have our hearts out. Where'd you leave it?"

"In the room. I'll get it."

Footsteps across the floor, then a low exclamation. "Somebody's been here! I never left those clothes like that!"

"Ah, nuts! How do you remember? Who would prowl a dump like this?"

"Somebody's been here, I say! I'm going to look around!"

They would be coming up the steps in a minute, and he had no chance of getting across that wide floor and opening the window, then climbing down between the walls. Even if the boards did not creak, the time needed for opening and closing the window and the risk of their hearing his feet scraping on the brick wall were too much. He glanced up toward the third floor. Swiftly, he mounted the steps to that unknown floor.

Morgan was fairly trapped, and he knew it. The weight of the .38 was reassuring, but he had no desire to shoot. A shot would bring the police and he had no right to be where he was.

Whatever was going on there was shrewdly and efficiently handled and, at the first hint of official interest, would quiet down so fast that no clue would be left. There were few enough as it was.

He could hear the two men stirring about down below. The blond man mumbling to himself, ignoring the protests of the taller, darker man. Twice, in the glow of their flashlights, Kip got a good look at them. Meanwhile, he was working fast. There was a window, and he eased it up. Down was impossible . . . but up?

He glanced up. The edge of the roof was there, only a few feet away and somewhat higher. Scrambling to the sill, his back against the window, he hesitated an instant, then jumped out and up.

It was a wild, desperate gamble, but the only alternative to a shootout, which he did not want. If he fell and broke a leg or was in any way disabled, they would find him and kill him.

He jumped, his fingers clawed for the edge of the parapet on the roof opposite, and caught hold. His toes scraped the wall, then he pulled himself up and swung his feet over the parapet just as the blond man reached the window. For a startled instant, their eyes met, and then he was up and running across the roof. He heard the sharp bark of a pistol shot, but the man could only shoot at where Morgan had been.

Crossing the roof, he looked down at the next one. Only a few feet. He dropped to that roof opposite, but this time he did not run. There was a narrow space there, and he could go down as he had come up. Bracing his back against one side, his feet against the other, he worked his way swiftly down.

He was almost down when he heard running feet on the roof above. Somehow, by a trap door, no doubt, they had reached the roof. "Where'd he go?" The voice was low but penetrating in the silence.

"Across the roofs! Where else! Let him go or we'll have the cops on us!"

"Let's get out of here!"

Dropping to the alley, Kip Morgan brushed himself off and walked to his car, almost a block away. He had barely seated himself when he saw a light gray coupe whisk by. The man nearest him was the blond man, and they did not see him.

Starting his car, he let the gray car get a start, then followed. Habitually, he went bareheaded, but in the car he kept an assortment of hats to be used on just such tailing jobs. He pulled on a wide-brimmed hat, tilting the brim down.

The gray car swung into Wilshire and started along the boulevard. It was very late, and there was little traffic. Holding his position as long as he dared, he came abreast only one lane away, and passing, turned left and off the street. When he picked them up again, he was wearing a cap and had his lights on dim. Moreover, his car now had a double taillight showing. He had rigged the car himself.

Shortly after reaching Beverly Hills, the gray car turned right, and Kip pulled to the curb, switched hats again, and turned his lights on bright. As the other car pulled up to the curb, he went by, going fast. Turning the corner, he pulled up and parked, then walked back to the corner, pausing in the darkness by a hedge and the trunk of a jacaranda tree.

Another car pulled up and stopped as the two men started across the street. A man and a woman got out. The blond man called out, "Mr. Villani? I got to see you!"

The man was tall and heavily built. He wore evening clothes, and as Morgan slipped nearer, staying in the shadows, he could hear the irritation in the man's voice. "All right, Gus, just a minute."

He turned to the girl he was with. "Would you mind going on in, Marilyn? I will follow in a minute."

The girl's face turned toward the light, and Kip's pulse jumped. *It was Marilyn Marcy!*

Drawing deeper into the shadows, he chewed his lip, scowling. This just did not make sense.

The two men had come up to Villani, who was speaking. "Gus? How many times have I warned you never to come near me? You know how to get in touch."

Gus's voice was low in protest. "But boss! This is bad news! That Morgan guy, he's been into the warehouse!"

"Inside?"

"Uh-huh. I don't know for sure if it was him, but I think it was."

"It was him," the dark man added, "but he got away and we had only a glimpse of him."

Morgan waited, hoping to see Villani's face. This was the boss, the man he had wanted to locate, and he knew Marilyn Marcy.

A low-voiced colloquy followed, but Morgan could hear nothing but the murmur of their voices. "All right, Vinson. Stay with him. We want no failure this time."

The two men started back to their car, and he started to follow them, then decided nothing would be gained. Rather, he wanted to know what was going on there.

As the gray car drove away, Morgan walked past the house into which Villani and Marilyn had disappeared, noting several other cars were parked outside. He went on down to the corner, crossed to a telephone booth and checked for Villani. It was there, the right name, the right address.

George Villani!

Marilyn had a date with George. That tied in, but what did it mean? If she was double-crossing Morgan, what could she hope to gain by it? On the other hand, suppose she did not know? That could be the way these crooks found out about Richards and about him as well. She had simply told her boyfriend.

Morgan walked back to his car, then stopped short, his mouth dry and his stomach gone hollow. The thin, dark man, Vinson, was standing by the tree, and he had a gun in his hand. "Hello, Morgan! Looks like we're going to get together, after all!"

He gestured. "Nice rig you got here—the hats and all. You had us fooled."

"Then what made you stop?" Kip asked pleasantly.

"Your car. It looked familiar, and it was like one we saw when we left the warehouse. For luck we had a look. You shouldn't leave your registration on the steering post."

"Well, so here we are." Morgan could not see the blond man, and that worried him. He had an idea that Gus was the tough one. This guy thought he was tough, and might be, but it was Gus who worried him. "You'd better put that rod away before somebody sees it."

"There's nobody around." Vinson liked that. He clearly thought he had the casual tough guy act down pat. "You've been getting in my hair, Morgan. We don't like guys who get in our hair."

Kip shrugged, and the gun tilted a little. This guy was hair-triggered, and that might be both good and bad. "Getting in people's hair is my business. Where's Tom Marcy?"

"Marcy?" The question surprised Vinson. "I never heard of anybody named Marcy. What's the angle?"

"Why, I am looking for him. That's my job." Morgan was alert and very curious. Obviously, the name surprised Vinson and puzzled him.

Vinson frowned. "I don't get it, pal. We figured you for a—" He paused, catching himself on the word. "We had you figured for the fuzz."

"Look," Morgan protested, "there's something screwy about this. I am looking for Marcy. If you don't know him we've no business together. Let's forget it. You go your way, and I'll go mine, and everybody'll be happy."

"Are you nuts? We're takin' you someplace where we can ask some questions, and we'll get answers." His eyes flickered. "Here comes—"

Morgan moved, swinging down and across with his left hand. He slapped the gun aside and came up under the barrel with his right, missed the grab, but followed through with the butt of his palm under Vinson's chin. The gangster's heels flipped up, and he went down hard, the gun flying from his hand.

From behind him Kip heard running feet, and he threw himself over a hedge, sprinting across the lawn. He ducked behind a huge old tree, grabbed a heavy limb, and pulled himself up. Almost at once, both men rushed on by.

Motionless in the tree, scarcely daring to breathe, he waited. "You fool!" Gus was saying. "You should have shot him!"

He heard them searching through the brush, but the branches above seemed never to occur to them. Nearby, a dog began to bark, and a light went on in a house. With a mutter of angry voices, the two men headed for their car. He heard it start.

Leaning back against the tree trunk, he waited. There was the chance it had been some other car starting or that they had driven but a short distance and were waiting, watching. He was in no hurry now. He had plenty to think about.

George Villani was the boss. In whatever was going on, he was the man who gave the orders and did the planning. When a serious problem came up, they had immediately gone to him. And George Villani was dating Marilyn Marcy.

The whys of that he did not know, but it seemed obvious that through him the killers had learned of Yin Richards, and it must have been Marilyn who told him Morgan was holed up in that hotel.

He lowered himself to the grass, waited an instant to see if he was unobserved, then went along the hedge to the alley.

His car could wait until daylight. If they were watching, and he returned now, they would kill him without hesitation. Once in the alley near the street, he paused.

Marilyn was still next door, and he could hear the sounds of music and laughter from the house. A small party was in the process.

He hesitated, half in the notion of crashing the party, but his shirt was rumpled, and his clothes were dusty from crawling through old buildings. Crossing several streets, he caught a cab and returned to his apartment. For this night the room at the hotel would stay empty.

As he considered the situation, he became convinced Tom Marcy must have come upon some hint of danger threatening his sister. Perhaps he had established a connection between Villani and the disappearances of Day and Russell. Only that seemed a logical explanation for his sudden breaking of old habits and his subsequent investigations. The danger of his sister marrying a murderer had started his interest in the warehouse and the street of missing men.

Back in his apartment he took off his shoes and sat on the edge of the bed. The next day would be soon enough, but at that time he would have to bear down. He must discover why those men had vanished and what had become of Tom Marcy.

He slept, dreaming a dream of flames, of a scream in the night, of—

He awakened suddenly. Vinson was standing over him, and Gus was standing with his back to the door, and they both had guns. He started to sit up, and Vinson hit him a full swing with a boot he had picked up. The blow caught him on the temple, and something exploded in his brain. He lunged to get off the bed, and another blow hit him. His feet tangled in the bedclothes, and he fell sprawling, taking another blow as he fell.

When he regained consciousness, he was lying on his face in the back of a van or delivery truck, and the first thing his eyes recognized was a shoe toe inches from his face. Closing his eyes, he lay still, pain throbbing in his skull.

Somehow they had traced him and gained access to his room without awakening him. Knocked out, he had been loaded in the truck and was being taken . . . where?

Listening, he decided by the lack of traffic sounds and the unbroken rate of speed that they were on a highway.

"What did he say to do with him?" Vinson was asking.

"Hold him. The boss needs to talk to him. He wants to know has he talked to anybody."

Tentatively, Kip tested his muscles. His hands were tightly bound. He relaxed, letting the hammers on his skull pound away. Suddenly, the truck made an abrupt turn, and the road became rough. A gravel road and badly corrugated. The truck dipped several times, then began to climb in slow spirals, higher and higher.

The air was clear and cool. The truck made another turn, ran on for a short distance, and then came to a stop. Morgan let his muscles relax completely.

"Haul him out," Vinson said. "I'll light up."

Gus opened the doors from within, dropped to the ground, then grabbed Morgan's ankles and jerked him to the ground. He hit the road with a thump, and it had been all he could do to keep from crying out when his head bumped on the tailboard, then the ground. Gus grabbed him by the shirtfront and dragged him to a dugout where he opened the door and threw him down the steps into darkness. The door closed, the hasp dropped into place, and he was alone.

For what seemed a long time, he lay still; the throbbing in his head became a great sea of pain where wave after wave broke over him. His head felt enormous, and every move generated new pain. Through it, fear clawed away tearing with angry fingers at the pain that drowned his awareness, hammering for attention at the portals of his consciousness.

They would come back, Vinson and Gus. The only way to escape more pain and even death was to endure the pain now while he had freedom from their watching eyes.

He lunged, bucking with his bound body, then rolling over three times until he found himself against a tier of boxes or crates. Hunching himself to a sitting position, he began sawing at the sharp edge of the box. In his desperation, he jerked too far, and the edge scraped his wrist. Wildly, his pain driving reason from his mind, he fought to cut loose the ropes that bound him. They were good ropes and drawn too tight.

He struggled on. The close confines of the dugout made him pant, and sweat soaked his shirt and ran into his eyes, smarting and stinging. His muscles grew heavy with weariness, but he fought on, to no avail. So intent was he that he failed to hear the approaching footsteps, failed to hear the opening door. Not until the light flashed in his eyes did he look up, startled and afraid.

"Finally woke up, did you?" Gus walked over and jerked him away from the boxes. "Tryin' to escape?" Gus booted him in the ribs.

With a knife, he slashed the ropes that bound Kip's ankles, then jerked him to his feet. Morgan's feet felt heavy, as though he wore diving boots. Gus put a hand between his shoulder blades and pushed him toward the door, and Morgan reached it in a stumbling run. The light of the flash shot past him, revealing the edge of a wash not fifty feet away.

A wash . . . or a canyon. Ten feet or two hundred. His stumbling run became a real run as he hurled himself, bending as far forward as he could, toward that edge and whatever awaited him.

There was a startled curse, then a yell, a momentary pause, and he veered sharply. A bullet slammed past him, and a gun barked. Kip left his feet in a long dive, hitting the edge in a roll that took him over the edge and sliding. He fell, brought up with a crunch and a mouthful of sand at the bottom of the wash. Lunging to his feet, wrists still bound behind him, he charged blindly into the darkness, down the wash. His feet were prickling with a thousand tiny needles at each step, but he ran, blindly, desperately, raw breath tearing at his lungs with each step.

Then, aware that his running was making too much sound, he slid to a stop, listening. There were running footsteps somewhere, and a shaft of light shot across the small plateau of a mine dump as the cabin door opened. He heard angry shouts; then a car started.

Kip Morgan had no idea where he was. His brain was pounding painfully, and he smarted from a dozen scratches and bruises. Yet he walked on, fighting his bonds with utter futility. The black maw of another wash opened on his right, and he turned into it. His feet found a steep path, and painstakingly he made his way up. Crouching to keep low, he crossed the skyline of the wash. He had no idea how far he walked, but he pushed on, wanting only distance between himself and his pursuers. As the first faint intimations of dawn lightened the sky, he crept around a boulder and, dropping to a sitting position, was almost immediately asleep.

The hot morning sun awakened him, and he staggered to his feet, aware of a dull throbbing in his hands. Twisting to get a look at them, he saw they were badly swollen and slightly blue. Frightened by the look of them, he looked around. Judging by the sun, he was on the eastern slope of a mountain. All about was desert, with no evidence of life anywhere. Not a sound disturbed the stillness of the morning.

Turning, he started to cross a shoulder of the mountain, sure he would find something on the western side. He must have been brought across to the eastern side during the night.

His mouth was dry, and he realized the intense heat, although only nine or ten o'clock was having its effect. Stumbling over and through the rocks, he saw a stretch of road. It was the merest trail with no tracks upon it, but it had to go somewhere, so he followed it. When he had walked no more than a mile, he rounded a turn in the road and found himself at an abandoned mine. There was a ramshackle hoist house and gallows frame. He stumbled toward it.

The door hung on rusty hinges, and a rusty cable hung from the shiv wheel. As he neared the buildings, a pack rat scurried away from the door.

The tracks of several small animals led toward the wall of the mountain beyond the small ledge on which the mine stood. Following them, he found a trickle of water running from a rusty pipe thrust into the wall. When he had drunk, he walked back to the hoist house, searching for something with which to cut his bonds. There was always, around such places, rusty tools, tin cans, all manner of castoffs.

On the floor was the blade of a round-point shovel.

Dropping to his knees, he backed his feet toward the shovel and got it between them. Holding it with his feet, he began to saw steadily. The pain was excruciating, but stubbornly he refused to ease off even for a moment, and after a few minutes the rope parted, and he stripped the pieces from his wrists. He brought his hands around in front of him and stared at them.

They were grotesquely swollen, puffed like a child's boxing gloves, with a tight band around his wrists showing where the ropes had pressed into his flesh. Returning to the spring, he dropped on his knees and held his wrists under the cold, dripping water.

For a long time, he knelt, uncertain how much good it was doing but enjoying the feel of the cold water. Slowly, very gently, he began to massage his hands. Finally, he gave up.

Taking a long drink, he turned away from the mine, glancing about for a weapon. He found a short length of rusted drill steel. He thrust it into his belt and headed down the road, carrying his arms bent at the elbows and his hands shoulder high because they hurt less that way. After he had walked a few miles, they began to feel better. A few steps farther, he glimpsed a paved highway, and the first truck along picked him up. "Not supposed to carry anybody," the trucker said, "but you look like you could use help. Filling station at the edge of town. Have to drop you there."

Back in Marcy's room, he ran the basin full of warm water to soak his hands. After a while, they began to feel better, and some of the swelling was gone. As they soaked, he considered the situation.

So far, he had learned little, but he seemed to have upset Villani and his men. No doubt they believed he knew more than he did. He was positive they had murdered Tom Marcy, but he had no evidence of any description beyond the presence of a pin-striped suit, which might or might not be Tom's.

He might go and swear out a warrant for kidnaping

and assault, but proving it would be something else with the kind of lawyers Villani would have.

What did he know? Three men had disappeared, at least two of them after answering ads to the warehouse. Vin Richards had been murdered, and undoubtedly the police were investigating that. Private detectives were not always popular with the police, but Vin Richards had himself been a police officer and a popular one. He had friends on the force who would not forget.

Digging out the clippings again, he studied them and once more he studied the clipping about the fire. That alone failed to fit. What could be the connection?

Suddenly, it hit him. What if the body in the fire had not been the owner, as was believed? *What if the owner was involved in a plot to rook the insurance companies? With Villani supplying the bodies?*

What about identification procedures? Fingerprints, teeth, measurements? Had the authorities checked out the bodies, or had they simply taken them for what they seemed to be? What did he mean, *bodies*? He had but one fire. Yet suppose there had been more?

Hastily, he dried his hands and took up the phone, dialing the number of the newspaper that published the item. In a matter of minutes, he had the name of the insurance company concerned. The city editor asked, "What's the problem? Is there anything wrong up there?"

Morgan hesitated. The papers had always given him a fair shake during his fighting days, and some of their reporters were better investigators than he was and had ready access to the files.

"I'm not sure, but something smells to high heaven, and somebody is so upset over my nosing around that they've given me a lot of trouble. Three men have disappeared off skid row in the last few months, and somebody doesn't seem to want it investigated."

"Who is this talking?"

"Kip Morgan. I used to be a fighter; now I'm a private investigator."

"I remember you. How about sending a man over to get your story?"

"Uh-uh. Just have somebody quietly check out George Villani, and two strongarm boys named Gus and Vinson." He mentioned the clippings he had found and the fire. Then he gave them the address of the warehouse. "It isn't much, but enough to make me think this may be insurance fraud."

As he hung up, he reflected with satisfaction that now, if anything happened to him, the newspapers at least would have a lead. He needed fifteen minutes by cab to the offices of the insurance company. He had heard a good deal of Neal Stoska, the insurance company's detective.

Stoska was a thin, angular man of fifty-odd, with shrewd, thoughtful eyes. "What is it, you wish to know?" He leaned back in his swivel chair, studying Kip's face, then his still-swollen hands.

"Your company insured a building up in Bakersfield that had a fire a short time ago. Is that right?"

"No," Stoska replied. "We insured Leonard Buff, the man who was burned. Tri-State insured the building. Why do you ask?"

"I'm working on something, and there seems to be a connection. Did it look all right to you? I mean, did you sense anything phony about it?"

Stoska was impatient. "Morgan, we can't discuss anything like that with just anybody who walks into this office. If I did suspect anything wrong, we'd be in no position to talk about it until we had some semblance of a case. Have you information for us?"

"Listen . . ." Kip sat back in his chair and told his story from the beginning. The Marcy case, the disappearance of Russell and Day, and what had happened to him. "It's a wild yarn," he added, "but it's true, and I could use some help."

"Your idea is that Marcy's body was in the fire?"

"No, I believe it was Russell's body. I think Marcy discovered something accidentally. My hunch is that he waited in the café for Russell when Slim applied for the job. Slim never came back, and it is possible Marcy saw Villani near the warehouse or with one of the men from the building. Something aroused his suspicions, and he was a man who loved his sister. In fact, his love for her was the only real thing in his life."

"It's all guesswork," Stoska agreed, "but good guesswork. You had something you wanted me to check?"

"A recheck, possibly. It is the size of Slim Russell and the body you found. Slim was a war veteran, so you can probably get his size that way or from the police. No doubt they picked him up from time to time, and they may have a description."

Stoska reached for the phone and at the same time pressed a button and ordered the file on Buff. "I want all we have on him," he added. "Also, put through a call to Gordon at Tri-State and ask him to come over. Tell him it's important."

A voice sounded on the telephone, and Morgan smiled, for the sharp, somewhat nasal sound had to be Mooney. In reply to Stoska's question, Mooney read off a brief description of Slim Russell. When Stoska hung up, he looked over at Morgan. "It fits," he said. "At least, it's close, very close."

Kip's cab dropped him at Marilyn Marcy's apartment, and he went up fast. She was alone, but dressed to go out.

"What is it?" She crossed the room to him. "You've found him? He's . . . he's dead, is that it?"

"Take it easy." He dropped into a chair. "Fix me a drink, will you? Anything wet." She was frightened of what he had come to tell her, and the activity might relieve the situation. "No, I haven't found him, but you have talked too much."

"I've talked?" She turned on him. "I've done no such thing! Why, I've—"

"Fix that drink and come over here. You did talk, and your talking got Vin Richards killed, and it almost got me killed. Right after you left my room, a guy attacked me with a knife in my hotel room. That was your doing, honey."

"That's nonsense! I told no one!"

"What about George?"

"What about him? Of course, I told him. I've told him everything. I'm engaged to him."

"You won't be for long," he replied grimly. "Now just

sit down and get this straight the first time. I haven't time to waste, and I don't want to go into any involved explanations. When I get through talking," he accepted the drink, "you'll probably call me a liar, but that's neither here nor there. You hired me to do a job."

"I don't like the way you talk," she said coldly, "and I don't like you. You're fired!"

"All right, I'm fired, but I am still on this case because it has become mighty personal since I last talked to you. Nobody puts the arm on me and gets away with it.

"Now just listen. You talked all right. You talked to George Villani about hiring Richards, and within a few days, Richards is dead. You told him about me, and somebody tried to kill me. Who else could have known where I was? Or that I was even hired? Who else knew about Richards?

"And get this: If your brother is dead, it was Villani who killed him or had him killed."

She sat down abruptly, her face pale, eyes wide. She tasted her drink and put it down. "I don't know what's the matter with me. I never drink scotch." She looked at him. "It just doesn't add up. How could George be involved? George didn't even know about Tom, as I'd never told him. And why should he kill him? Why should he kill anybody?"

"Tom loved you. You were his little sister." Morgan watched her over the glass, and he could see she was thinking now. Her anger and astonishment had faded. "What if Tom saw you with somebody he knew was bad? Don't ask me how he knew, but Tom Marcy had been around, and he was always skating along the thin edge of the underworld. People down there hear things and they see things and nobody notices them, they're just a bunch of outcasts and drunks.

"I don't believe," he added, "that Villani knew Tom Marcy was your brother. If he knew him it was only as somebody who was interfering. Or that's how it could have been at first. When you told him about Richards and your brother being missing he may have put two and two together."

Briefly he explained but said nothing about talking to the newspapers or the insurance company. "What does Villani do?" he asked then.

"Do?" she shrugged. "He's a contractor of some sort. I have never talked business with him, but he seems prosperous, has a beautiful home in Beverly Hills, and owns some business property there."

"Well, don't ask him any questions now, just be your own sweet, beautiful self and leave him to me."

The buzzer sounded and she came quickly to her feet. "That's George now. He is coming to pick me up and I'd forgotten!"

"Don't let it bother you, and be the best actress you can be. If he got suspicious now he might start on you. When a man kills as casually as he has he never knows when to stop."

There was a tap on the door and Marilyn crossed to it, admitting George Villani.

He was a big man, broad-shouldered and deep in the chest. His eyes went to Morgan and changed perceptibly. "George? I want you to meet Kip Morgan. He's the detective who is looking for my brother."

"How do you do?" Villani was all charm. "Having any luck?"

"Sure." Unable to resist the needle, Morgan added, "We hope to break the case in a matter of hours."

Villani smiled, but there was no humor in it. "Isn't that what detectives always say?"

Kip Morgan was irritated. He did not like this big, polished, easy-looking man, and some devil within him made him push it further. He had been hit, dragged, and banged around. A good suit of clothes had been ruined and he had a knot on the back of his head. All his resentment began to well to the surface. He knew it was both foolish and dangerous but he could not resist baiting him. Maybe it was this big man who was dating Marilyn, and maybe it was something else.

"Maybe," he replied carelessly. "I don't know what detectives say. I know this one is a cinch. This guy," he was enjoying Marilyn's tenseness, "has been a dope all along. We think he's been supplying bodies to folks who want to collect insurance. He's been getting his bodies off skid row where there are men nobody is supposed to be interested in."

"Seems rather farfetched," Villani said, no suggestion of a smile now. "Wouldn't the insurance companies become suspicious?"

Kip felt good. He had never been much of a hand at beating around the bush. He was a direct action man and he liked to bull right into the middle of things and keep crowding until a crook acted without thinking. Careful planning is often foolproof until the planner is pushed so fast he has to ad lib his actions and his talking.

"Of course, the insurance companies are suspicious. I helped to make them suspicious. So are the newspapers. Now all we have to do is pick up the boys this man has been working with and make them talk. Once they let their hair down, we will have the man behind it, and fast."

Villani did not like that. He did not like it a bit. Suddenly, he did not want to be going on a date, and it showed. Villani had no reason to believe he was suspected, but he would want to cover up fast, and his next move would be to rid himself of the two who might talk. That done he would be in the clear.

Villani had come to the same conclusion. He turned to Marilyn. "I had no idea you were so busy. Why don't we just skip dinner tonight? I've a few things that need attention and you could finish your conference with Mr. Morgan."

"Why . . . !" Marilyn started to speak but Morgan interrupted.

"That would be a help, although I don't like to intrude. There are several things we have to discuss."

"Fine!" Villani was relieved. "I'll call you, dear." He turned to Morgan. "I wish you success. I hope you find your men."

As the door closed behind Villani, Marilyn turned to Morgan. "He couldn't get away too fast, could he? What is the trouble?"

"No trouble for us. As for Gus and Vinson, I wouldn't

want to be in their shoes. He's going to kill them, you know. He'll be headed right for them, right now!"

He finished his drink and got up, real regret in his eyes. "There's nothing I'd like better than to spend the evening with you, but I must follow him."

She caught up her coat. "Then what are we waiting for? Let's go!"

"Not you," he protested. "You can't go."

"Tom Marcy was my brother," she said, "and I am going. If George Villani is all you say he is I want to see for myself."

He hesitated no longer and had already delayed longer than he should. "It's your funeral, and it could be just that. Remember, I warned you this was no place for you."

Villani was just starting his car when they reached the street, and Marilyn tugged Morgan back into the shadows by the door. "Come on! My car's in the driveway!"

As they turned into the street Villani's car was rounding the corner into the boulevard and traveling fast. Following at a distance, they saw Villani turn off the boulevard and head for his own place.

"We'll switch to my car," Morgan suggested. "He will recognize yours."

They made the switch, then sat in darkness waiting for Villani to emerge. Both were tense. Before this night was over there could be serious trouble, for Villani was not a man who was willing to lose. He had too much at stake.

Gus was dangerous, and so was Vinson, in his own

way, and he had no business allowing Marilyn to come although he doubted if he could have stopped her and had not wasted breath trying.

Villani left his house on the run and jumped into his car. He did a fast U-turn in the middle of the street, and his headlights sprayed across their car. Kip, seeing what was to come had ducked down in the seat pulling Marilyn down with him so they could not be seen. Her lips were invitingly near so he kissed them, quickly but effectively.

When the lights were gone he moved out from the curb and rounded the corner on two wheels. After half a mile Kip fell behind another car, switched his lights to dim and put on another hat. Gus knew all about his hats but it was unlikely he'd had the chance or thought to mention it to Villani.

Villani seemed to glance back once but gave no indication that he knew he was being followed, and they chanced it. He headed over the pass toward the Valley and Kip tailed him at a safe distance.

At a filling station near a motel where there were booths, Kip swung to the curb. "Take this number and call Stoska. Tell him what has happened and that we're headed for an abandoned mine in this vicinity—" he drew a quick circle on the map and handed it to her, "and ask him to get hold of the sheriff and get him out there!"

Marilyn slid from the seat and even as she took her first step away, Kip was gone, traveling fast after Villani. He overtook him as he was swinging off into the hills, and followed, his lights on bright again. After a short distance he turned into a side road that led to some houses, switched to his dimmers again, and backed out, following again. He turned again, then followed without lights.

Gus and Vinson must still be at the mine, or Villani was expecting them soon. When the car ahead turned off on the mine road Kip followed but a little farther, then turned off on some hard-packed sand among the cacti and parked. From a hidden panel under the dash he took a .45 caliber Colt automatic and followed up the hill. His car was now hidden and to get out, Villani would have to come this way.

All was still at the old mine. The car stood in the open space near the gallows frame, but the delivery truck was nowhere in sight. There was a light in the shack.

Kip Morgan moved into the darkness of the hoist house and waited. Without doubt, Gus and Vinson would be there. Villani had made his rendezvous at a place where their bodies were not likely to be discovered. He could shoot first and fast, then drop the bodies down the old shaft and drive away. The scheme had every chance of succeeding.

What little Kip knew would not constitute evidence tying Villani to the crimes. Unless more evidence could be discovered or Gus and Vinson talked, Villani would go free or not even be accused.

He heard the car for several minutes before it arrived. It was the truck.

Vinson and Gus got out. They whispered together for a minute or two, then walked to the shack and went in.

Kip moved away from the hoist house and to the wall of the shack. Voices sounded and he pressed his ear to a crack.

"I don't know," Vinson was saying, sullenly, "so don't blame me. He's a hard guy to hold."

Kip found a crack and peered in. Vinson was seated at the table and Villani was pacing. On the shelf behind Vinson lay a piece of drill steel. Vinson's eyes were on his hands. "Gus was there, too!" he protested. "Don't blame me!"

Where was Gus?

Villani stopped pacing, and his hand reached for the drill steel. He lifted it clear off the shelf and—

Gravel crunched at the corner of the house, and Morgan turned sharply. A gun flamed not a dozen feet away, and only his sudden movement saved him. Instantly, he fired in return. Gus caught himself in midstride and fired again. That bullet thudded into the wall, and Kip fired a second and third time and Gus went down on the gravel.

Flattening against the wall, Morgan peered through the crack. Instantly, he turned his head away, sick to his stomach. There was no sign of Villani inside the shack, but the door stood slightly open. Vinson was surely dead for no man could survive a skull crushed as was his.

Villani had sent Gus out while he got rid of Vinson, planning to finish Gus later or when he returned. The shots would have warned him that Gus had found something or somebody. Now Villani would know he had at least one man to kill, possibly two.

The slightest move might bring a shot. Kip moved

despite the risk, going toward the front of the building, reasoning that Villani would come around the other side as Gus had done. At the front of the house, he took three quick steps to the truck and crouched behind it.

A slow minute dribbled away, then another. Every sense alert, he waited, but there was no nearby sound. Faintly, somewhere far off, he could hear a car. The sound seemed miles away in the clear night air.

"Morgan!" It was Villani. "Is that you out there? Let's talk business!"

Kip kept very still, waiting. For a few seconds there was no sound, then Villani spoke persuasively. "Morgan, you're being foolish. What Marilyn can pay isn't worth the risk. I've done well and I've got money. A thousand dollars if you just drive away and forget all this!"

Morgan offered no reply. He could dimly see the area from which the voice came. Only Gus's body was visible, if Gus was actually dead. He had no way of knowing.

"A thousand dollars is a lot of money. You've not found Marcy so all you'll get is expense money. I am offering a thousand dollars. You say the word and I'll toss it to you."

"And have you shoot me while I'm in the open? No, thank you!"

Deliberately, he was prolonging the discussion to better locate Villani. Also the sheriff should be on his way.

"I'll wrap it around a stone and toss it to you. You're in no danger."

"You're talking peanuts," Kip said. "Marilyn Marcy

might not pay that much but the insurance company will."

There was a brief silence. Was he moving closer? In the vague gray light it was hard to see. There was no moon, only the stars.

"Five thousand might sound better." Morgan held his mouth close to the car, hoping to give it a muffled sound.

Suddenly they both heard the crunch of feet on gravel, and Kip looked around. He started to yell a warning but she was already within sight. Marilyn Marcy was walking fast and she was unaware of the situation.

"Marilyn!" Kip yelled. *"Get back! Get back quick!"*

"No, you don't!" Triumph was hoarse in his tone. "Stay right where you are or I'll kill you!"

Villani was in control, unless—

Kip left the ground in a running dive for the shelter of the building. A gun roared, a hasty shot that missed, and he fired at a dark shadow looming near the corner of the building and heard his shot ring on metal, an old wheelbarrow turned on its side! And then Villani came up from the ground several feet away, and they both fired.

Both should have scored hits and neither did, but Kip felt a sharp tug at his sleeve, and then Villani's descending gun barrel knocked his gun from his hand. As the gun fell he knotted his fist, whipping it forward and up and Villani took it with a grunt, then threw a short hook to the neck, purposely keeping the blow low to avoid hurting his tender fist. The blow staggered Villani, and

Kip followed through with his elbow, over, then back, slamming Villani against the building. His gun roared into the ground, the bullet kicking gravel over Kip's shoes. Another blow to the mid-section and Villani dropped his gun, reached to grab it off the ground and met Kip's knee in the face. Villani staggered forward and Kip rabbit-punched him behind the neck and the bigger man fell.

Kip scooped both guns off the ground, the fallen man gasping for breath.

Marilyn ran to him. "Kip? Are you hurt? Are you all right?"

"Did you get word to them?"

"They're coming now. I can hear the cars." She came closer. "They told me to wait but I thought I might help. Was I wrong?"

He looked at her, exasperated, then he shrugged. "No, you were all right. It was okay."

Villani started to get up.

"Stay where you are," Morgan advised. "Lie down flat. There . . . that's better."

"That offer stands." Villani's words were muffled by battered lips. "I've got twenty thousand here. I'll give you half to let me go."

"What became of Tom Marcy?"

"Suppose you find out? You've nothing on me!"

Two cars were pulling into the yard. "No? I've murder against you. You killed Vinson. Your fingerprints will be on that drill steel you used to kill him."

Stoska, Mooney, and a half dozen other men came

from the cars, pulling Villani to his feet. During the hurried explanations Marilyn stood beside Kip.

He was beginning to feel it now, sore in every muscle, his swollen fists hurting from the fighting and all the tension of the past few days.

"We checked that burned body again," Stoska said, "and there were discrepancies, although they were few. Now we're going to check several other doubtful cases."

Mooney came over to Marilyn. "We found your brother. It was Morgan's tip that started us looking. I'm afraid . . . well . . ."

"He's dead?"

"No, he's not dead, but he's in bad shape. He must have had a run-in with Gus. He took a bad beating and he's in a hospital. They found him last night when a couple of wino friends of his came to the police. They found him and were taking care of him, but they thought he'd just gotten drunk and fallen. When he didn't regain consciousness they got worried and came to us."

"He's all right? Is he conscious?"

"He's conscious, but I won't lie to you. He's in bad shape." Mooney glanced at Kip. "He spotted you. He had been staying away from his old hideouts, tailing Villani and his boys. He saw you in some grease joint across from the warehouse. He almost came to you."

"I wish he had." Kip took Marilyn's arm. "Let's go home."

When they walked almost to the car he commented, "That's why his eyes looked familiar. They were like your eyes. He was sitting there all the time and must have heard me asking questions of the waitress. He couldn't have known why I was interested. Let's go see him."

"Tomorrow. He will be asleep now and sleep will do him more good than anything else. In the meantime you need to get cleaned up, rest a little and have a drink."

"Well," he agreed, "if you twisted my arm."

"Consider it twisted," she said.

AUTHOR'S NOTE

STAY OUT OF MY NIGHTMARE

The idea that poverty is a cause of crime is a lot of nonsense. It is one of those clichés that is accepted because it seems logical.

Crimes are committed by people who have some money and want more.

More often they are committed by somebody who wants to have money to flash around, to buy fancy clothes, or spend on women, drugs, or whiskey.

In proportion to their numbers, there are just as many poor people who are honest as there are rich people who are.

Dashiell Hammett once commented that he had never known a man capable of turning out first-rate work in a trade, profession, or art who was a professional criminal.

This may have been his experience, but there have been exceptions to that rule.

STAY OUT OF MY NIGHTMARE

When I walked in, Bill was washing a glass. "There's a guy looking for you. A fellow about twenty-five or so. He said to tell you it was Bradley."

"What did he want? Did he say?"

My eyes swept the bar to see if any of my friends were around. None of them was, but about four or five stools away sat a fellow with slicked-back hair and a pasty face. He looked as if he were on the weed.

"He wanted to see you, and he wanted you bad."

Bill brought a bourbon and soda, and I thought it over. Sam Bradley had been a corporal in my platoon overseas, but we had not seen each other since our return. We had talked over the phone but had never gotten together. I knew that if he wanted me badly, there was something definitely wrong.

A nice guy, Sam was. A good, reliable man and one of

the most decent fellows I'd ever met. "I'll look him up," I said. "He's a right guy, and maybe he's in trouble."

"You never can tell." The man with the sickly face intervened. "Right guys can turn wrong. I wouldn't trust my best friend."

The interruption irritated me. "You know your friends better than I do," I told him.

He looked around, and there was nothing nice about his expression. Looking directly into his eyes made me change my mind about him. This was no casual bar rat with a couple of drinks under his belt and wanting to work off a grouch. This guy was poison.

That look I'd seen before, and the man who had it was usually a killer. It was the look of a man who understands only brutality and cruelty. "That sounded like an invitation," he said.

"Take it any way you like. I didn't ask you into this conversation."

"You're a big guy." He watched me like a snake watching a bird. "And I don't like big guys. They always think they've got an edge. Maybe I should bring you down to my size."

He was getting under my skin. I had no idea of anything like trouble when I walked into the Plaza. Now Sam Bradley was on my mind, and I'd no idea of messing around with such a specimen as this. "Your size?" I said. "Nothing is that small."

When he came off that stool, I knew he meant business. Some men bluff. This torpedo wasn't bluffing. He was going to kill me. He was only a step away when I saw the shiv. He was holding it low down in his right hand, and nobody in the bar could see it but me. He might be on the weed or all coked up, but he was still smart.

"Put the shiv away, chum." I had not moved from my stool. "You come at me with that and they'll be putting you on ice before dark. I don't like steel."

He never said a word, but just looked at me from those flat, ugly eyes. Bill heard me speak of the knife and came down the bar, always ready to stop anything that meant trouble and to stop it before it started.

"Don't do it, pal," I said. "They've got a new carpet on the deck. I don't want to smear it with you."

He came so fast he nearly got me. Nearly, but not quite. His right foot was forward, and when that knife licked out like a snake's tongue, I chopped his wrist to deflect the blade. My hand closed on his wrist, jerking him toward me, off balance. Then I shoved back quick and at the same time caught him behind the knee with my toe.

He went down hard, the knife flying from his hand as his head thudded against the brass rail. Picking up the knife, I tossed it to Bill. "Put that in your collection. I've got mine."

Getting off the barstool I walked into the sunlight. Cops might come around, and there was no use straining Mooney's friendship further. Grabbing a cab, I headed for Bradley's place.

It was a single off Wilshire and a nice place. When I pressed the bell, nothing happened. Ellen must be shopping. Bradley was probably at work. I tried the bell again for luck; I was turning away when I saw the edge of a business card sticking out from beneath the door. It was none of my business, but I stooped and pulled it out. It read, Edward Pollard, Attorney-at-Law.

Under it in a crabbed, tight-fisted script were the words:

> *Was here at eight as suggested. If you return before 10* P.M. *meet me at Merrano's. Don't do anything or talk to anyone until I see you.*

Pollard was a shyster who handled bail bonds and a few criminal cases. We had never met, however. I knew Merrano's, a sort of would-be night club on a side street, a small club but well appointed and catering to a clientele on the fringe of the underworld.

What impressed me about the card was that neither Sam nor his wife had been home since the previous night. Where, then, was Sam? And what had become of Ellen?

Reaching the walk, I thrust the card into my coat pocket.

At that moment, a car wheeled to the curb, and a man spilled out in a run. Brushing by me without a glance, he went to Bradley's door. He did not ring the bell or knock, but stooped quickly and began looking for something on the step or under the door. Not finding it, he got to his feet and tried the door. Only then did he ring the bell. Even as he did so, he was turning away as if he were sure it would not be answered.

He gave me a quick glance as he saw me watching him, then went on by. "Hello, Pollard," I said.

He stopped as if struck and turned sharply. His quick, ratty eyes went over me. "Who are you? I never saw you before."

His voice was quick and nervous, and I was talking to a very worried man.

"I was just wondering why a man would try a door before ringing the bell."

"It's none of your business!" he said testily. "It strikes me you've little to do, standing around and prying into other people's affairs."

He did not walk away, however. He was waiting to see what my angle was. So far, he had not decided what I meant to him or what to do about it.

For that matter, neither had I. Actually, I'd no business bothering him. Sam and Ellen might be visiting. There was no sense in building elaborate plots from nothing, yet the fact that Sam had come looking for me and that I had found the card of a man like Pollard under his door was disturbing.

Two facts had been evident. Pollard had not expected Sam to be home, and he had wanted to pick up his card. He could not have been looking for anything else.

If Pollard knew Sam was not at home, it might imply he knew where he was. And why go to all this trouble to pick up a business card unless something was wrong?

"Look, pal," I said, "suppose you tell me where Sam is and why you were so sure Sam was not home. Come on, give!"

"None of your business!" he snapped, and was getting into the car before I spoke.

"Sam Bradley is a friend of mine. I hope nothing has

happened to him or will happen. From your actions, I am beginning to wonder, and if anything has happened, I am going to the police. Then I shall start asking questions myself, and buddy, I'll get answers!"

He rolled down the window and leaned as if to speak, then started off with a jerk. There was just time to catch his license number before he got away.

Standing in the street, I thought it over. I had nothing to go on but suspicions, and those without much foundation. Telling myself I was a fool and that Sam would not appreciate it, I went back to the door. The lock was no trick for me, as I'd worked as a locksmith for several years, and in something over a minute, I was inside.

The apartment was empty. Hoping Sam would forgive me, I made a hurried check. The beds were unslept in, the garbage unemptied, yet there were no dirty dishes.

Looking through the top drawer of the bureau, I found something. It was a stack of neatly pressed handkerchiefs, but some had been laid aside and something taken from between them. There was a small spot of oil and the imprint of something that had been lying there for some time. That something might have been a .45 army Colt.

My thoughts were interrupted by the rattling of a key in the door. Hurriedly closing the door, I reached the bedroom door just in time to see the door close behind a girl.

Her eyes caught me at the same instant. She was uncommonly pretty, and that contributed to my surprise, for I had seen Ellen Bradley's picture, and this was not she.

My eyes followed as she moved to pick up her dropped bag, and then I looked up into the muzzle of a .32 automatic. "Who are you?" she demanded. "And what are you doing here?"

It had been a neat trick, as smooth a piece of deceptive action as I'd ever seen. Her bag had been dropped purposely to distract my attention. There was nothing deceiving about that gun. It was steady, and it was ugly. Whoever she was, she was obviously experienced and had a quick, agile brain. "Who are you?" she repeated.

"Let's say that I am an old army friend of Sam Bradley's."

Her eyes hardened. "Oh? So you admit you're one of them?" Before I could reply, she said, "I'll just call the police."

"It might be the best idea. But why don't you put that gun down and let's talk this over. Sam left word he wanted to see me, and if you're a friend of his, we should compare notes. When he said he was in trouble, I hurried right over."

"I'll bet you did! Now back against the wall. I am going to use the telephone, and if you have any doubts whether I'll use this gun, just start something."

I had no doubts.

She took the receiver from the cradle and dialed a number. I watched the spots she dialed and filed it away for future reference. From where I stood, I heard a voice speak but could distinguish no words.

"Yes, Harry, I'm at Sam's . . . no sign of him, but

there's somebody else here." She listened, and I could hear someone talking rapidly. She looked me over coolly. "Big fellow, over six feet, I'd say, and broad-shouldered. Gray suit, gray shirt, blue tie. Good-looking but stupid. And," she added, "he got in without a key."

She listened a moment. "Hold him? Of course. I'll not miss, either. I always shoot for the stomach; they don't like it there."

"I don't like it anywhere," I said.

She replaced the telephone. "You might as well sit down. They won't be here for ten minutes." She studied me as if I were some kind of insect. "A friend of Sam's, is it? I know how friendly you guys are. What are you trying to do? Cut in?"

"Cut in on what?" I asked.

She smiled, not a nice smile. "Subtle as a truck. As if you didn't know!"

"And who," I asked, "is Harry?"

"He's a friend of mine, and from what he said over the phone, I think he knows you. And he doesn't like you."

"I'm worried. That really troubles me. Now give. What's this all about? Where's Sam? Where's Ellen? What's happened to them?"

"Don't play games, mister."

Her tone was bitter, and it puzzled me. Not to say that I wasn't puzzled about the whole action. Sam Bradley was in plenty of trouble, without a doubt, but what sort of trouble?

Although something in her attitude made me wonder if she was not friendly to Sam and Ellen, she had come in with a key, and she had not called the police. Moreover, she was handling the situation with vastly more assurance than the average woman, or man, for that matter. It was an assurance that spoke of familiarity with guns and the handlers of guns. Another thing I knew: The number she called had not been that of the police department.

"Look," I said, "if you're a friend of Sam's, we'd better compare notes. When he left here, he took a gun. If Sam has a gun, you can bet he's desperate, because it isn't like him."

At the mention of the gun, her face tightened. "A gun? How do you know?"

I explained. "Now tell me," I finished by asking, "what is this all about?"

Before she could reply, hurried footsteps sounded on the walk, and she stepped back to the door. She opened it, but in the moment before she did, her eyes showed uncertainty, even fear.

Three men stepped into the room, and when I saw them, every fiber turned cold. There wasn't a cop in the country who wouldn't love to get his hands on George Homan. He was the first man through the door, and when I saw him, I lost the last bit of hope that this girl might be friendly. No girl who knew Homan could be a friend to any decent man. Homan was a brutal killer, utterly cold-blooded, utterly vicious.

The second man was tall, with a wiry body and broad shoulders, his features sharp, his eyebrows a straight black bar above his eyes. Then I saw the last man through the door, and he was my friend from the bar, the one who tried to knife me. Now I knew why he wanted my scalp. It was because he had heard me say I was going to find out what Sam's trouble was.

"This is the man, Harry," the girl was saying. "He claims he's a friend of Sam's."

Harry walked over to me, his bright, rodentlike eyes on mine, the hatred in them sharpened by triumph.

"Nice company you keep." I looked past him at the girl. "Did he ever show you the frogsticker he carries? Now I know where you stand, honey. No friend of Sam's would know this kind of rat!"

"Shut your face!" Harry yelled, his mouth twisting. As he spoke, he swung.

It was the wrong thing to do, for gun or no gun, I was in no mood to get hit. For a second, Harry had stepped between me and the gun, but as he stepped in, throwing his right, I dropped my left palm to his shoulder, stopping the punch; then I threw an uppercut from the hip into his belly that had the works on it.

His mouth fell open, and his face turned green as he gasped for air.

Before he could fall, I closed with him, shoving him hard at Homan. The third man I did not know, but George was no bargain, and I wanted him out of the play. I went for my gun fast. Hatchet face yanked his, too, but neither of us fired. We stood there, staring at each other. It was a Mexican standoff. If either fired at that range, both would die.

The girl's gun had dropped to her side. She seemed petrified, staring at me as if a light had flashed in her eyes.

Homan had backed away from Harry, who was groaning on the floor. Hate was in Homan's eyes. "Kill him, Pete! Kill him!"

"Sure"—I was cool now—"if he kills me, we ride the same slide to hell. Shoot and I'll take you all with me. I'm a big guy, and if you don't place them right, it's going to take a lot of lead, and until I fold, I'm going to be shooting."

Harry was on the floor, living up to expectations. He was being disgustingly sick. Homan stepped distastefully away from him. "I'm surprised, George." I was keeping an eye on Pete. "Playing games with a weed head. You know they're unreliable, and you're a big boy now."

"Who is this guy, George?" Pete's eyes were on me. "He's not fuzz."

"Harry had a run-in with him this morning. I saw it, but the guy didn't see me. Harry popped off, and this lug didn't like it. He's Kip Morgan."

That brought a sudden intake of breath from the girl, but my eyes were on Pete, as I was realizing Pete was top man here. Pete was my life insurance.

"That's right. I am Kip Morgan. If the name means anything to you, you'll know I am just the kind of damned fool who will shoot if you push me. Take that buzzard off the floor and back out of here. Back out fast."

Pete was a careful man, and Pete was not ready to die. Not yet.

"What if I say nothing doing? What if I tell you to beat it?"

"Then don't waste time—just start shooting. I'll get George and Harry, Pete, but I'll get you first. I don't know how good you are with that thing, but I've shot expert on every course I've run. No matter what happens after, you're cold turkey, and I'll bet a thousand bucks I can blow a kidney right out of your back from here."

"All right." I had guessed Pete would be smart. I'd gambled on it. "We'll go, but we'll do a retake on this one, Morgan. But there's one thing I want to know. What's your angle?"

"Sam Bradley was in my outfit overseas. He was a good guy and a good friend. Anything else?"

"All right. You've proved you're a great big lovable guy. Now get smart and bow out. There's no percentage for you."

"I didn't come into this for laughs," I said. "When Sam Bradley and his wife are back home and in the clear, then I'll bow out. Until then, I'm in."

"What if I told you he was dead?" Pete said. "And his wife, too?"

That brought another little sound from the girl. I was beginning to wonder about her and just where she belonged. "I wouldn't believe you unless I saw the bodies, and then I'd never rest until you three were dead or in the gas chamber."

"George?" Pete said. "Pick up Harry, put his arm over your shoulder, and walk him to the car. I'll follow. This is no place to settle this." He smiled at me. "There's more of us, and Morgan here has to move around. He can run, and he can hide, but we'll find him."

Homan picked up Harry and started for the door. Harry looked back at me, and his look gave me a chill. I would rather he'd said something.

Pete backed toward the door, keeping his gun on me. "You, too," I told the girl.

She started to protest, but I cut her short. "Get going! Do you think I want you around to shoot me in the back?

"And Pete? Play it smart. If Sam and his wife aren't back in their apartment by midnight, I'm coming for you. I will give you until then."

They went out, and the girl didn't look back. I felt sorry for her, but that might have been because she was pretty. She did not look like a crook, but then, who does?

When they had gone I started after them. I was no closer to knowing what it was all about. Whatever it was, Bradley and Ellen, if not already dead, were in danger. If Pete whoever-he-was was playing with men like George Homan and Harry, he was playing for keeps, and for money, big money.

Before I could move, I had to know what was going on, and I had to find out who the girl was and her connection. Actually, I'd little reason to care. She was a gun moll, as they used to call them, or tied in with it all somehow.

Come to think of it, there was a clue. It was her attitude toward Sam's army friends. What had she meant by her remarks?

Turning around, I began to give that apartment a going-over. In the writing desk, I got my first lead.

It was a circular, or rather, a stack of them. Beside

them was a bunch of envelopes and a list of names, several of which I recognized as veterans.

Opening the circular, I glanced over it.

BOOM DAYS BOOM AGAIN
Faro . . . CHUCKALUCK . . . Poker
CRAPS
Come one! Come all!
Proceeds to Wounded Veterans

Dropping into a chair, I read it through; an idea began to germinate.

Where there is gambling, there are sure-thing operators. They flock to money like bees to sugar, and unless I was mistaken in my man, Pete was a cinch player. Moreover, I had picked up some talk lately of various gamblers moving in on the vets and taking them for considerable loot. No doubt they had spotted their own players in the crowds and might even have been running the games themselves. Sam Bradley was on several veterans' committees.

Pete! . . . *Pete Merrano!* Owner of the Merrano Club! A bookie and small-time racketeer wanting to reach for the big time! Already he had a hand in the numbers and was reported to be financing the importation of cocaine, although keeping free of it himself.

Suppose somebody had brought Merrano in to operate their games? Known as an expert and occasionally donating money, they might have been gullible enough to invite him in. Suppose he had been skimming the games and Sam Bradley discovered it? No sooner did the idea come to mind than I was sure it was the answer.

Now I needed evidence. Leaving the apartment by the service entrance, I went down the back stairs. Once I reached my car, I checked over the list of names I had brought with me. One, Eugene Shidler, lived not far away. Starting my car, I swung around the corner and headed along the street.

Shidler came to the door in his shirt-sleeves with a newspaper in his hand. He was a short, stocky man, partly bald. Showing him the circular, I asked what he knew about it.

"Only what we all know. We need to raise money to give some of the boys a hand, and Earl Ramsey suggested a real, old-time gambling setup. It would last a week, sponsored by us. He said he knew just the man to handle it, a man who had a lot of gambling equipment he had taken in on a loan. He was pretty sure this man could also provide the dealers, equipment, and refreshments for a small cut of the proceeds.

"Naturally, it looked good to us. We had to do nothing at all when the games started but to come and bring our friends. As we were busy men, that was a big item. Time was the one thing none of us could spare."

"Pete Merrano?"

"He's the one." Shidler looked at me thoughtfully. "What's the matter? Is something wrong?"

There seemed to be something underlying his question, so I said, "Yes, I believe so, but first tell me how it all came out? Did the vets make money?"

"We cleared about a thousand dollars, although

some of the boys figured it should have been more. In fact, there was a lot of talk about something crooked, but shucks, you know Sam as well as I do! There isn't a crooked bone in his body!"

"You're right," I said, and then I laid it out for him, all I knew and what I suspected. "Sam and his wife have vanished completely. Merrano hinted that Sam was dead, but I don't believe that. Anyway, something has Merrano worried, and what it is I have no idea."

Shidler got to his feet. Angrily, he jerked the cigar from his mouth, staring at it with distaste. Glancing toward an inner door, he dropped to the sofa beside me. "If my wife hears of this, I'll never hear the last of it, but I got rooked in that game, but plenty! They took me for five hundred bucks. I owe that to Merrano."

"Then it makes sense. Merrano probably took the lot of you for plenty, and he's counting on you being good sports and keeping your mouths shut. I'd bet he took every one of you for at least as much as you lost."

He nodded. "I lost about a hundred, then drifted into a little side game that Pete was running. I dropped about forty more, then gambled on credit. Merrano holds my IOU for the five hundred."

"Get a few of the boys on the phone and do some checking. Tell them what the story is. Maybe we can get that money back. In the meantime, I am going to find out what became of Sam Bradley."

It was after nine when I returned to my car. The best thing was to talk to Mooney in homicide. He knew me and could start the wheels turning even though it lay outside his department. Although, I reflected, by this time it might not.

First, I would do some checking. There was Earl Ramsey, who had suggested Merrano to run the games and could be in it up to his neck. If Ramsey could be persuaded to tell what he knew, we might be on the track. Before anything else, I must think of Sam and Ellen.

It seemed strange to be riding down a brightly lit street, with all about me people driving to or from home, the theater, dinner, and to realize that somewhere among these thousands of buildings a man and his wife might be facing death. Yet without evidence I could do nothing, and all I had was a hunch that they were still alive.

Checking the list, I found Ramsey's name. The address was some distance away, but worth a visit. If Ramsey were not tied in with the crooks, he might talk.

It was a large, old-fashioned frame dwelling on a corner near a laundry. Parking the car, I got out and went up the steps. As there was a light in one of the rear rooms, I pressed the bell. Three times I rang with no response; then I saw the door was not quite closed. It was open by no more than a crack.

Had it been closed when I arrived? My impression was that it had. That meant someone had opened the door while I stood there! An eerie feeling crept over me, and suddenly I was wishing the street were not so dark. I rang again.

For the second time that day, I pushed open a door I had no right to touch. It swung open, and I peered into a dark living room. "Hello? Mr. Ramsey?"

Silence, then a subdued whispering, not voices but a surreptitious movement.

A clock ticked solemnly, and somewhere I could hear water running in a basin. Uncomfortably, I looked around me. The street was dark and empty except for my own car and another that was parked in darkness farther along the street. Momentarily distracted from the house, I stared at that car. I had not noticed it when I first drove up.

Suddenly, a hand from the darkness grasped my arm. I started to pull away, but the grip tightened. A voice from the shadows, a voice so old you could almost hear the wrinkles in it said, "Come in, won't you? Did you wish to see Earl?"

It was an old woman's voice, but there was something else in it that set my nerves on edge, and I am not easily bothered.

"Yes, I want to see him. Is he in?"

"He's in the kitchen. He came home to eat, and I put out a lunch for him. Maybe you would like something? A cup of coffee?"

The house was too warm, the air close and stuffy. She walked ahead of me toward a dim rectangle of doorway. "Just follow me. I never use the lights, but Earl likes them."

She led me along a bar hall and pushed a door open. As the door opened, I saw Earl Ramsey.

He was seated at a kitchen table, his chin propped on his hand, the other hand against the side of his face. There was a cup before him and an untasted sandwich on his plate. He was staring at me as I came through the door.

"Are you Mr. Ramsey?"

He neither spoke nor blinked, and I stepped past the old woman and stopped abruptly. I was staring into the eyes of a dead man.

Turning, overcome with horror, I looked at the old woman who was puttering among some dirty dishes. "Don't mind him," she said. "Earl was never one for talking. Only when he takes the notion."

My skin crawled. She turned her head and stared at me with expressionless eyes. Gray hair straggled about a face that looked old enough to have worn out two bodies, and her clothing was drab, misshapen, and soiled. She fumbled at her pocket, staring at me.

It gave me the creeps. The hot, stuffy room and this aged and obviously imbecilic woman and her dead son.

Stepping past the table, I saw the knife. It had been driven into the left side of his back, driven up from below as he sat at the table, and driven to the hilt. I touched the hand of Earl Ramsey. It was cold.

The old woman was puttering among the dishes, unaware and unconcerned.

"Have you a telephone?"

She neither stopped nor seemed to hear me, so I stepped past her to the hallway and found a switch. The telephone was on a stand in the corner. I needed but a minute to get Mooney.

"Morgan here. Can you come right over? Dead? Sure he's dead! Yes, I'll wait."

Walking back to the kitchen, I looked around, but

there was nothing that might be a clue. Nothing I could see, but then I wasn't a cop. Only, I was willing to bet the killer had come in the door behind Ramsey, dropped a hand on his shoulder, then slammed the knife home. The knife was a dead ringer for the one I'd taken from Harry only that morning.

Several steps led down from that open door behind Ramsey to a small landing. It was dark down there, and a door that would probably let a man out into the narrow space between the house and the laundry next door. I went down the steep steps and grasped the knob to see for myself.

There was a whisper of movement in the darkness, and I started to turn. Something smashed against my skull, and my knees folded under me. As I fell, my arm swept out and grabbed a man around the knees. There was an oath and then a second blow that drove the last vestige of consciousness from me. I seemed to be sliding down a steep slide into unbelievable blackness.

Yet even as consciousness faded, I heard a tearing of cloth and the sound of a police siren, far away.

When next I became aware of anything, I was lying on a damp, hard floor in absolute darkness. Fear washed over me in a cold wave. With a lunge, I came to a sitting position. My head swam with pain at the sudden movement, and I put both hands to it, finding a laceration across my scalp from one of the blows. My hair was matted with blood. Struggling to my knees, I was still shaky, and my thoughts refused to become coherent.

The events of the night were a jumble, the hot, close air of the kitchen, the hallway, the dead man, the weird old woman, my call to the police, and the blows on the head.

Somehow I had stumbled into something uglier than expected. A man had been murdered. Perhaps Bradley, too, was dead.

Feeling for my shoulder holster, I discovered my gun was missing. That was to be expected. The floor on which I knelt was concrete, and there was no light. The room had a dank, musty smell, and I believed for a moment I must be in the basement of the murder house. Then I placed another smell, one that I knew well. It was the smell of the sea.

So I had been taken from the house and dumped here? Why? Had they believed me dead? Or had they lacked time to kill me?

Getting up, I waited an instant, then took four careful steps before encountering a wall. Feeling along the wall, I found three stone steps and at the top a door. My hands quested for the knob or latch. There was none. Not even a hinge or a finger hold anywhere. The door was fitted with admirable precision.

Working cautiously, for I knew not what lay ahead, I worked my way around the room, keeping my hands on the wall. The room was about ten feet wide by twenty feet long and appeared to be empty, although I had not been down the center of it. At the far end, there was an opening in the wall not much above floor level. It was perhaps three feet wide and covered with a grating of iron bars. They were not thick bars, but definitely beyond the power of my unaided muscles.

Dropping to my knees, I peered out and could make

out a faint line of grayness some distance away and below the level of the floor. My fingers found damp sand around the grate.

Fumbling in my pockets for a match, I found everything gone from my pockets. Feeling for my inside coat pocket, I found it torn. The labels had been torn from my clothes! That could mean but one thing. I was marked for murder.

The pieces began to fall into place, and as each one fit, I felt a mounting horror. The grate near the floor, the smell of the sea, that damp sand *inside* the window, the faint line of gray! At high tide, this place was under water!

Rushing across the room, I hurled myself at the door, grasping and tearing at the edges, but nowhere could I get a handhold. The door was of heavy plank, a door built to stay where it was placed. In all probability, a watertight door.

I shouted and pounded, but there was no sound. Pausing, gasping for breath, sweat trickling down my face and body, I listened. All was a vast and empty silence. No movement, no sound of traffic. I was alone, then. Alone in a deserted place with no chance of outside help. Then, very slightly at first, I heard a sound. It was a faint rustling, ever so soft, ever so distant. It was the sea. The tide was coming in.

They had known I was alive. They had left me to be drowned by the inflowing water, probably believing I would still be unconscious. Once drowned, they would simply drop my body in the sea, and as it would have all the signs of drowning, my death would be passed off as a suicide or an accident.

How many times, I wondered, had this place already been used for just that purpose? How many had died there, with no chance to escape?

The killers had evidently returned to Earl Ramsey's house and found me there, and when I inadvertently walked into their hands, they simply slugged me and dumped me there. That car parked outside in the dark must have been the car they came in and in which I had been carried away.

Yet I had called Mooney, and Mooney would know something had gone wrong when I was not present, as I had promised I would be.

For the first time in my life, I found myself in a spot that seemed to offer no solution. I had no idea how high the tide would rise in that room. Nor did I know how high were the tides along this coast. It had been years since I looked at a tide table. There had been, however, a number of items about higher tides and waves due to a Pacific storm. As I had no beach property, such news was usually skimmed and left for others more concerned. That the tide would he high enough to drown me, they had no doubts.

Seated on the steps, I tried to puzzle a way out, searching for some means to get the door open or to get past that grate. Yet even as I sat, the room seemed to grow lighter, but for several minutes, the reason did not occur to me. Then I realized the tide was rising and the added light was reflected from the water.

It was only a faint, gray light, but on my knees by the

grate I could peer out. The opening was under a wharf or dock, and beyond a short stretch of sandy beach was the lapping water of the incoming tide.

Crossing the room through the middle, I glimpsed something I had not seen before. Putting up a tentative hand, I discovered it was a chain dangling from a beam overhead. It was a double chain. Pulling on it, I heard it rattle in a block above me.

A chain hoist?

No doubt the room had once been used for overhauling boat engines or something of the kind. Running my hand down the chain, I found it ended in a hook. Suddenly there was hope. The chance was a wild one, an absurd one, really. Yet a chance was a chance.

Hauling the chain over to the grate, I hooked in the crossbars and hauled the chain tight. The chance of pulling that grate loose was pitifully small, but I was in no position to pass up any chance at all. My weight was a muscular two hundred pounds, and I gave it all I had. The grate held. Again and again, I tried, hoping the action of the sea water might have weakened the grate or the concrete in which it was set.

No luck. Panting, my shirt soaked with perspiration, I stopped and mopped my face. The water was almost to the edge of the window. It meant little that the water might not rise high enough to drown me. If they returned and found me, I would be killed in any event. I tried again, then gave up the attempt as useless.

Kneeling, I studied the concrete in which the grate was set. There seemed little enough to hold it in place, but it was too much for my strength. With a sledge hammer now—But I had no sledge hammer or anything like it. Moreover, as the grate was set closer to the inside edge, the power must be applied from outside to be most effective. It was useless to consider it.

Or was it? Suddenly, I saw something long and black moving upon the water outside the window. It was some distance away, but each movement of the sea brought it closer. At first, I thought it a man's body. Then I recognized it as timber, much the size of a railroad tie, all of six-feet long and perhaps six by six.

The water lapped at the sill below the grate, then retreated. Each time the ripples curled in, the timber came closer.

In an instant, I was on my feet, and recovering the chain from its block, I carried it back to the opening and thrust it through the bars. I made a loop of it; then I waited.

The beam came closer. I tried to snag it with the loop but failed. Again and again, I tried. Sweat poured down my face and body. I wiped it from my brow with the back of my hand. I tried to grasp the timber with my hands by reaching through the crossbars, but failed. Then it actually bumped against the sill, and I grabbed it with both hands. That time, when the water retreated, I held the timber. After a few minutes of struggle, I managed to get a half hitch around the timber. If this did not work, I'd be finished.

Roughly estimating the time, I guessed I might have as much as thirty minutes, perhaps less.

If by that time I had not been successful, the water would have risen so high the timber would be above the opening, and I would be knee-deep in water with my last chance gone.

The waves returned, and that time water spilled over to the floor. Grasping the chain in my hands, I waited for the next wave. When it came, with the beam floating on it, I heaved with all my strength, and the butt of the timber crashed against the iron bars. Relaxing when the wave rolled in next, I gave a second heave. The waves retreated less, and I got in three smashing blows with my crude battering ram before the water rolled back. By now, there was always some water trickling over the sill, and my feet were covered with it.

Water was coming in, and the timber was floating. Again and again, I smashed it against the bars. My muscles ached, and my breath came in gasps. Once, something seemed to give, but there was too little light to see. Feeling with my fingers, my pulse gave a leap. One of the bars had broken free!

Letting go of the chain but anchoring it with a foot, I seized the bars in my hands and gave a tremendous heave. Nothing happened. A second heave and a second bar broke through the crumbling concrete. Now I could bend the bars upward, and using the timber again, I worked on the remaining two bars. When they were bent inward, I grasped them with my hands and pulled them higher. Water was pouring through, but there was room enough for my body. Grasping the sill, I pulled myself through the hole, then lifted my hands to the opening's top and got my feet out. Then I stood up, waist-deep in the dark water. Some distance off was the dim outline of a ladder. I splashed toward it and crawled up to the surface of the dock. Then I sprawled out, exhausted.

It was there she found me.

How long I had been lying there, I do not know, but probably not more than a few minutes. The sound of a car's motor snapped me to awareness. A car meant trouble. Then heels were clicking on the dock, and I came to my feet, staggering. Drunk with fatigue, I stood swaying, ready for battle.

It was the girl, the girl I had met at Sam's. When she saw me, she stopped running. "Oh, you're free! You're safe!"

"You bet I'm free, but it isn't your fault or that of your friends."

"They are not my friends! It wasn't until a few minutes ago somebody made a comment that let me know where you were. I knew they had left you somewhere, but I had no idea where."

"What about Bradley? And his wife?"

"We haven't found them. Nobody seems to know where they are."

"I'll bet your friend Merrano knows!"

She was puzzled. "He might," she admitted. "He acts funny about her. He's looking for Sam, I know."

I had no reason to trust her and did not; however, she did have a car, and I needed transportation. "Let's get back to town. I've got to get some clothes."

She handed me a gun. "It's yours. I stole it back from them."

That didn't make sense, not any way I could look at it. One minute she was with them, sticking me up at gunpoint, and the next she was giving me a gun. I checked the clip. It was loaded, all right.

"How did I rate this trip of yours?" I asked. "Did you come to see if I was drowned?"

"Oh, be still! We're on the same side!" She glanced at me as we got into the car. "My name is Pat Mulrennan."

"That's just ducky," I said. "Now that we're properly introduced we might even start holding hands. No thanks, honey. I'm not turning my back on you."

She sounded honest, and she might be, but nothing about the setup looked good to me except her. She looked as if she were shaped to keep me awake nights, but I couldn't forget how chummy she had been with Pete Merrano and Harry, to say nothing of that big-time torpedo, George Homan.

"To be honest, I was not sure you were there, but from a comment, I thought you might be, and I know that Pete has been using that place for something. How I could get you free, I had no idea, but I came, anyway. Then I saw something or somebody lying on the dock."

There was nothing I could think of to say, so I just sat still and listened. "You were closer to being killed than you know," she added. "The police had a running gun battle with the car you were in, and it was badly shot up. They switched you to another car."

At my apartment, I tried to call Sam, never taking my eyes off Pat. I'll say this for her. I did not trust her, but she was easy to watch. In fact, I was beginning to enjoy it. "If you're so friendly, why not tell me where Sam is?"

"I don't know." She sounded sincere. "Please! Forget about yesterday morning! I had no idea you were a friend of Sam's. For all I knew, you were somebody trying to cut in on Pete's deal."

"And you were acting for Pete?"

"No, I was with him, but I had a job of my own to do. Pete means nothing to me."

She finished saying it as Pete appeared in the door of my bedroom. He had his gun in his hand, and this time, mine was still in its holster. Where he came from, I couldn't guess, unless from the fire escape outside my window. A moment before, I had been in there picking up a clean shirt and had not seen him.

"Is that so?" Pete was watching me but talking to her. "So I mean nothing to you? All right, chick, have it your way. You mean nothing to me, then. When this lad goes out, you go with him."

Not for a second did his eyes leave mine, and believe me, I was doing some fast thinking. "This is no place for a bump-off, Pete." I spoke casually. "There's too many people around. You'd have them all over the place before the sound of the shot died out."

"What if I use a shiv? What if I borrow a note from Harry?" he said, chuckling. "They might even think Harry did it. I hear they're fingering him for the Ramsey killing."

"So that's it? You let your boys take the rap for your killings?"

"Why not? Why have killers unless they are some use to me? I do my own killing, but everybody knows what George Homan and Harry are like. Naturally, they take the rap."

"You're probably right," I agreed, "and I must say

you've played it the smart way except for one thing. How did Sam get away with the money?"

That was a guess, simply a guess, but it figured to be something like that.

"How do you know he's got the money?" Merrano asked. His gaze was intent. "Maybe you know where the money is? Do you?"

"Why should I be looking for him if I did? Anyway, if I did know, I'd keep it under my hat, the way things stand."

"No?" My guess had been right. Somehow Sam had laid hands on the money and disappeared. Knowing Sam, I knew he was saving it for the vets. But it was no wonder Pete Merrano wanted him. "If I turn you and the babe loose, will you tell me where he is?"

"Suppose you do? That isn't enough."

"Suppose, then"—he was watching me—"I turn Ellen loose, too. I've been hanging onto her but haven't been able to let Bradley know I have her."

Another point cleared up, but doubt seemed to come into his mind.

"Enough talk," he said irritably. "How do I know you know anything? Turn around."

I turned.

It was still early, and in a matter of minutes, the milkman would be coming. "Look," I said, "Mooney is to meet me here in a few minutes. I just called him."

Gambling that he had seen me on the phone, I was hoping the bluff might work. He could have seen me, and I knew from experience that somebody in the bedroom could not hear what was said unless the speaker purposely talked loud.

"You wouldn't tell me if you knew he was coming," Pete said, but there was doubt in his tone.

"Am I a damned fool? Do you think I want you guys swapping lead with me in the middle? You better take it on the lam while you can, but you turn Ellen loose and I'll see you get your money."

"What's she to you?"

My answer was quick and a lie. "She's my sister. Not that she's proud of it."

That made sense. "All right, but get this. She's being watched by George Homan. He will kill her if he's approached. If the police find her, he'll kill her and skip. We've got a getaway all set."

"What about your club?"

He shrugged. "I still owe money on it, and there's fifteen to twenty thousand in that bag Sam's got."

He was moving, toward my bedroom door, I believed.

"All right, you get the dough and call me at home. I'll tell you where to bring it. You've got until noon."

We stood facing the wall, and I counted a slow one hundred, then lowered my hands a little. Nothing happened, so I turned around. Pete was gone.

Undoubtedly, he had been searching the apartment and retreated to the fire escape when he heard me at the door. A glance at my desk drawers and closet showed he had given the apartment a shaking down.

Pete Merrano was worried. His plan for a big cleanup had gone sour when somehow Bradley had realized what was happening and had gotten away with the money. He had put the snatch on Ellen, which had done him no good at all, because he couldn't threaten Sam with her. Then I barged into the picture and messed everything up by nosing around in all the wrong places. Evidently, Ramsey had gotten cold feet, so they killed him when he wanted out. At least that was how I had it figured.

The next question was what to do now? I'd made a promise I could not back up because I had no idea where Sam was, and I believed Pete was telling the truth when he said George was watching Ellen. That left the situation a nasty one, yet there was, I believe, a way.

"Pat, I'm going to trust you. Get hold of Mooney and tell him what's happened. Tell him I am following my inclinations, and he will know what to do." Knowing Mooney, I could bet on that.

"All right," she said reluctantly, "but be careful. Those boys aren't playing for fun."

She was telling *me*?

We parted, but when I glanced back she was watching me go. For a minute, I thought she looked worried, but that made no sense. My own car was still near Ramsey's, if it hadn't been towed away or stolen, so I hailed a cab.

Pete Merrano had been doing all right for himself. He lived in a picturesque house overlooking Sunset Strip. Leaving the cab a few doors away, I walked up the hill. Skirting the house, I glimpsed a Filipino houseboy coming down the steps from the back door. Turning on the sprinkler to water the lawn, he went around the house. As soon as his back was turned, I went into the house.

There was a pot of coffee on the range, so I took up a cup, filled it, and drank a couple of swallows, then started up the hall with the coffee in my left hand.

Harry was snoring on a divan in the living room, and Pete was sprawled across the bed with only his shoes and tie off.

The houseboy was working around the yard, so I cut a string from the venetian blinds and very cautiously slipped a loop over Harry's extended ankles. Drawing it as tight as I dared, I tied it.

His gun in its shoulder holster lay on the floor, and with a toe I slid it back under the sofa. Picking up his handkerchief, I placed it within easy reach. Very gently, I took his wrist by the sleeve, lifted it, and placed it across his stomach. I'd just lifted the second to bring it into tying position when he opened his eyes.

By his breath, the glass, and bottle nearby, it was obvious he'd had more than a few drinks before passing out on the divan. His awakening could not have been pleasant. Not only was he awakening with a hangover, but with a man bending over him, he had every reason to believe he was dead or dying.

For one startled instant, he stared. Then his thoughts came into focus, and his mouth opened to yell. The instant he opened his mouth, I shoved the handkerchief into it. He choked, gagged, and grabbed at my wrist, but I jerked a hand free and gave him four stiff fingers in the windpipe.

Grabbing him by his pants at the hips, I jerked him up and flopped him over on his face. He struggled, but he was at least fifty pounds lighter than I and in no condition to put up much of a fight. With my knee in his back, I got a slip knot over one wrist, then the other. In less than a minute, he was bound and gagged.

Pete's voice sounded from the bedroom. Goose flesh ran up my spine. "You sick again, Harry? For the luvva Mike, get into the bathroom! That carpet's worth a fortune!"

Taking my knee from Harry's back, I started for the bedroom, keeping out of line with the door. Merrano was muttering angrily, and I heard his feet on the floor, then his slippers. At the moment, I was thinking of Sam and Ellen and how he had planned to murder me by drowning. There was no mercy in me.

Merrano came through the door scratching his stomach and blinking sleep from his eyes, and I never gave him a chance. Grabbing his shirt-sleeve, I jerked him toward me and whipped one into his belly. The blow was wicked and unexpected, and his mouth fell open, gasping for air, his eyes wide with panic. As he doubled up, I slapped one hand on the back of his head, pushing his face down to meet my upcoming knee.

That straightened him up, blood all over his face and his fingers clawing for his gun. Ignoring the reaching hand, I stepped closer and threw two punches to his chin. His knees sagged, and he hit the floor. Reaching over, I slid the gun from his pocket, then jerked him to his feet.

He was not out, but he had neither the wind nor the opportunity to yell. Grabbing him by the shirt collar, I stood him on his toes. "All right, buddy, you like to play rough. You started bouncing me around, and I don't like it! Now where's Ellen?"

He gasped; the blood running from his broken nose splashed on my wrist. He'd had no chance to assemble his thoughts. Pete Merrano was like all of his kind who live by fear and terror. When that failed, they're backed into a corner. He had been sure he would win. He had still been sure when things started going against him because he simply believed he was too smart. He had forgotten the old adage that cops can make many mistakes, a crook need only make one.

Pete Merrano had made several, and he was realizing that all people can't be scared.

"Where is she?" I insisted.

"Try and find out!" he said past swollen lips.

It was no time for games, so I slugged him in the belly again. "Look, boy," I said, "if that woman's been harmed, the gas chamber will be a picnic compared to what I do to you. Where is she?"

His eyes were insane with fury. "You'd like to know, wouldn't you?" he sneered. "You think you can make *me* talk? Why, you—!"

He jerked away from me, and I let go. He took a roundhouse swing at me, and I stepped inside of it and hit him with both hands. The punches he'd taken before were kitten blows compared to those. The first smashed his lips into his teeth, which broke under the impact; the second lifted him out of his slippers. He hit the floor as though he'd been dropped off a roof. Jerking him to his feet, I backed him against the wall and began slapping him. I slapped him over and back, keeping my head inside his futile swings, and my slaps were heavy. His head must have been buzzing like a sawmill.

When I let up, there was desperation in what I could see of his eyes. "How does it feel to be on the wrong end of a slugging? You boys dish it out, but you can't take it.

"Now where is she? I don't like crooks. I don't like double-crossers. I don't like crooks who pick on women. I'm in good shape, Pete, and I can keep this up all day and all night. Three or four hours of it can get mighty tiresome."

He glared at me, hating and scared. Then something else came into his eyes, and I knew he'd had an idea. "She's at the club," he said, "but you'll never get her. You just find Bradley, get the money, and we'll turn her loose."

Shoving him back on the bed, I let go of him. "Get your coat," I said. "We'll go over there together."

He did not like that, not a little bit, but my gun was in my hand, and he started for the door, glancing at Harry, still lying tied on the divan, as we passed.

We stopped the car a few doors from the club. There was nobody in sight. It was too early for the bar to be open, so I kept the gun in my pocket while Merrano fumbled with his keys.

It was all I could do to keep my eyes open. My muscles felt heavy, and I was dead tired. The long fight to escape from the cellar had taken it out of me, and all I'd needed to have weariness catch up with me was that ride in the car.

If Ellen was actually there, Homan would be watching over her, and that, I believed, was what Merrano was depending on. He was planning on my walking into Homan, and both of us knew what that would mean. George would ask no questions. He was trigger-happy and kill-crazy. Nor would Merrano's presence stop him. If he figured he was due for arrest, he would willingly kill Merrano to get at me.

We started across the polished floor. It was shadowed and cool, the tables stacked with chairs, the piano ghostly in the vague light. We headed toward a door that led backstage from the orchestra's dais. Pete went through the door ahead of me, and a girl screamed. I sprang aside, but not quite enough, for I caught a stunning blow on the skull from a blackjack. George Homan had been waiting right behind the door.

My .45 blasted a hole in the ceiling as I went down, but I was only stunned and shaken by the blow, not knocked out. Scrambling to my feet, I was just in time to see Homan grabbing for a sawed-off shotgun.

That was one time I shot before I thought. That shotgun and his eyes were like a trigger to my tired brain, and I got off three fast shots. Another shot rang out just as my first one sounded. I saw Homan jerk from the impact of the first bullet, smashing his right hand and wrist and going through to the body. The next two bullets caught him as he was falling. The other shot had come from a side door or somewhere.

Leaping over Homan's body, I started after Merrano. Ellen Bradley was tied to a chair in the office, and Merrano was grabbing for a desk drawer behind her. Pete got his gun but chose not to fight and dove through a door in the corner behind some filing cabinets. His feet clattered on a stair, and I jumped past the filing cabinets and after him.

A dozen steps led down to a street door, and at the bottom, Merrano turned and snapped a hurried shot that missed by two feet; then he jerked the door open as my gun was coming into line. Outside, there was a shout, then a hammering of gunfire from the street.

Standing there gripping my gun, I waited, hesitant to leave Ellen tied and wondering what happened outside. Then the door was blocked by a shadow, and Mooney appeared. "Put it away, Kip," he said. "Merrano ran into the boys. He's bought it."

"How did you get here?" I asked.

Two more men came through the door, and with them was Pat Mulrennan. Our eyes met for an instant, and I thought I saw relief there, but could not be sure. "Where does she fit in?" I asked.

"This is Sergeant Patricia Mulrennan," Mooney said. "She's been working undercover for us. She knew Ellen Bradley, so it was a big help to us."

As he spoke, I began to untie Ellen, but scarcely had I begun when Sam Bradley came in and took the job from my hands. In a moment, they were in each other's arms, laughing or crying, I couldn't tell which.

"You were already on this case? You knew about Merrano?"

"We knew what was going on but had no evidence. It was your tip on the Ramsey killing that gave us a break. Ramsey was a small-time crook, not quite right in the head, but nobody in the service groups knew him as anything but a quiet ex-soldier, and that was usually the case. He had done time, however, and he worked with Pete on small jobs, but when Merrano put the snatch on Ellen Bradley, Ramsey got cold feet. He was going to talk to us, so they killed him.

"That gave us a direct lead because we knew who he had been working with. They killed him, but somehow Merrano found out Ramsey had written a letter to the D.A. telling him all he knew, so they came back to search the house for it. Then they ran into you."

Mooney gave me a sour smile. "You had a close shave in that car. We found it in Redondo shot full of holes."

"You lost us?"

"Unfortunately. In the meanwhile, Sam Bradley found out his wife wasn't with her sister, so he came to us and filled us in. After you left Sergeant Mulrennan, she gave us the rest of the story."

Suddenly, I remembered Harry and told Mooney. He ducked out to send men after him, and Ellen came over and said, "Thanks, Kip. Sam told me all you have done."

Mooney had returned, and Pat was standing by the door when Edward Pollard walked in. He had taken three running steps before he saw Mooney and the other officers. The police cars had been at the side or in back, and he had missed them.

He stopped abruptly. From where I stood, he could not see me, and his eyes were on Mooney.

"It would seem I am a bit late, lieutenant, or is Mr. Merrano in? He asked me to represent him in a criminal case."

"Merrano?" Mooney shook his head. "No, he's out of trouble."

"Oh, I'm sorry. Well, nothing for me, then. I'll be going. Good morning."

As he turned, I was moving. That briefcase in the lawyer's hands had begun to seem awfully heavy. He was walking rapidly for the front door when I ducked out the side, and I reached his car just as he did.

Mooney and others had followed, stopping on the walk while I confronted Pollard.

"Take your hand off the door!" he demanded. "I've no time to waste!"

"No, you haven't, Ed, but in a few weeks you will have plenty of time. You'll be doing time."

"I've got the card you left at Bradley's, Ed. You were asking him to come down and walk right into a trap. That card should help to convict you, but I've a hunch we'll find more in the briefcase."

His eyes were desperate. "Get out of my way!"

Mooney had come up behind him. "Maybe we should have a look at the briefcase, Mr. Pollard."

All the spirit went out of him. His face looked gray and old as he turned on Mooney. "Let me go, lieutenant. Let me go. I'll pay. I'll pay plenty."

Mooney opened the briefcase and began leafing through the papers. "You should have thought of this before you planned to gyp a lot of vets out of their money." He glanced up at me. "Morgan, unless I'm mistaken, this is the man who engineered the whole affair. From the looks of this, he was coming to settle up with Merrano."

"Lieutenant, you work it out any way you like. I am

going to buy Pat a drink as soon as she's off duty, and then I'm going home and sleep for a week."

"She's off duty as of now," Mooney said, but as we started to walk away, he called after us. "Sergeant? You'd better watch that guy! He's a good man in the clinches!"

Pat laughed, and we kept going. In the clinches, I had an idea Pat could take care of herself.

AUTHOR'S NOTE

COLLECT FROM A CORPSE

Joe Ragan, career police officer, plays a central role in the next two stories. I have a great deal of respect for the kind of twentieth-century lawman he represents.

The police have an extremely tough job. We Americans accept laws because we know they're necessary, but nobody likes them very much. We're a people who are kind of freewheeling, used to going our own way and the police officer has a difficult time because he's coping with people who are committing crimes or who are about to do so. In addition, very few people will tell an officer the truth. Nine out of ten people will tend to tell the officer, "Well, I wasn't really speeding, officer, I just missed that stoplight."

Yet, even though they do not get a very good view of human nature, a great many of the police are honorable people. Like Joe Ragan they're hard-working men and women who stay with their jobs. An awful lot of police work is done just by sheer legwork. They have to get around, know their town, know their people, know where things happen.

COLLECT FROM A CORPSE

Pike Ambler called the department from the Fan Club at ten in the morning, and Lieutenant Wells Ryerson turned it over to Joe Ragan. "Close this one fast," he said, "and give me an airtight case."

With Captain Bob Dixon headed for early retirement, Ryerson was acting in charge of the burglary detail. If he made a record, his chance of taking Dixon's job was good.

Ragan knew the Fan Club. A small club working in the red, it had recently zoomed into popularity because of the dancing of Luretta Pace. Ragan was thinking of that when he arrived at the club with Sam Blythe and young Lew Ryerson. Sam was a veteran, Lew a tall young man with a narrow face and shrewd eyes. He had been only four months in the department.

Sam Blythe glanced at the hole chopped in the ceiling

and then at the safe. "An easy one, Joe. Entry through the ceiling, a punch job on the safe, nothing touched but money, and the floor swept clean after the job was finished." He walked over to the wastebasket and took from it a crumpled wad of crackly paper. "And here's the potato-chip sack, all earmarks of a Pete Slonski job."

Ragan rubbed his jaw but did not reply. Obviously, he was puzzled.

"Slonski, all right. It checks with the *modus operandi* file, and it's as open and shut as the Smiley case. I'll call headquarters and have them put out a pickup on Slonski."

"Take it easy," Ragan said. "Let's look this over first."

"What's the matter?" Lew Ryerson was like his brother, too impatient to get things done. "Like Sam said, Slonski's written all over it."

"Yeah, it does look like it."

"It is his work. I'm going to call in."

"It won't do any good," Ragan said mildly. "This job would even fool Slonski, but he didn't do it."

Sam Blythe was puzzled, Ryerson irritated. "How can you be sure?" Ryerson demanded. "It's obvious enough to me."

"This isn't a Slonski job," Ragan said, "unless ghosts can crack safes. Pete Slonski was killed last night in Kansas City."

"*What?*" Ryerson was shocked. "How do you know that?"

"It was in the morning paper, and as we have a charge against him, I wired the FBI. They checked the fingerprints. It was Slonski, all right, dead as a herring. And dead for a couple of hours before they found him."

Blythe scowled. "Then something is funny. I'd have sworn Slonski did this job."

"So would I," Ragan said, "and now I am wondering about Smiley. He swears he's innocent, and if ever I saw a surprised man, it was Smiley when I put the cuffs on him."

"They all claim to be innocent," Ryerson said. "That case checked out too well, and you know as well as I do you can identify a crook by his method of operation as by his fingerprints."

"Like this one?" Ragan asked mildly. "This looks like a Slonski job, but Slonski's dead and buried."

"Smiley had a long record," Blythe said uneasily. "I never placed any faith in his going straight."

"Neither did I," Ragan admitted, "but five years and no trouble. He'd bought a home, built up a business, and not even a traffic count against him."

"On the other hand," Ryerson said, "he needs money. Maybe he's just been playing it smart."

"Crooks aren't smart," Ragan objected. "No man who will take a chance on a stretch in the pen is smart. They all make mistakes. They can't beat their own little habits."

"Maybe we've found a smart one," Ryerson suggested. "Maybe he used to work with Slonski and made this one look like him for a cover."

"Slonski worked alone," Blythe said. "Let's get some pictures and get on with it."

Joe Ragan prowled restlessly while Ryerson got his

pictures. Turning from the office, he walked out through the empty bar and through the aisles of stacked chairs and tables. Mounting the steps from the street, he entered the studio, from which entry had been gained to the office below.

Either the door had been unlocked with a skeleton key, or the lock had been picked. There was a reception room whose walls were covered by pictures of sirens with shadows in the right places and bare shoulders. In the studio itself, there was a camera, a few reflectors, a backdrop, and assorted props. The hole had been cut through the darkroom floor.

Squatting on his heels, Joe Ragan studied the workmanship. A paper match lay on the floor, and he picked it up. After a glance, he put it in his pocket. The hole would have taken an hour to cut, and as the club closed at two A.M. and the personnel left right after, the burglar must have entered between three and five o'clock in the morning.

Hearing footsteps, Ragan turned his head to see a plump and harassed photographer. Andre Gimp fluttered his hands. "Oh, this is awful! Simply awful! Who could have done it?"

"Don't let it bother you. Look around and see if anything is missing and be careful you don't forget and walk into that hole."

Ragan walked to the door and paused, lighting a cigarette. He was a big man, a shade over six feet, with wide, thick shoulders and big hands. His hair was rumpled, but despite his size, there was something surprisingly boyish about him.

Ryerson had borrowed him a few days before from the homicide squad, as Ragan had been the ace man on the burglary detail before being transferred to homicide.

Ragan ran his fingers through his hair and returned to the club. He was remembering the stricken look on Ruth Smiley's face when he arrested her husband. There had been a feeling then that something was wrong, yet detail for detail, the Smiley job had checked as this one checked with Slonski.

Leaving Lew Ryerson and Sam Blythe to question Ambler, he returned to headquarters. He was scowling thoughtfully when he walked into Wells Ryerson's office. The lieutenant looked up, his eyes sharp with annoyance.

"Ragan, when will you learn to knock? What is it you want? I am very busy."

"Sorry." He dropped into a chair. "Are you satisfied with the Smiley case?" Briefly, he explained their discoveries at the Fan Club.

Wells Ryerson waited him out with obvious irritation. "That has nothing to do with Smiley. The man had no alibi. He was seen in the vicinity of the crime within thirty minutes of its occurrence. We know his record, and we know he needs money. The tools that did the job came from his shop. The D.A. is satisfied, and so am I."

Ragan leaned his thick forearms on the chair arms. "Nevertheless," he said, "I don't like it. This job today checks with Slonski, but he's dead, so where does that leave us with Smiley? Or with Blackie Miller or Ed Chalmers?"

Ryerson's anger and dislike were evident as he replied. "Ragan, I see what you're trying to do. You know Dixon is about to retire, and if you can mess up my promotion, you can step up yourself.

"Well, you go back to homicide. We don't need you or anybody like you. As of this moment, you are off the burglary detail."

Ragan shrugged. "Sorry you take it this way. I don't want your job. I asked for the transfer to homicide, but I don't like to see innocent men go to prison."

"Innocent?" Ryerson's tone was thick with contempt. "You talk like a schoolboy! Jack Smiley was in reform school at sixteen and in the pen when he was twenty-four. He was short of cash, and he simply reverted to type. Go peddle your papers in homicide."

Joe Ragan closed the door behind him, his ears burning. He knew how Ryerson felt, but he could not forget the face of Ruth Smiley or the facts that led to the arrest of her husband. Smiley, Miller, and Chalmers had all been arrested by virtue of information from the M.O. file.

It was noon and lunch time. He hesitated to report to his own chief, Mark Stigler. He was stopping his car before the white house on the side street before he realized it.

Ruth Smiley wore no welcoming smile when she opened the door. He removed his hat, flushing slightly. "Mrs. Smiley, I'd like to ask a few questions if I may. It might help Jack if you answer them."

There was doubt, but a flicker of hope in her eyes. "Look," he explained, "something has come up that has me wondering. If the department knew I was here, they wouldn't like it, as I am off this case, but I've a hunch." He paused, thinking ahead. "We know Jack was near the scene of the crime that night. What was he doing there?"

"We told you, Mr. Ragan. Jack had a call from the Chase Printing Company. He repaired a press of theirs once, and they asked him to come not later than four o'clock, as they had a rush job that must begin the following morning."

"That was checked, and they said they made no such call."

"Mr. Ragan, please believe me," Ruth Smiley pleaded. "I heard him talking. I heard his replies!"

Ragan scowled unhappily. This was no help, but he was determined now. "Don't raise your hopes," he said, "but I am working on an angle that may help."

The Chase Printing Company could offer no assistance. All their presses were working, and they had not called Smiley. Yes, he had repaired a press once, and an excellent job, too. Yes, his card had been found under the door when they opened up.

Of course, the card could have been part of an alibi, but that was one thing that had bothered him all along. "Those guys were crooks," he muttered, "yet not one of them had an alibi. If they had been working, they would have had iron-clad alibis to prove themselves elsewhere."

Yet the alternative was a frame-up by someone familiar with their working methods. A call had taken Smiley from his bed to the vicinity of the crime, a crime that resembled his working ways. With the records each man had, there was no way they could escape conviction.

He drove again to the Fan Club. Pike Ambler greeted him. "Still looking? Any leads?"

"A couple." Ragan studied the man. "How much did you lose?"

"Two grand, three hundred." His brow furrowed. "I can't take it, Joe. Luretta hasn't been paid, and she'll raise a squawk you'll hear from here to Flatbush."

"You mean Luretta Pace? Charlie Vent's girl?"

Ambler nodded. "She was Vent's girl before he got himself vented." He smiled feebly at the pun. "She's gone from one extreme to the other. Now it's a cop."

"She's dating a cop? Who?"

"Lew Ryerson." Ambler shrugged. "I don't blame him. She's a number, all right."

Ragan returned to the office, reported in, and completed some routine work. It was late when he finally got to bed.

He awakened with a start, the telephone jangling in his ears. He grabbed it sleepily. "Homicide calling, Joe. Stigler said to give it to you."

"To me?" Ragan was only half-awake. "Man, I'm off duty."

"Yeah"—the voice was dry—"but this call's from the Fan Club. Stigler said you'd want it."

He was wide awake now. "Who's dead?"

"Pike Ambler. He was shot just a few minutes ago. Get out there as fast as you can."

Two patrol cars were outside, and a cop was barring the door. Joe had never liked the word "cop," but he had grown up with it, and it kept slipping back into his thinking. The officer let him pass, and Joe walked back to the office.

Ambler was lying on his face beside the desk, wearing the cheap tux that was his official costume. His face was drained of color now, his blue eyes vacant.

Ragan glanced at the doctor. "How many times was he shot?"

"Three times, and damned good shooting. Right through the heart at close range. Probably a .45."

"All right." Ragan glanced up as a man walked in. It was Sam Blythe. "What are you doing here?"

"Prowling. I was talking to the cop on the beat when we heard the shots. We busted in here, and he was lying like that, with the back window open. We went out and looked around but saw nobody, and we heard no car start."

"Who else was in the club?"

"Nobody. The place closed at two, and the last to leave was that Pace gal. What a set of gams she's got!"

"All right. Have the boys round 'em all up and get them in here." He dropped into a chair when the body had been taken away and studied the situation. A little bit of thinking sometimes saved an awful lot of shoe leather. Blythe watched him through lowered lids.

He got up finally, making a minute examination of the room, locating two of the three bullet holes and digging them from the wall with care to add no scratches. They were .45s and he studied them thoughtfully.

"You know," Blythe suggested suddenly, "somebody could be playing us for suckers, kicking this *modus operandi* stuff around like they are."

"Could be." What was Blythe doing there at this hour? He got off at midnight. "Whoever it is has established a new method of operation. All those jobs—Smiley, Chalmers, and Miller—including the burglary here, all between three and five A.M. The technique is that of other men, but the working hours are his own."

"You think those jobs were frames? Ryerson won't like it."

Ragan shrugged. "I'd like to see his face when he finds I'm back on this job."

"You think it's the same one?" Blythe asked quickly.

"Don't you?"

"I wouldn't know. Those were burglaries. This is murder."

"Sure," Ragan agreed, "but suppose Ambler suspected somebody otherwise unsuspected? Wouldn't the crook have a reason for murder?"

A car slowed out front, and then a door slammed open. They heard the click of angry heels, and Luretta Pace swept into the room. Her long, almond-shaped eyes swept the room, from Blythe to Ragan. "You've got a nerve! Getting me out of bed in the middle of the night! Why couldn't you wait until morning?"

"It is tomorrow," Ragan said. He took out a crumpled pack of cigarettes. "Have one?"

She started to refuse, but something in his amused gray eyes made her resentment flicker out. She turned abruptly, seating herself on the arm of a chair. "All right, ask your questions!"

She had green eyes and auburn hair. Ragan found

himself liking it. "First," he suggested, "tell us about the fight you had with Ambler."

Luretta stiffened, and the warmth left her face. "Listen! Don't try to frame me! I won't stand still for it! I was out of here before he was shot, and you know it!"

"Sure, I know it. And I don't think you slipped around back and shot him through the window, either." He smiled at her. "Although you could have done it."

Her face paled, but Luretta had been fighting her own battles too long. "Do you think I'd kill a guy who owes me six hundred bucks? You don't collect from a corpse! Besides, Pike was a good lad. He was the first guy I'd worked for in a long time who treated me right.

"You'll hear about it, anyway," Luretta said. "Joe owed me money and couldn't pay up. The money he figured on paying me was in that safe, so when he was robbed, I figured I was working for nothing. I can't afford that, so we had some words, and I told him what he could do with his night club."

"Did he give you any idea when he could pay? Or tell you when he might have the money?"

"Yes, as a matter of fact, he said he would have it all back, every dime. He told me he would pay me tomorrow. I didn't believe him."

"Where do you think he planned to get it?"

"How should I know?" She shrugged a lovely shoulder.

"Then," Ragan asked gently, "he said nothing about knowing who robbed him?"

Sam Blythe sat up abruptly, his eyes on Ragan's, and Luretta lost her smile. She was suddenly serious. "No, not exactly, but I guess what I told you could be taken that way. Do you think that was why he was killed? Because he knew and tried to get his money back?"

It was a theory and a good one. Suppose Ambler possessed information not available to the police and believed he could get his money returned by promising not to turn in the thief? If he contacted the criminal that could be a motive for murder. Joe understood there could be other reasons for murder, but he believed the relationship between Ambler and Luretta was strictly business . . . but suppose someone else had not?

The only admirer of Luretta's he knew was Lew Ryerson, and that was ridiculous. Or was it?

Such a girl as Luretta Pace could have many admirers. That Sam Blythe thought she was something was obvious. For that matter, he did himself.

It was almost noon when he left the club and walked into the sunlight, trying to assemble his thoughts and assay the value of what he had learned. He was standing on the curb when Andre Gimp came up to him. "Mr. Ragan? Only one thing is missing, and that seems strange, for it was only a picture."

"A picture?" Joe Ragan knew what was coming. "Of whom?"

"Luretta Pace . . . in costume!"

There it was again. The burglary, Luretta Pace, the murder. He drove back to headquarters and found Stigler pacing the floor with excitement. "Hey!" Stigler exploded. "You've got something! The gun that killed Ambler was the same gun that killed Charlie Vent!"

"I thought so when I had them checked. It was a hunch I had."

"You think this ties in with those burglaries?" Stigler asked. Then he smiled. "Wells Ryerson called up, boiling mad. Said you'd been questioning people. I told him homicide was involved now. He shut up like a clam, but he was sure sore." Stigler rolled the cigar in his jaw and asked, "What next?"

"A little looking around and another talk with Luretta Pace."

In the alley in back of the Fan Club, he found where a man had been standing behind a telephone pole watching Ambler through the window. A man who smoked several cigarettes and dropped paper matches. Ragan picked up a couple of them; each match stub had been divided at the bottom by a thumbnail and bent back to form a cross. Such a thing a man might do subconsciously, while waiting. Many people, Ragan had noticed, have busy fingers of which they are scarcely aware. Some doodle, and usually in the same patterns.

Ragan placed the matches in a white envelope with a notation as to where they were found. In another envelope, he had an identical match, and he knew where others were to be found.

Later, he went to a small target range in the basement at headquarters and fired a couple of shots, then collected all the bullets he could find in the bales of cotton that served as backstop for the targets.

Luretta met him at the door when he arrived, and he smiled at her questioning glance.

"Wondering?" he asked.

"Wondering whether this call is business or social." She took his hat, then glanced over her shoulder. "Drink?"

"Bourbon and soda." He hesitated. "Better not; I'm still on duty. Just a cup of coffee."

She was wearing sea-green slacks and a pale yellow blouse. Her hair was down on her shoulders, and it caught the sunlight. He leaned back in the chair and crossed his legs, watching her move about.

"Ever think about Charlie?" he asked suddenly.

The hand that held the cup hesitated for the briefest instant. When she came to him with his cup and one for herself, she looked at him thoughtfully. "That's a curious thing to ask. Charlie's been dead for nearly five months."

"You didn't answer my question."

She looked over her cup at him. "Occasionally. He wasn't a bad sort, you know, and he really cared for me. But why bring him up?"

"Oh, just thinking!" The coffee tasted good. "I was wondering if your recent company made you forget him."

Luretta looked him over carefully. "Joe, you're not subtle. Why don't you come right out and ask me what you want to know. I'm a big girl now, and I've been coming to the point with people for a long time."

"I wasn't being subtle. The trouble is, I've a finger on something that is pure dynamite. I can't do a thing until I know more, or the whole thing is liable to fly up and hit me in the face.

"This much I can say. Two things are tied up with the

killing of Pike Ambler. One of them is the burglaries; the other one is you."

"*Me?*" She laughed. "Oh, no, Joe! Don't tell me that! There was nothing between Pike and me, and you don't for the minute think I double in safecracking?"

"No, I don't. Nor do I think there was anything between you and Pike. It's what somebody else may have thought. Moreover, you may know more than you realize, and I believe if I could get inside your mind and memory, I could put the pieces together." He got to his feet and put his cup down. "If anybody should ask you, this call was purely social. If you always look as lovely as you do now, that would be easy to believe."

The buzzer sounded from the door, and when she opened it, Lew Ryerson was there. His eyes went from Ragan to her. He was about to speak, but Ragan beat him to it. "Hi, Lew! Good to see you!"

Ryerson came on into the room, his eyes holding Ragan's. "Heard you were all wrapped up in a murder case?"

"Yeah, just took time off to drop around for coffee."

"Looks like I've got competition." There was no humor in the way he spoke, and his eyes were cold and measuring.

"With a girl like Luretta, you will always have it."

Ryerson glanced at her, his lips thinned down and angry. "I guess that's so, but it doesn't make me like the idea any better."

She followed Ragan to the door. "Don't mind him, and do come back."

There was ugly anger in Ryerson's eyes. "Luretta," he said, "I want you to tell him not to come back!"

"Why, I'll do nothing of the kind!" She turned on Lew. "Please remember we are only dating occasionally. I told you after Charlie was killed that it wouldn't be any different. I just do not intend to tie myself down. If Mr. Ragan wants to come by, he's welcome."

"Thanks, honey." Ragan turned to Lew. "See you later, Lew. It's all fun, you know?"

Ryerson glared. "Is it? I'm not so sure."

Sam Blythe was waiting for him when he walked into the office at homicide. His face was dark and angry. "What goes on here?" he demanded. "Who gave you the right to have my gun tested by ballistics?"

"Nobody," Joe admitted cheerfully. "I knew you didn't carry this one off duty, so I had it checked. I had mine checked, too, as they will tell you, and Stigler's."

"What?" Stigler glared. "You had my gun checked?"

"Sure!" Ragan sat on a corner of the desk. "I needed some information, and now I've got it."

"Aside from this horsing around, what have you done on the Ambler case? Have you found the murderer?"

"Sure, I have."

Stigler jumped, and Blythe brought his leg down from the arm of the chair. "Did you say—you have? You know who did it?"

"That's right. I know who did it, and that means I know who killed Charlie Vent, too."

He scowled suddenly, and taking the phone from its cradle, he dialed a number. Luretta answered. "Joe here. Still busy?"

"Yes."

"Luretta, I meant to tell you but forgot. The same man who killed Pike Ambler killed Charlie Vent."

"*What?*" He heard her astonished gasp, but before she could ask questions, he interrupted.

"Honey, don't ask questions now or make any comments, but you do some thinking, keep the thinking to yourself, and call me any time of the day or the night, understand?"

He replaced the phone and turned back to Stigler, who took his cigar from his mouth. "All right, give! Who did it?"

"Stigler, you'd call me a liar if I told you. Nor do I have evidence for a conviction, but I've set a trap for him if he will only walk into it. Also, he pulled those jobs for which Blackie Miller, Ed Chalmers, and Jack Smiley are awaiting trial."

"That's impossible!" Stigler said, but Ragan knew he believed. Sam Blythe sat back in his chair watching Ragan but saying nothing, his eyes cold and curious.

"What happens now?" Stigler asked.

"We sit tight. I've some more prowling to do."

"What if your killer skips? I want this case sewed up, Ragan."

"Just what Wells Ryerson told me. You'll both get it." Ragan studied his shoes. "Anything about Charlie Vent's murder ever puzzle you, chief? You'll recall he was shot three times in the face, and that's not a normal way to kill a man."

"I've thought of that. If I hadn't thought it to be a gang killing, I'd have said it was jealousy."

"My idea, exactly. Somebody wanted to muscle in, all right, but on Charlie's girl, not his other activities."

"That doesn't make sense," Blythe protested. "Lew Ryerson's going with her."

"And how many other guys? She belongs to nobody. She's a doll, that one, but she's got a mind of her own, and for the time, she's playing the field."

"Yeah," Sam agreed. "I could name three of them right now."

The phone rang, and Ragan dropped a hand to it. "Joe? This is Luretta. I think I know what you mean. Can you come over about ten tonight?"

"I will, and not a minute late." He hung up, glancing from one to the other. "Ten o'clock, and I think we'll get all the evidence we need. If you guys can sit and wait in a car for a while, I'll give you a murderer."

It was dark under the row of trees that lined the curb opposite the apartment house where Luretta Pace lived, and the dark, unmarked car was apparently empty. Only a walker along the park fence might have seen the three men who waited in the car.

"You're sure this thing is set up, Joe? We can't slip up now!"

"It's set. Just sit tight and wait."

Rain began to fall, whispering on the leaves and on the car top. It was almost 8:40 when Ragan suddenly touched Stigler on the sleeve. "Look!" he whispered.

A man had come around the corner out of the side street near the apartment house. He wore a raincoat, and his hat brim was pulled down. He stepped quickly to the door.

Mark Stigler sat straight up. "Man, that looked just like—!" His voice faded as Ragan's hand closed on his arm.

"It was!" Ragan replied grimly.

A curtain in an apartment-house window went up and down rapidly, three times. "Let's go," Ragan said. "We've got to hurry!"

An officer in uniform admitted them to the apartment next door to that of Luretta Pace. A recording was already being made, and through the hidden mike in the next apartment, they could hear the voices clearly.

"I don't care who he is!" A man was speaking, a voice that stiffened Sam Blythe to the same realization that had come to Mark Stigler on the outside. "Keep him away from here!"

"I don't intend to keep anybody away whom I like, but as a matter of fact, I don't care for him."

"Then tell him so!"

"Why don't you tell him?" Luretta's voice was taunting. "Are you afraid? Or won't he listen to you?"

"Afraid? Of course not! Still, it wouldn't be a good idea. I'd rather he did not know we were acquainted."

"You weren't always so hesitant."

"What do you mean by that?"

"Why, you never approved of Charlie, either. You knew I liked him, but you did not want me to like him."

"That's right. I didn't."

"One thing I'll say for Charlie: He was a good spender. I don't care whether a man spends money on me or not, but it helps. And Charlie did."

"You mean that I don't? I think I've been pretty nice lately."

"Lately. Sometimes I wonder how you do it on your salary."

"I manage."

"As you managed a lot of other things? Like Charlie, for instance?"

For a moment, there was no sound, and Joe Ragan's tongue touched dry lips. Nerve, that girl had nerve.

The tone was lower, colder. "Just what do you mean by that?"

"Well, didn't you? You didn't really believe I thought Charlie was killed in some gang war, did you? Nobody wanted Charlie dead, nobody but you."

He laughed. "I always did like a smart girl! Well, now you know the sort of man I am, and you know just how we stand and what I can do to you or anyone! The best of it is, they can't touch me."

There was a sound like a glass being put down on a table. "Luretta, let's drop this nonsense and get married. I'm going places, and nothing can stop me."

"I won't marry you. This has gone far enough as it is." Luretta's voice changed. "You'd better go now. I never knew just what sort of person you were, although I suspected. At first, I believed you were making things easy for me by not allowing too many questions. Now I realize you were protecting yourself."

"Naturally. But I was protecting you, too."

Joe Ragan got up and took his gun from its holster and slid it into his waistband. Blythe was already at the door. There was a hard set to his face.

"I neither wanted nor expected protection." Luretta was speaking. "I cared for Charlie. I want you to understand that. No, I was not in love with him, but he was good to me, and I hadn't any idea that you killed him. If I had, I would never have spoken to you. Now, get out!"

The man laughed. "Don't be silly! We're staying together, especially now."

"What do you mean?"

"Why, I wouldn't dare let you go now. We'll either get along or you will get what Charlie got." There was a bump as of a chair knocked over, then a shout. *"Stay away from that door!"*

Ragan was moving fast. He swung into the hall and gripped the knob, but it was locked. There was a crash inside, and in a sudden fury of fear for the girl inside, Ragan threw himself against the door. The lock broke, and he stumbled inside.

Lieutenant Wells Ryerson threw the girl from him and grabbed for his gun. Ragan was moving too fast. He slapped the gun aside and hooked a wicked right to the chin, then a left. Ryerson fell back, his gun going off as he fell. He scrambled to his feet, lifting his gun.

Sam Blythe fired in the same instant, and the bullet slammed Ryerson against the wall. The gun dribbled from Ryerson's fingers, and he slid to the floor.

His eyes opened, and for a moment they were sharp, clear, and intelligent. "I told you," he said hoarsely, "to close this one up fast, an airtight case."

His voice faded, and then he struggled for breath. "It looked so . . . easy! The file, those ex-cons on the loose. I could make a record . . . the money, too."

Mark Stigler shook his head. "Ryerson! Who would have believed it?" He glanced at Ragan. "What tipped you off?"

"It had to be somebody with access to the files, and who could be out between three and five A.M. It couldn't be you, Mark, because you're at home with your family every chance you get and your wife would know. Sam, here, likes his sleep too much.

"What really tipped me off was this." Ragan picked up a paper match split into a cross. "It was a nervous habit he had when thinking. Many of us do similar things.

"Matches like that were found on the Smiley and Miller jobs and in the alley near Ambler's office."

"Did Lew know his brother liked Luretta?"

"I doubt it."

"What about Ambler?"

"I think he knew, and somehow he discovered it was Ryerson who cracked his safe. He must have called him. Ryerson did not dare return the call, for then there might be somebody else who knew his secret."

When the body had been taken away, Stigler looked over at Ragan. "Coming with us, Joe? Or are you staying?"

"Neither. We're going to drive over to see Ruth Smiley. I want that to be the first thing we do—turn Jack Smiley loose so he can go back to his family."

Later, in the car, Luretta said, "She'll be so happy! It must be wonderful to make somebody that happy!"

"That's something," Joe Ragan said, "that we ought to talk about."

AUTHOR'S NOTE

I HATE TO TELL HIS WIDOW

One part of writing detective stories that I like very much is the different backgrounds and elements I get to work into the stories. I enjoy the "language" of detective writing especially.

Each genre has its phrases that are particularly colorful, but detective stories of this period have more than their share—terms that appear in these pages such as "punch jobs," "torpedos," "shivs," and numerous others that almost make up a second criminal language.

Some police officer friends of mine had helped arrange for me to be able to interview a whole group of men who were in the penitentiary at one point in my writing, as well as many others associated with crime who were out of prison. At one point I even interviewed a group of men who specialized in grand larceny when I was researching the subject of the "economics of crime."

From these discussions and from many books I accumulated over the years, I became somewhat of an expert on criminal slang. You never know when that kind of knowledge can come in handy.

Here is just one example, which also shows how nobody learns from history. In the late 1800s through 1910, cocaine was a very big thing in this country. It was used by nearly all of the criminals, and criminals who used it were called "snowbirds."

I HATE TO TELL HIS WIDOW

Joe Ragan was drinking his ten o'clock coffee when Al Brooks came in with the news. "Ollie's dead." He spoke quietly. "Ollie Burns. Shot."

Ragan said nothing.

"He was shot twice," Al told him. "Right through the heart. The gun was close enough to leave powder burns on his coat."

Ragan just sat there holding his cup in both hands. It was late and he was tired, and the information left him stunned and unbelieving. Ollie Burns was his oldest friend on the force. Ollie had helped break him in when he first joined up after the war. Ollie had been a good officer, a conscientious man who had a name for thoughtfulness and consideration. He never went in for the rough stuff, knowing the taxpayers paid his salary and understanding he was a public servant. He treated people with consideration and not as if they were enemies.

"Where did they find him?" he said at last. "How did it happen?"

"That's the joker. We just don't know. He was found on a phoned-in tip, lying on the edge of a vacant area near Dunsmuir. What he was doing out there in the dark is more than anybody can guess, but the doc figures he'd been dead more than an hour when we found him." Brooks hesitated. "They think it was a woman. He smelled of perfume and there was lipstick on his cheek and collar."

"Nuts!" Ragan rose. "Not Ollie. He was too much in love with his wife and he never played around. I knew the guy too well."

"Well," Brooks said, "don't blame me. You could be right. It wasn't my idea, but what Stigler's thinking."

"Where's Mary? Has she been told?" Ragan's first thought was for her. Mark Stigler was not the type to break such news to anyone.

"Uh-huh. Mark told her. Your girl, Angie Faherty, is with her. They were to meet Ollie at a movie at nine, so when he didn't show up she got worried, so they went home. Ollie had been anxious to see this show with Mary, and they arranged to go together. She called the station when he wasn't at home, and a couple of minutes after she called, somebody told us there was a body lying out there in the dark."

"Who called?"

"Nobody knows. The guy said he didn't want to get mixed up in anything and hung up."

"Odd, somebody seeing the body so soon. Nobody walks around there much at night."

Stigler was at his desk when Ragan came in. He looked up, unexpected sympathy in his eyes. "Do you want this case?"

"You know I do. Ollie was the best friend I had in the world, and you can forget the woman angle. He was so much in love with Mary that it stuck out all over him. He wasn't the type to play around. If anything, he was overly conscientious."

"Every man to his own view." Stigler tapped with a pencil. "This is the first man we've had killed in a year, and I want the killer brought in with evidence for a conviction. Understand?"

"Will I work with the squad?"

Stigler shook his head. "You've got a fresh viewpoint and you've worked with Ollie. You can have all the help you need, but we'll be working on it too."

Joe Ragan was pleased. This was the way he wanted it but the last thing he expected from Mark Stigler. Stigler was a good homicide man but a stickler for the rulebook, and turning a man loose to work on his own was unheard of from him.

"Mark, did Ollie say anything to you about a case he was working on? I mean, in his spare time?"

"No, not a word." Stigler tapped with the pencil. "On his own time? I didn't know that ever happened around here. You mean he actually went out on his free time and worked on cases?"

"He was a guy who hated loose ends. Ask Mary sometime. Every tool had a place, every magazine was put back in a neat pile on the shelf, every book to its place. It wasn't an obsession, just that he liked things neat, with all the ends tied up. And I know he's had some bug in his bonnet for months now. What it was I have no idea."

"That's something," Stigler agreed. "Maybe he was getting too close to the right answer for somebody's comfort." He lit a cigar, then put it down. "My wife's trying to get me to smoke a pipe," he explained.

"You're right about him being overly conscientious. I recall that Towne suicide, about a year ago. He was always needling me to see if anything new had turned up.

"Hell, there wasn't anything new. It was open-and-shut. Alice Towne killed herself and there was no other way it could have happened. But it seems Ollie knew her and it bothered him a good deal."

"He was like that." Ragan got up. "What have you got so far?"

"Nothing. We haven't found the gun. Ollie's own gun was still in its holster. He was off duty at the time and, like we said, was meeting his wife to go to a show."

"Why didn't he go? I knew about that because my girl was going with them."

"Somebody called him just before eight o'clock. He answered the phone himself and Mary heard him say, 'Where?' A moment later he said, 'Right away.' Then he hung up and asked them if he could meet them in front of the theater at nine. He had an appointment that wouldn't keep."

"I see." Ragan rubbed his jaw. "I'll look into it. If you need me during the next hour, I'll be at Mary's."

"You aren't going to ask her about it now, are you?"

"Yes, I am, Mark. After all, she's a cop's wife. It will be better to get her digging into her memory for facts than just sitting around moping.

"I know Mary, and she won't be able to sleep. She's the kind of woman who starts doing something whenever she feels bad. If I don't talk to her, she'll be washing the dishes or something."

Angie answered the door. "Oh, Joe! I'm so glad you've come! I just don't know what to do. Mary won't lie down and she won't rest. She—"

"I know." Joe squeezed her shoulder. "Mary's like that. We'll have some coffee and talk a little."

Walking through the apartment, he thought about what Stigler had said. Lipstick and perfume. That didn't sound like Ollie. Stigler had never known Ollie the way Ragan had. Ollie had never been a chaser. If there had been lipstick and perfume on him when he was found, it had been put there to throw off the investigation.

And the call. That was odd in itself. It might be that somebody had *wanted* the body found, and right away. But why? The man on the phone might have been the killer, or somebody working with him. If not, what would a man be doing in that area at that hour? For that matter, what was Ollie doing there? It was a dark, gloomy place, scattered with old lumber and bricks among a rank growth of weeds and grass. And right in the middle of town.

"On that call, Angie? Did Ollie say anything else? Give you any idea of what it was all about?"

"No, he seemed very excited and pleased, that was

all. He told us he would not be long, but just to be sure to give him until nine. We went to dinner and then to the theater to meet him, but he never showed. He was driving his own car. Mary and I were driving yours."

At the sound of a step in the hall, Ragan looked up. He had known Mary Burns even longer than Ollie. There had been a time when he liked her very much. That was before he had met Angie or she had met Ollie.

She was a dark-eyed, pretty woman with a round figure and a pleasant face. If anyone in the world had been perfectly suited for Ollie, it was Mary.

"Mary," Ragan said, "this may not seem the best time, but I need to ask you some questions. You know that every minute counts in these investigations, and you'll feel better with your mind occupied. I need your help, Mary."

"I'd like that, Joe, I really would." Her eyes were red and swollen but her chin was firm. She sat down across the table, and Angie brought the coffeepot.

"Mary, you're the only person who knew Ollie better than I did. He was never one to talk about his work. He just did what was necessary. But he had that funny little habit of popping up with odd comments that were related to whatever he was thinking or working on. Unless you knew him, those comments were incomprehensible."

"I know." She smiled, but her lips trembled. "He often did that. It confused people who didn't know him."

"All right. We know Ollie was working on something on his own time. I have a hunch it was some case the rest of us had forgotten about. Remember that Building & Loan robbery? He stewed over that for a month without saying anything to anybody, and then made an arrest and had all the evidence for a conviction. Nobody even knew he was thinking about the case.

"Well, I think he was working something like that. I think he was so close on the trail of somebody that they got scared. I think, somehow, they led him into a trap tonight. We've got to figure out what it was he had on his mind."

Mary shook her head. "I have no idea what it could be, Joe. He was working on something, I do know that. I could always tell when something was on his mind. He would sit staring across the top of his newspaper or would walk out in the yard and pull a weed or two. He never liked to leave anything until it was finished. What it was this time, I do not know."

"Think, Mary! Think back over the past few weeks. Try to remember any of those absentminded little comments he used to make. One of them might be just the lead we need."

Angie filled their cups again. Mary looked up doubtfully. "There was something just this morning, but it doesn't tell us a thing. He looked up while he was drinking his coffee said, 'Honey, there's just two crimes worse than murder.' "

"Nothing more?"

"That was all. He was stewing about something, and you know how he was at times like that. I understood and left him alone."

"Two crimes worse than murder?" Ragan ran his fingers through his hair. "I know what one was. We'd talked about it often enough. He thought, as I do, that narcotics peddling was the lowest crime on earth. It's a foul racket. I wonder if that was it?"

"What could the other crime be?"

He shook his head, frowning. Slowly, carefully then, he led Mary over the past few days, searching for some clue. A week before, she had asked him to meet her and go shopping, and he had replied that he was in the Upshaw Building and would meet her on the corner by the drugstore.

"The Upshaw Building?" Ragan shook his head. "I don't know anything about it. Well"—he got up—"I'm going to adopt Ollie's methods, Mary, and start doing legwork and asking questions. But believe me, I'll not leave this case until it's solved."

Al Brooks was drinking coffee when Ragan walked into the café the next morning. He dropped on the stool beside the vice-squad man and ordered coffee and a side order of sausage.

Al was a tall, wide-shouldered man with a sallow face. He had an excellent record with the force. He grinned at Ragan, but there was a question in his eyes. "I hear Stigler has you on the Burns case. What gives?"

Ragan did not feel talkative. Morning coffee with Ollie Burns had been a ritual of long standing, and the ease and comfort of the big man was much preferred to the sharp, inquisitiveness of Al Brooks.

"Strange, Stigler putting you on the Burns case."

"Not so strange." Ragan sipped his coffee, hoping

they'd hurry with the sausage. "He figured that being a friend of Ollie's, I might know something."

After a moment, Brooks looked around at him. "Do you?"

Ragan shrugged. "Not that I can think of. Neither does Mary, but we'll find what it was. Ollie was working on something, I know that."

"I still think it was a woman." Brooks was cynical. "You say he never played around. Hell, what man would pass up a good-lookin' babe? Ollie was human, wasn't he?"

"He was also in love with his wife. The guy had ethics. He was sincere and conscientious as anyone I ever knew."

Al was disgusted. "Where did all that lipstick come from? Do you think he cornered some gorilla in that lot and the guy kissed him? Are you kidding?"

"You've judged him wrong, Al, you really have. My hunch is that was all for effect. The killer wanted us to think a woman was involved.

"Besides," he added, "something they didn't count on. He had a date with his wife and my girlfriend. He was to meet them at nine. Allowing time for going and coming, he wouldn't have had much more time than to say hello and good-by."

Al stared at him for a moment, then shrugged. "Have it your way, but take a tip from me and be careful. If he was working on something that was serious enough to invite killing, the same people won't hesitate to kill again. Don't find out too much."

Ragan chuckled. "That doesn't sound like you, Al.

Nobody on the force stuck his neck out more than you did when you pinched Latko."

"That's another thing. I had him bottled up so tight he didn't have a chance. None of his friends wanted any part of it. I had too much evidence."

Ragan got to his feet. "What the hell? We're cops, Al. Taking risks is expected of us. Only if they tackle me, they will have a different problem than with Ollie."

"What do you mean?"

"Why, I'm sort of a rough type, Al. I like it the hard way. If they start shooting, I'll be shooting too. If they start slugging, I'll meet them halfway. I like to play rough, Al, and when it comes to Ollie's killer, I'll be out for blood."

Al Brooks lifted a hand and walked out. Ragan looked after him. He had never liked Al Brooks, but he was one of the best men on the force. The way he had broken the Latko gang was an example. Aside from a few petty vice raids, it had been Brooks's first job. Two months later he followed it with the arrest of Clyde Bysten, the society killer.

Stigler met him in the hall and motioned him into the office. "Joe, you knew them. How did Ollie get along with his wife?"

Ragan's head came around sharply. "They were the most affectionate people I ever knew. They lived for each other."

Stigler looked up from the papers on his desk. "Then how do you explain that he was shot with his own gun?" Shock riveted Ragan to the floor. "Shot with *what*?"

"Not with his issue pistol, but another gun he kept at

home. It was a .38 Smith & Wesson. We've found the gun, and the ballistics check. The gun is on our records as belonging to Ollie."

"Oh, no!" Ragan's mind refused to accept what he had heard. "Anyway," he added, "Mary was with Angie all the time, from seven until I left them, long after midnight."

Stigler shook his head. "No, Ragan, she wasn't. Your loyalty does you credit, but Mary left Angie at the table to go to the powder room. She was gone so long Angie was afraid she'd gotten sick and went to the rest room. Mary wasn't there."

Ragan dropped into a chair. "I don't get it, Mark, but I'd swear Mary can't be guilty. I don't care whose gun Ollie was shot with."

"What are you trying to do, Joe? Find a murderer or protect Mary?"

Ragan's face flushed. "Now see here, Mark. Ollie's the best friend I ever had, but I'm not going to stand by and see his wife stuck for a crime she could no more commit than I could. It's absurd. I knew them both too well."

"Maybe that was it, Joe. Maybe you knew them too well. Maybe that led to the killing."

Ragan stared at Stigler, unwilling to believe he was hearing correctly. "Mark, that's the most rotten thing that's ever been said to me, and you're no half-baked rookie. You must have a reason. Give it to me."

Stigler looked at him carefully. "Joe, understand this. We have almost no evidence to prove this theory. We do have a lot of hearsay. I might also add that I never dreamed of such a thing until we found that gun in the weeds, and even then I didn't think of you. That didn't come up until Hazel Upton."

"Who's she?"

"She's secretary to George Denby, the divorce lawyer."

"*Divorce lawyer?*" Ragan stared. "Who would want a divorce lawyer?"

"Miss Upton called us to say that Mary Burns had called when her boss was out, but Mary told her she wanted a divorce from Ollie."

"Somebody is crazy," Ragan muttered. "This is all wrong!"

"We've got a statement from her. We've also got a statement from a friend of Mary's, a Louella Chasen, who said Mary asked her what her divorce had cost and who her lawyer had been. She also implied there was another man."

Ragan was speechless. Even before this array of statements, he could not believe it. He would have staked his life that Ollie and Mary were the happiest couple he had ever known. He looked up. "Where do I come in?"

"You were a friend of the family. You called often when Ollie was away, didn't you?"

"Well, sure! But that doesn't mean we were anything but friends. Good Lord, man . . ."

For several minutes he sat without speaking. He knew how a word here and there could begin to build a semblance of guilt. Many times he had warned himself against assuming too much, and here it was, in his own life.

There was that old affection for Mary, never serious, but something they would bring up. He knew what a hard-hitting district attorney could do with the fact that he had known Mary before she met Ollie. They would insinuate much more than had ever existed between them. Ragan could see the net building around them, and there were two aspects he could not explain. Ollie had been shot with his own pistol, and Mary Burns had no alibi. Worse still was the one thing he could not understand, that Mary had actually spoken of divorce.

"Mark," he said slowly, "believe me, there is something very wrong here. I don't know what it is or where I stand with you, but I know as well as I am sitting here that Mary never wanted a divorce from Ollie. I was with them too much. And as for Mary and me, we were never more than friends.

"Mary knows I am in love with Angie and would marry her tomorrow if she'd have me. She knows that somehow or other we've gotten into the middle of something very ugly."

"Keep on with the case, Joe. If you can find out anything that will help, go ahead. I am afraid Mary Burns is in a bad spot. You can't get around that gun, and you can't escape those statements."

"They lied. They lied and they know they lied."

"For what reason? What would they gain? Why, they didn't even know why we wanted the information! Mary Burns was seen coming out of Denby's office, so we made inquiries. That was when we got the statement from Denby's secretary. Denby was out of the office, so he knew nothing about it."

"Who saw her come out of that office?"

Stigler compressed his lips. "I can't say. It was one of our men and he had a hunch there was something in back of it. As his hunches paid off in the past, we asked him to look into it."

"Al Brooks?"

"Don't start anything, Ragan. Remember, you're not in the clear yourself. You make trouble for Al and I'll have you locked up as a material witness." His face softened. "Damn it, man, I don't want to believe all this, but what can I do? Who had access to that gun? She and you. Maybe your girlfriend too. There isn't anybody else."

"Then you've got three suspects. I wish you luck with them, Stigler."

Nevertheless, when he got outside he felt sick and empty. He knew how much could be done with so little. Still, where had Mary gone? And what about this divorce business?

For a moment he thought about driving out to see just what had happened, then he decided against it. Nobody needed to see him and Mary again now. Besides, there was much more to do.

Mary had said Ollie had called her from the Upshaw Building. There was no reason why that should mean anything, but it was a place to begin, so he drove over and parked his car near the drugstore where Ollie had met Mary to go shopping.

No matter what had happened since, his every instinct told him to stick to the original case. If Ollie had begun to close in on somebody, all the troubles might stem from that.

The Upshaw Building had a café on the ground floor across the hall from a barbershop. Upstairs there were offices. In the foyer of the building there was a newsstand. Walking over, he began to study the magazines. There was a red-haired girl behind the counter and he smiled at her, then bought a package of gum. He was a big young man with an easy Irish smile, and the girl smiled back.

"Is there something I can find for you? Some particular magazine?"

"I was sort of watching for a friend of mine, a big guy with a wide face. Weighs about two-twenty. Has a scar on his jaw."

"Him? Sure, I remember him. He comes by a lot, although I don't know what for."

"Maybe to see you?" Joe smiled. "I couldn't blame him for that."

"He's nice. Married, though. I saw the ring on his finger. He was talking to me about Nebraska."

"Are you from there? I used to work out in a gym in Omaha. I was a fighter for a while."

"You sure don't look it. I mean, you're not banged up a lot. You must have been pretty good."

"Fair." Ragan peeled a stick of gum. So Ollie had been here more than once? And just standing around? "He's a friendly guy, my friend is. Likes to talk."

"Yes, he is. I like him. He's sort of like a big bear, but don't you tell him I said so."

"All warm and woolly, huh?"

She laughed. "He did talk a lot, but he's a good listener too." She glanced at Ragan again, appraising his shoulders. "What business is he in? He told me he was looking for an office in this neighborhood."

"He's a lawyer, but he doesn't handle court cases. He works with other lawyers, prepares briefs, handles small cases. He likes to take it easy." Ragan paused. "Did he find an office?"

"I don't know. They're full up here, though he was interested in that office on the fourth floor. Nobody is ever around there, and he was hoping they'd move out. I told him I couldn't see why anybody would want an office they didn't use."

"Does seem kind of dumb, when you're paying rent. That's like buying a car and leaving it in the garage. It doesn't make a lot of sense."

"It sure doesn't. I think Mr. Bradford has been in no more than twice all year. I think he comes over to do his work in the evening. Old Lady Grimes, she cleans up in there, and she says he's been here several times at night. I asked her about the office, thinking maybe I could find out something for your friend. She said they had a special lock on the door, and their own cleaning man who comes once a week."

Joe Ragan steered the talk to the latest movies and her favorite songs, then strolled to the elevator and went to the fourth floor.

He had no idea what he was looking for, except that Ollie Burns had been interested, and Ollie was not a man who wasted his time. Getting off the elevator, he walked briskly down the hall as if looking for a particular place, his eyes scanning the names on the doors.

A closed door with a frosted-glass upper panel was

marked JOHN J. BRADFORD, INVESTMENTS. There was a mail slot in the door.

Opposite was an open door where a young man sat at a desk. He was a short, heavyset young man with shoulders like a wrestler. He looked up sharply and there was something so intent about his gaze that Ragan was puzzled by it. He went on down the hall and into the office of JACOB KEENE, ATTORNEY-AT-LAW.

There was no receptionist in the outer office, but when he entered, she appeared. She was not a day over twenty, with a slim and lovely body in a gray dress that left little to the imagination, but much to think about and more to remember.

"Yes?"

Ragan smiled. "Now that's the way I like to hear a girl begin a conversation. It saves a lot of trouble. Usually they only say it at the end of the evening."

"Oh, they do?" She looked him over coolly. "Yes, for you I imagine they would." Her smile vanished. "Now may I ask your business, please?"

"To see Mr. Keene. Is he in?"

"Just a minute." She turned, and her figure lost nothing by the move. "A gentleman to see you, Mr. Keene."

"Send him in." The voice was crabbed and brusque.

Joe Ragan stepped by the girl as she stood in the doorway, her gaze cool and unresponsive. Then she stepped out and drew the door shut.

Jacob Keene was a small man who gave the appearance of being a hunchback, but was not. His face was long and gray, his head almost bald, and he had the eyes of a weasel. He took Ragan in at a glance, motioning to a chair. "Can't get girls these days that don't spend half their time thinking about men," he said testily. "Women aren't like they were in my day." He looked up at Joe, and suddenly the hatchet face broke into a lively smile and his eyes twinkled. "Damn the women of my day! What can I do for you?"

Ragan hesitated, then decided against any subterfuge. "Mr. Keene, I don't think I'm going to fool you, so I am not going to try. I'm looking for information and I'm willing to pay for it."

"Son!"—Keene's eyes twinkled with deviltry—"your last phrase touches upon a subject that is close to my heart. Pay! What a beautiful word! Money, they say, is the root of all evil. All right, let's get to the root of things!"

"As a matter of fact, I don't have much money, but what I want will cost you no effort. Shall we say"—Ragan drew ten dollars from his pocket—"a retainer?"

The long and greedy fingers palmed the ten. "And now? This information?"

"I want to know all you know about John Bradford and his business."

Keene's little eyes brightened. Their light was speculative. "Ah? Bradford? Well, well!"

"Also, I'd like to know something about the business across the hall from Bradford, and about the young man at the desk."

Keene nodded. "Sit down, young man. We've much to talk about. Yes, yes, that young man! Notices everything, doesn't he? Most odd, I'd say, unless he's paid to notice. That could be, you know. Well, young man, you have paid me. A paltry sum, but significant, significant.

"Bradford is a man of fifty, I should say, although his walk seems to belie that age. He dresses well, conservative taste. He calls at his office about once a month. The cleaning man takes away the mail."

"The cleaning man?" Ragan was incredulous.

"Exactly. An interesting fact, young man, that has engaged my fancy before this. Ah, yes, money. We all like money, and my guess would be that our friend down the hall has found a shortcut. People come to his door but they never knock or try to enter, they just slip envelopes through the mail slot."

Keene glanced at his calendar. "Wednesday. Four should come today, but they will not arrive together. They never arrive together. Three are women, one a man."

He drew a long cigar from a box in a drawer and bit off the end. "Nice place I have here, son. I see everyone and everything in that hallway. Two doors here, you see. The one you came in has my name on the door; the outside of this one is just marked 'Private.' If you noticed, there are mirrors on both sides of that door, and they allow me to see who is coming to my office before they arrive. If I don't want to see them, I just press a buzzer and my girl tells them I am out.

"Not much business these days, young man. I tell people I am retired, but I handle a few accounts, longstanding. Keeps me busy, and seeing what goes on in the hallway helps to while the time away."

Keene leaned forward suddenly. "Look, young man, here comes one of the women now."

She was tall, attractive, and no longer young. Ragan's guess was she was no longer fifty. She walked directly to the door of Bradford's office and dropped an envelope into the slot. Turning then, she went quickly down the hall as if in a hurry to be away. He was tempted to follow her, but on second thought he decided to wait and see what would happen.

It was twenty minutes before the second woman came. Joe Ragan sat up sharply, for this woman was Mary's acquaintance, Louella Chasen: the woman who, according to Stigler, Mary had asked about a divorce lawyer. She, too, walked to the door of Bradford's office and dropped an envelope through the slot.

Keene nodded, his small eyes bright and ferretlike. "See? What did I tell you? They never knock, just drop their envelopes and go away. An interesting business Mr. Bradford has, a very interesting business!"

Three women and a man, Keene had said, and that meant another woman and man were still to come. He would wait. Scowling thoughtfully, Ragan shook out a cigarette and lighted it. He rarely smoked anymore, and intended to quit, but once in a while . . .

"Look into the mirror now," Keene suggested.

The big-shouldered young man had come into the hall and was looking around. He threw a sharp, speculative glance at Keene's office, then returned to his own.

A few minutes later a tall young man, fair-haired and attractive, dropped his envelope into the slot and left. It was almost a half hour later, and Joe was growing sleepy, when he glanced up to see the last visitor of the day.

She was young and she carried herself well, and Ragan sat up sharply, unbelieving. There was something familiar . . . She turned her face toward Keene's office. It was Angie Faherty, his own girlfriend. She dropped a letter into the slot and walked briskly away.

"Well," Keene said, "you've had ten dollars worth. Those are the four who come today. Three or four will come tomorrow, and so it is on each day. They bunch up, though, on Saturday and Monday. Can you guess why?"

"Saturday and Monday? Could be because they draw their pay on Saturday. They must be making regular investments."

Keene chuckled. "Investments? Maybe. That last young lady has been coming longest of all. Over six months now."

Ragan heaved himself from the chair. "See you later. If anything turns up, save the information for me. I'll be around."

"With more money," Keene said cheerfully. "With more money, young man. Let us grease the wheels of inflation, support the economy, all that."

Angie was drinking coffee at their favorite place when Ragan walked in, and she looked up, smiling. "Have a hard day, Joe? You look so serious."

"I'm worried about Mary. She's such a grand person, and they are going to make trouble for her."

"For Mary? How could they?"

He explained, and her eyes darkened with anger. "Why, that's silly! You and Mary! Of all things!"

"I know, but a district attorney could make it look bad. Where did Mary go when she left you, Angie? Where could she have been?"

"We'll ask her. Let's go out there now."

"All right." He got up. "Have you eaten?"

"No, I came right here from home. I didn't stop anywhere."

"Been waiting long?"

"Long enough to have eaten if I'd thought of it. As it was, all I got was the coffee."

That made the second lie. She had not been here for some time, and she had not come right here from home. He tried to give her the benefit of the doubt. Maybe the visit to the Upshaw Building was so much a habit that she did not consider it. Still, it was out of her way in coming here.

He wanted to believe her. Maybe that's why cops get cynical—they are lied to so often.

All the way out to Mary's, he mulled it over. Another idea kept coming into mind. He had to get into that office of Bradford's. He had to know what those letters contained.

Yet what did he have to tie them to Ollie's death? No more than the fact that Ollie had loitered in the Upshaw Building and had an interest in the fourth floor. Louella Chasen, who came to that office, had volunteered information. She had stated that Mary Burns was asking about a divorce. It was a flimsy connection, but it was a beginning.

He had no other clue to the case Ollie had been working on, unless he went back to the Towne suicide.

Mark Stigler had mentioned that Ollie was interested in the Towne case, and it was at least a lead. The first thing tomorrow, he would investigate that aspect.

He remembered Alice Towne. Ollie had known her through an arrest he'd made in the neighborhood. She had been a slender, sensitive girl with a shy, sweet face and large eyes. Her unexplained suicide had been a blow to Ollie, for he liked people and had considered her a friend.

"You know, Joe," he had said once, "I've always thought that might have been my fault. She started to tell me something once, then got scared and shut up. I should have kept after her. Something was bothering her, and if I'd not been in so much of a hurry, she might have told me what it was."

Mary opened the door for them. Joe sat down with his hat in his hand. "Funeral tomorrow?" he asked gently.

Mary nodded. "Will you and Angie come together?"

"I thought maybe you'd like to have Angie with you," he suggested. "I'll be working right up to the moment, anyhow."

Mary turned to him. "Joe, you're working on this case, aren't you? Is there any way I can help?"

Ragan hated it, but he had to ask. "Mary, where did you go when you left Angie the night Ollie was murdered?"

Her face stiffened and she seemed to have trouble moving her lips. "You don't think I am guilty, Joe? You surely don't think I killed Ollie?"

"Of course not! I know better, Mary, but they are asking that question, and they will demand an answer."

"They've already asked," Mary said, "and I've refused to answer. I shall continue to refuse. It was private business, in a way, except that it did concern someone else. I can't tell you, Joe."

Their eyes held for a full minute and then Joe got up. "Okay, Mary, if you won't tell, you've got a reason, but please remember: That reason may be a clue. Don't hold anything back. Now let me ask you—did you ever think of divorce?"

"No." Her eyes looked straight into Ragan's. "If people say that, they are lying. From what Mr. Stigler has said, I believe someone is saying that. It is simply not true."

After Ragan left them, he thought about that. Knowing Mary, he would take her word for it, but would anybody else? In the face of two witnesses to the contrary and the fact that Ollie was shot with his own gun, Mary was in more trouble than she realized.

Moreover, he was getting an uneasy feeling. Al Brooks was hungry for newspaper notices and for advancement. He liked getting around town and liked spending money. A step up in rank would suit him perfectly. If he could solve the murder of Ollie Burns and pin it on Mary, he would not hesitate. He was a shrewd, smart man with connections.

Ragan now had several lines of investigation. The Towne case was an outside and remote chance, but the Upshaw Building promised better results.

What had Angie been doing there? What did the mysterious letters contain? Who was Bradford?

Taking his car, Ragan drove across town to the Upshaw Building. He had his own ideas about what he would do now, and the law would not condone them. With the meager evidence he had, a search warrant was out of consideration, but he was going to get into the Bradford office or know the reason why.

In Keene's office he had noticed the fire escape at his window extended to that of Bradford's office. The lock on the Bradford office door was a good one, and there was no easy way to open it in the time he would have.

After parking his car a block away, he walked up the street to the Upshaw Building. The night elevator man was drowsing over a newspaper, so Ragan slipped by him and went up the stairs to the fourth floor. He paused at the head of the steps, listening. There was not a sound. He walked down the hall to Keene's office and tried the door. It opened under his hand. Surprised and suddenly wary, he stepped inside.

The body of a man was slumped over Keene's desk.

He sat in a swivel chair, face against the desk, arms dangling at his sides. All this Ragan saw in sporadic flashes from an electric sign across the street. He closed the door behind him, studying the shadows in the room.

All was dark and still; the only light was that from the electric sign across the street. The corners were dark, and shadows lay deep along the walls and near the safe.

Ragan's gun was in its shoulder holster, reassuring in its weight. Careful to touch nothing, he leaned forward and spoke gently.

No reply, no movement. With a fountain pen flash he studied the situation.

Jacob Keene was dead. There was a blotch of blood on his back where the bullet had emerged. There was, Ragan noted as he squatted on his heels, blood on Keene's knees and on the floor under him, but not enough. Keene's body, he believed, had been moved. Flipping on the light switch, he glanced quickly around the office to ascertain that it was empty. Then he began a careful search of the room.

Nothing was disturbed or upset. It was just as he had seen it that afternoon, with the exception that Keene was dead. Careful to touch nothing, he knelt on the floor to examine, as best he could, the wound. The bullet had evidently entered low in the abdomen and ranged upward at an odd angle. The gun, which he had missed seeing, lay on the floor under Keene's right hand.

Suicide? That seemed to be the idea, but remembering the Keene of that afternoon, Ragan shook his head. Keene was neither in the mood for suicide nor the right man for it. No, this was murder. It was up to Ragan to call homicide, but he hesitated. There were other things to do first.

The first thing was to see the inside of that office of Bradford's. He believed Keene had been murdered elsewhere and brought here. He might have been killed trying to do just what Ragan was about to attempt.

Absolute silence hung over the building. Ragan put his ear to the wall, listening. There was no sound. Carefully he eased up the window. Four stories below, a car buzzed along the street, then there was silence. The windows facing him were all dark and empty. As he stepped out on the fire escape, a drop of rain touched his face. He glanced up at the lowering clouds. That would be good. If it rained, nobody would be inclined to glance up.

Flattened against the wall, he eased along to the next window. It was closed and there was no light from within. He tested the window, hoping it was unlocked. It was locked. He took the chewing gum from his mouth and plastered it against the glass near the lock, then tapped it with the muzzle of his gun. The glass broke but could not fall, as it stood against the lock itself. Easing a finger into the hole, he lifted the glass out very carefully, then unlocked the window and lifted it.

Slipping inside, he moved swiftly to the wall and waited, listening. Using utmost care, he began a minute examination.

For an hour he went through the office and found exactly nothing. Nothing? One thing only: a large, damp place where the floor had been wiped clean. Of blood? But blood can never be washed completely away in such a hurried job. Ragan knew what a lab test could prove.

The office was similar to any other, except that nothing seemed to have been used.

There was a typewriter, paper, carbons, extra ribbons, paperclips. The blotter on the desk was also new and unused. The filing cabinets contained varied references to mines and industries. Except for that damp place on the floor, all was as one might expect it to be.

Then he noticed something he had missed. A tiny,

crumpled bit of paper lying on the floor under the desk, as though somebody had tossed it to the wastebasket and missed. Retrieving it, Ragan unfolded it carefully and flashed his light upon it.

Ollie Burns's phone number!

Here was a definite lead, but to where? Ragan stood in the middle of the office, wondering where to turn next. Somewhere nearby was the clue he needed. Suddenly there returned to his mind one of the titles of the mining companies he had glimpsed in leafing through the files. Wheeling about, he took a quick step to the filing cabinets and drew out the drawer labeled *T.*

In a moment he had it. *Towne Mining & Exploration.* Under it was a list of code words, then a list of sums of money indicating that fifty dollars per month had been paid until the first of the year, when the payments had been stepped up to one hundred dollars a month. Four months later there was this entry: *Account closed, 20 April.*

His heart was pounding. The suicide of Alice Towne had been discovered on the nineteenth of April!

Towne Mining & Exploration—was there such a firm?

A quick survey showed that on several of the drawers the names of well-known firms were listed, but no payments on any of them. They must be used as a blind, probably for blackmail.

What had Ollie told Mary? *There were just two crimes worse than murder.* Dope peddling and blackmail.

Who else had come to this office? Louella Chasen.

Ragan drew out the drawer with the C, thumbing through it to a folder marked *Chasen Shipping.* A quick check showed that payments had progressed from ten dollars a month to one hundred over a period of four years.

Louella Chasen was the one who said she had recommended a divorce lawyer to Mary Burns. Would she lie to protect herself? If blackmail could force continual payments, would she not also perjure herself?

Hazel Upton, secretary to Denby, the divorce lawyer. Her name, thinly disguised, was here also.

It was the merest sound, no more than a whisper, as of clothing brushing paper, that interrupted him. Frozen in place, Ragan listened. He heard it again. It came from the office of Jacob Keene, where the murdered attorney still lay.

Ragan's hand went to his gun, a reassuring touch only. This was neither the time nor the place for a gun. The window stood open, and so did the window in the Keene office. If someone was there, he would see the open window, and if that someone leaned out, a glance would show this window to be open too. And if the man who was in the next room happened to be the murderer . . .

Even as he thought of that, Ragan realized there was something else in the files he must see: the file on Angie Faherty.

There was no time for that now, and the door to the hall was out of the question. The only exit from the office was the way he had come.

Like a wraith, he slipped from the filing cabinet to

the deep shadow near the safe, then to the blackness of the corner near the window. Even as he reached it he heard the scrape of a shoe on the iron of the fire escape. The killer was coming in.

It was very still. Outside, a whisper of rain was falling and there was a sound of traffic on wet pavement. The flashing electric sign did not light this room, and Ragan waited, poised for action.

A stillness of death hung over the building. The killer on the fire escape was waiting, too, and listening for some movement from Ragan.

Did he know Ragan was there? And who he was? It was a good question.

With a quick glance at the window, Ragan gauged the distance to the telephone. Moving as softly as possible, he glided to the phone. With his left hand he moved the phone to the chair, then lifted the receiver.

Holding the phone, he waited. Tires whined on the pavement below and he spoke quickly. "Police department! Quick!"

In a moment, a husky voice answered. Ragan spoke softly. "Get this the first time. There's a prowler on the fire escape of the Upshaw Building!"

His voice was a low whisper, but the desk sergeant got it, all right. Ragan repeated it and then eased the receiver back on the cradle. From his new position he could see the dim outline of a figure on the fire escape, as whoever it was edged closer.

The police would be here in a minute or two. If only the man on the fire escape would—

He heard the wail of sirens far off, and almost smiled.

It would be nip-and-tuck now. The siren whined closer and Ragan heard a muffled curse. Cars slid into the street below and he heard the clang of feet on the fire escape, running down.

For a breath-catching instant he waited, then ducked out of one window and into the next, even as the police spotlight hit the wall. A moment before the glare reached him, he was safely inside. From below he heard a shout. "There he is!" They had spotlighted the other man.

Ragan ducked out the door and ran down the hall, taking the back stairs three steps at a time. When he reached the main floor he saw the watchman craning his neck at the front door, trying to see what was happening. On cat feet, Ragan slipped up behind him. "Did they get him?" he asked.

The watchman jumped as if he'd been shot. He turned, his face white, and Ragan flashed his badge. "Gosh, Officer, you scared the daylights out of me! What's going on?"

"Prowler reported on the fire escape of this building. I'm looking for him."

Sergeant Casey came hurrying to the door. When he saw Ragan he slowed down. Casey was one of Ragan's buddies, for this was a burglary detail. "Hi, Ragan! I didn't know you were here!"

"Did you get him?"

"We didn't, but Brooks almost did."

"Al Brooks?" Ragan's scalp tightened. What had Brooks been doing here? Tailing him? Ragan hadn't thought they might put a tail on him, but Brooks was just the man to do it.

"He was on the street and saw somebody on the fire escape. He started up after him just as we drove up. Fellow got away, I guess."

"Ain't been nobody here," the watchman said. "Only Mr. Bradford, and he left earlier."

"What time was he here?" Ragan asked.

"Maybe eight o'clock. No later than that."

Eight? It was now almost one A.M., and Keene had not been dead long when Ragan found him. Certainly no more than an hour, at a rough guess. His body hadn't even been cold.

Al Brooks came around the corner with two patrol-car officers. He stopped abruptly when he saw Ragan. He was suddenly very careful. Ragan could see the change. "How are you, Joe? I wasn't expecting to see you."

"I get around." Ragan shook out a cigarette.

Casey interrupted. "We'd better go through the building, Joe, now that we're here. The man might be hiding upstairs."

"Good idea," Ragan said. "Let's go!"

Everything was tight and shipshape all the way to Keene's office. Ragan was letting Casey and a couple of his boys precede him. It was his idea to let them find the body. It was Casey who did.

"Hey!" he called. "Dead man here!"

Ragan and Brooks came on the run. "Looks like suicide," Brooks commented. "I doubt if this had anything to do with the prowler."

"Doesn't look like he even got in here," Casey said.

"But the window's op—" Brooks stared. The window was closed. "You know," he said, "when I started up the fire escape, I'd have sworn this window was open."

He returned to the body at the desk. "Looks like suicide," he repeated. "The gun's right where he dropped it."

"Except that it wasn't suicide," Ragan said quietly. "And, Al, you'd better leave this one for homicide." He smiled. "The autopsy will tell us for sure, but this man seems to have been stabbed before he was shot."

"Where do you get that idea?" Brooks demanded.

"Look." Ragan indicated a narrow slit in the shirt, just above the wound. "My guess is he was killed by the stab wound, then shot to make the bullet follow the stab wound. I'll bet the gun belongs to Keene."

Brooks looked around. "How did you know his name?"

"It's on the door. Jacob Keene, attorney-at-law. We don't actually know this is Keene, of course, but I'm betting it is."

Brooks shut up, but the man was disturbed and he was angry. Al Brooks had a short fuse, and it was burning.

Ragan was doing some wondering. What about that prowler? What had become of him? He was carrying on a swift preliminary examination of the office, without disturbing anything, when Mark Stigler arrived. He glanced from Ragan to Brooks. "Lots of talent around," he said. "What is it, murder or suicide?"

The slit in the material of the shirt was barely visible,

but Ragan indicated it. "A clumsy attempt to cover up a murder," Ragan commented.

"Could be," Stigler agreed. "Seems kind of far-fetched, though. Who was this guy?"

"From his files, he was a sort of shyster, handling a good many minor cases in the past, but he changed here lately, or seemed to. He's semiretired, handling only a few legal affairs for various people."

Stigler's crew went to work while Stigler chewed on a toothpick, listened to the talk, and studied the situation. Al Brooks shoved his hat back on his head and took over.

He had been down on the street when he looked up and saw a prowler outside a window on the third floor. Just as he started up, he heard sirens and the patrol cars appeared. "And just about that time I ran into Joe Ragan. He was already here."

Stigler glanced at Ragan. "How are you coming on the Burns job?"

"Good enough. I'll have it in the bag by the end of the week."

Stigler eyed him thoughtfully. "We've got a strong case against his wife. Brooks thinks she did it. She or somebody close to her."

That meant Ragan, of course.

"Brooks doesn't know what he's talking about. Mary loved her husband, loved him in a way Brooks couldn't even understand."

Brooks's laugh was unpleasant. "For your sake, I hope you are right, but Mary Burns is in this up to her neck, and there *might* just be somebody else involved!"

Ragan walked over to him. "Listen, Al, you do your job and we'll do ours, but just be sure that if you try to pin anything on any friends of mine, you can prove your case. If you've got the goods, all right, but you start a frame and I'll bust you wide open!"

"Cut it out, Ragan!" Stigler said sharply. "Any more talk like that and you'll draw a suspension. I won't have fighting on any job of mine."

"Anyhow," Brooks said quietly, "I don't think you could do it."

Ragan just looked at him. Someday he would have to take Brooks, and he would take him good. Until then he could wait.

Ragan repeated what little he had to Stigler, saying nothing about his previous entry. However, he lingered after Brooks had gone to add a few words.

"I talked to Keene," he said, "and he was a cagey old bird. He gave me the impression that something was going on here that wasn't strictly kosher. He was suspicious of some of the activities on this floor."

"Suspicious? How? Of what?"

"That I don't know, except that the office next to him seems to have been used rarely, and then at night. Although people did come to the door and drop envelopes through the slot."

"So? There's a law says somebody has to use an office because he pays rent?"

Ragan turned away, but Stigler stopped him. "Stay away from Al Brooks, do you hear?" Then, in a rare bit of confidence, he added, "I don't like him any better than you do, but he's been making points with the Commissioners."

Ragan walked back to his car, approaching with care. From now on he must walk cautiously indeed. He was learning things, and he had a feeling it was realized. What he wanted now was to be away where he could think, if he could only—An idea came to him that was insane, and yet . . .

Where had Al Brooks come from? What was he doing in this area, at this hour? His explanation was clear and logical enough, yet a prowler had been on the fire escape, and when the spotlight came on, it had picked up Al Brooks.

Ragan considered that and a few other things about Al Brooks. He dressed better than any man on the force, drove a good car, and lived well. Ragan shook his head. He must be careful and not be influenced by his dislike for Brooks or by Brooks's obvious dislike for him. And the man did have a good record with the department.

It was Al Brooks, however, who had first suggested that Mary Burns might have killed her husband. It was also Al Brooks who had reported seeing Mary coming out of a divorce lawyer's office.

Now that he was thinking about it, a lot of ideas came to mind. Stopping his car at the curb in front of his apartment, Ragan got out and started for the door. There was a strange car parked at the curb a few doors away, and for some reason it disturbed him. He walked over to it. There was no one inside, and it was not locked. He looked at the registration. *Valentine Lewis, 2234 Herald Place.*

The name meant nothing to him, and he turned away and walked to his private entrance and fitted the key into the lock. As he opened the door he was wondering what the blackmailer could have that would influence both Hazel Upton and Louella Chasen to start the divorce rumor, and if Brooks—

He stepped through the door, and the roof fell on him.

Wildly, grabbing out with both hands, Ragan fell to his knees. He had been slugged and he could not comprehend what was happening, then there was a smashing blow on his skull and he seemed to be slipping down a long slide into darkness.

When he fought his way out of it, he was lying on the floor and his head felt like a balloon. Gray light was filtering into the room. It must be daylight.

He lay still, trying to focus his thoughts. Then he got to his hands and knees, and then to his feet. He staggered to the sofa and sat down hard.

His skull was pounding as if an insane snare drummer were at work inside. His mouth felt sticky and full of cotton. He lifted his head and almost blacked out. Slowly he stared around the room. Nothing had been taken that he could see. He felt for his handkerchief and realized his pockets had been turned inside out.

Staggering to the door, he peered into the street. The strange car was gone.

"Val Lewis," he muttered grimly, "if you aren't guilty, you'd better have a mighty good story, and if you slugged me, God help you!"

Somehow he got out of his clothes and into a shower,

and then tumbled into bed. His head was cut in two places from the blows, but what he wanted most was sleep.

It was well past noon when he was awakened by the telephone.

It was Angie. "Joe!" She sounded frightened and anxious. "What's happened? Where are you?"

"I must be home. When the phone rang, I answered it. Where are you?"

"Where am *I*?" Her tone was angry. "Where would I be? Don't you remember our luncheon date?"

"Frankly, I didn't. I got slugged on the head last night, and—"

"At least," she interrupted, "that's an original excuse!"

"And true. I was visiting an office in the Upshaw Building, and then—"

Her gasp was audible. "Joe? Did you say the Upshaw Building?"

"That's right." Suddenly he remembered her visit there while he and Keene had watched. "Some people up there play rough, honey. A lawyer was murdered up there last night. He knew too much and was too curious about somebody named Bradford."

She was silent. "The slugging," he added, "happened after I got home. I think somebody wanted to find out if I'd carried anything away from that building."

That idea had come to him while he was talking, but it made sense. What other reason was there? Thinking it over, it struck him as remarkable that he had not been killed out of hand. They had probably killed Ollie Burns for little more, or even for less.

She still did not speak, so he asked, "How's Mary? Is she all right?"

"Joe!" She was astonished. "You didn't know? She was arrested this morning. I believe it was Al Brooks."

Brooks? Ragan's grip tightened on the phone until his fist turned white. "So he arrested her, did he? All right, that does it. I'm going to blow everything loose now."

"What are you going to do?" Her voice sounded anxious.

"Do? Their whole case is built on a bunch of lies and perjury. I know that Hazel Upton and Louella Chasen were forced into this by a blackmailer."

"Joe, did you say a . . . blackmailer?"

"Yes, Angie, a blackmailer. The same people who hounded Alice Towne to death murdered Ollie Burns and Jacob Keene."

"You mean you *know* all that? Can you prove it?"

"Maybe not right now, but I will, honey, I will!"

It was not until after he hung up that he realized he was still groggy from the blows on the head, and that he had talked too much. He was still suffering from the concussion, but he was mad, also. He had been a damned fool to say so much. After all, she had been blackmailed, too.

He dressed halfway and then went into the bathroom to shave. His Irish face had been altered somewhat some years back, when he stopped a right hook with his nose. The hook had broken his nose, not flattened it, and what had happened to the other guy was in the record books. He lost by a knockout in the fourth round.

His razor smoothed the beard from his face while he turned the case over in his mind. He decided to start with Val Lewis, then work his way to Hazel Upton and Louella Chasen. Also, he was going to talk with that luscious job Keene had for a secretary. And with the sharp-eyed lad who kept an eye on Bradford's door.

For the next two hours Ragan was busy. He visited and questioned several people and spent time checking the files of the *Times*. Also, he visited the address that Valentine Lewis had.

The door was answered by a dyspeptic-looking blonde with the fading shadow of a black eye. She wore a flowered kimono that concealed little.

"I'm looking for Valentine Lewis." Ragan spoke politely. "Is he in?"

"What do you want to see him for?"

"Veteran's Administration," Ragan said vaguely.

"That's a lousy joke," she replied coldly. "Val was in San Quentin during the war. Come again."

"Police department." Ragan flashed his badge and started to push by her.

She yelled, strident and angry. "You get out of here, copper! You got no search warrant!"

Ragan took one from his pocket. She didn't get a chance to see more than the top of it, for it was just a form, partly filled out.

She stepped back and asked no more questions, muttering to herself. Ragan needed only a glance around to see that Lewis had enough guns to start World War III.

It was all he needed. He called headquarters and suggested they come down with a warrant for Val Lewis. Any ex-convict with a gun in his possession was on his way back to jail.

Blue Eyes stood there looking mean. "You think you're smart, don't you?"

"Whatever I am," he said, "I am not foolish enough to buck the law."

"No," she said, sneering. "You're just a dope. You cops aren't smart enough to make any money, you just crab it for others."

"An officer doesn't have to be smart," Ragan said gently, "although the fact that he's on the side of the law shows he's far from as dumb as you seem to think. We've got organization, honey: records of crimes, methods of operation, fingerprints, and cooperation from other cities.

"We have a lot of very bright men at headquarters, and some other very bright boys in the patrol cars, but best of all is the organization."

"You'd better have them all with you when you go after Val," she said venomously. "I'd like to see you try it!"

The police cars were arriving. "Lady," Ragan said, "that is just what I am going to do. He works in the Upshaw Building, doesn't he?"

Her surprise showed him he was right. "I am going to send you to headquarters, and then I'm going after your Val. In case you don't know, he slugged me last night. Now it will be my turn."

"Oh? So you're Joe Ragan?" Her face stiffened, realizing she'd made a miscue. "I hope he burns you down!"

Mark Stigler was with them when they came in. He glanced grimly at the assortment of guns. "What is this?" he asked Ragan. "I thought you were working on the Burns murder."

"This is part of it," Ragan said. "See what the girl has to say. I doubt if she wants to be an accessory."

She was really frightened now, but Stigler ignored her. "You think this Val Lewis did it?"

"If he didn't, he knows who did."

All the way to the Upshaw Building, Mark Stigler chewed on his dead cigar while Ragan laid it out for him. He built up the blackmail background, reminded him how Ollie had been bothered by the Towne suicide, and how Ollie had worried the case like a dog over a bone. He told Stigler of his idea that Ollie had been murdered because he had stumbled into the blackmail ring.

He explained about the Bradford office and the letters dropped there and who dropped them. The one thing he did not mention was Angie. She was still his girl, and if she was being blackmailed, he'd cover for her if she wasn't otherwise involved.

"You think there was money in those envelopes?"

"That's right. I believe all those records in the filing cabinets, with the exception of a few obvious company names, are blackmail cases. From what I can remember—and I had only a few hasty glances—the income must run to thousands of dollars a month.

"They weren't bleeding just big shots, but husbands

and wives, clerks, stenographers, beauty operators, everybody. I think Bradford, whoever he is, is a smart operator, but he had somebody else with him, somebody who knew Ollie."

"Somebody who could get close to him?"

"Yes, and somebody who believed Ollie was getting close to a solution. Also, it had to be somebody who could get into his house or his locker for that gun."

Stigler rolled his cigar in his lips. "You're telling a good story, but do you have any facts? It all sounds good, but what we need is evidence!"

At the Upshaw Building, Stigler loitered around the corner and let Ragan go after Val Lewis. Lewis was sitting at the open door, as usual. As Ragan turned toward the door of the Bradford office, Lewis got up and came around his desk. "What do you want?" he demanded.

"What business is it of yours?" Ragan asked. "I want into this office. Also"—he turned, with some expectation of what was coming—"I want you for assault and murder!"

Lewis was too confident and too hotheaded for his own good. He started a punch and it came fast, but Ragan rolled his head and let the punch go around it, and hooked a wicked right to the solar plexus that dropped Lewis's mouth open in a desperate gasp for breath. The left hook that followed collapsed the bridge of Lewis's nose as if it were made of paper.

He was big, bigger than Ragan, built like an all-American lineman, but the fight was knocked out of him. Stigler walked up. "You got a key to this place?"

"No, I ain't. Bradford's got it."

"To hell with that!" Ragan's heel drove hard against the door beside the lock. It held, a second and a third time, then he put his shoulder to it and pushed it open. While an officer took Lewis to a patrol car, Ragan went to the filing cabinet.

It was empty.

A second and third were empty too. Mark Stigler looked from Ragan to the smashed door. "Boy, oh, boy! What now?"

Ragan felt sick. The files had been removed sometime after he left the place. By now they were hidden or destroyed, and there would be a lot of explaining to do about this door.

Stigler glared at him. "When you pull a boner, you sure pull a lulu!"

"Mark," Ragan said, "get the lab busy on that floor. This is where Keene was murdered. Right there."

"How do you know?"

Ragan swallowed. "Because I was in here last night after the murder."

Stigler's eyes were like gimlets. "*After* the murder? Were you the prowler?"

"No." Ragan filled him in on the rest of it. His meeting with Keene, his return, the discovery of the body, and the mysterious watcher outside.

"Have you any idea who that was?" Stigler fixed him with a cold eye.

"I might have, but I'd rather not say right now."

Oddly, Stigler did not follow that up. He walked around the office, looking into this and that. He was still puttering about when Ragan looked up to see Keene's receptionist standing in the door. "Hi, honey," she said cheerfully. "This is the first time I ever saw this door open."

"Who are you working for now?"

She smiled. "Nobody. Came up to clear my desk and straighten up some work that's left. I'll be out of a job. Need a secretary?"

"Lady," Ragan said, "I could always find a place for you!"

Stigler turned and looked at her from under his heavy brows. "What do you know about this Bradford?" he asked.

"Bradford?" She smiled. "I wondered if you'd ever ask." She indicated Ragan. "Will it do him any good if I talk?"

"Plenty," Stigler said with emphasis.

"All right." She was suddenly all business. "I know that the man who has been calling himself Bradford for the past three months is not the Bradford who opened this office. He is a taller, broader man.

"Furthermore, I know he was in my office after closing time last night, and must have been there after Mr. Keene was murdered."

Stigler took the cigar from his mouth. "How do you figure that?"

"Look." She crossed to the wastebasket below the water cooler and picked out a paper cup. "The man who calls himself Bradford has strong fingers. When he finishes drinking, he squeezes the cup flat and pushes the bottom up with his thumb. It is a habit he has."

She picked up the wastebasket and showed a half-dozen cups to Stigler. He glanced at them and walked next door to Keene's office. She picked up the basket from the cooler and said, "See? One cup left intact, one crushed. On top of the cup that Mr. Keene threw away in this crushed one."

She paused. "I don't know anything about such things, but you might find fingerprints on those cups."

Stigler chewed on his cigar. "We could use you," he said, "in the department."

Outside in the street, Stigler said little. He was mulling something over in his mind. Ragan knew the man and knew he was bothered by something. Finally, Stigler said, as much to himself as to Ragan, "Do you think those records were destroyed?"

"I doubt it. If what that girl says is true, he hasn't been running this business that long. He would need the files to use for himself. I have a suspicion," Ragan added, "that whoever he is, he muscled in."

Stigler nodded. He took the cigar from his teeth. "Joe, I don't know exactly where you're going, but I won't push this case against Mary Burns until I hear more from you. In the meantime, I think we'll check the dead and missing for the last few months."

Stigler got into his car and rolled away, and Ragan stared after him, then realized somebody was at his elbow. It was the receptionist with the figure. "Can I help? I've some free time now."

"Not unless you can remember something more about Bradford and that setup. Did Keene know any more about them?"

"He was curious about a girl who came there, and he had me follow her once."

"What sort of girl?"

"A slender girl with red hair. She wore a green suit and was quite attractive."

For a moment Ragan just stood there. It made no sense, no sense at all.

His eyes turned to the blonde. "What's your name, honey?"

"I was wondering if you even cared," she said, smiling. There was no humor in her eyes, just something wistful, somehow very charming and very young. "I'm Marcia Mahan, and I meant what I said about helping."

Ragan did not know what to do. There was little evidence against Mary. They had the testimony of Hazel Upton and Louella Chasen, but how would they stand up under severe cross-examination? Angie Faherty agreed she had gone to the rest room but had not been there at the time of the killing.

The gun was Ollie's own, so with work they might build a stiff case against Mary. The worst of it was that if she was tried and acquitted, a few would always have their doubts.

He could not stop now. Ollie would have done it for him. Now he was beginning to see where the arrows pointed, and it made him feel sick and empty. One can control events only up to a point.

Other things were clicking into place now. His memory was a good one and had been trained by police work. He remembered something he had overlooked. In those files there had been one with the title BYSTEN PACKING COMPANY.

One of the big cases Al Brooks had broken was that of Clyde Bysten, a blackmail case.

Ragan threw his cigarette into the gutter. He was smoking too much since this case began. "All right, if you really want to help, you can." He wrote an address on a slip of paper. "This is where Alice Towne worked. I want a list of the employees at that office during the time she worked there. Can you do that?"

Marcia nodded. "No problem."

"And meet me at the Peacock Bar at four."

Grabbing a cab, he headed for the bank. Within minutes he was closeted with a vice-president he knew and a few minutes later was receiving the information needed. When he left the bank, he felt he had been kicked in the stomach.

Yet his job was only beginning, and from then until four, he was going through files of newspapers, and using the telephone to save his legs, to say nothing of gasoline. He called business firms, and people he knew, and checked charge accounts and property lists. By four o'clock he had a formidable list of information, blackening information that left him feeling worse than he had ever felt in his life.

Outside the cocktail lounge he waited, thinking over what lay before him. He could see no end in sight. Once more he was going to enter an apartment without a search warrant, only this time he was hoping to find nothing. He was, in fact, planning to enter two apartments.

Marcia was waiting for him, a cup of coffee before her. She placed the list on the table and Ragan scanned it. His heart almost stopped when he saw the name, the one he was positive he would see, and feared to see.

"You look as if you lost your best friend," Marcia said. "Can I help?"

"You help just by being here," he said.

When Ragan came into homicide, Stigler was behind his desk. "I think I've got it." He shoved a card at Ragan. "Sam Bayless. He did two terms for con games but was hooked into one blackmailing offense that could not be pinned on him. Smooth operator, fits the description we have of Bradford."

"Dead?"

"Found shot to death in the desert near Palmdale. Shot four times in the chest with a .38. We have one of the slugs."

"Good! Can you check it with that gun?"

"We will—somehow. Have you got anything more?"

"Too much." Ragan hesitated. "He's not in this alone. There's a woman."

Stigler rolled his cigar in his lips. He did not look at Ragan. "I had a hunch," he said. "Do you know who she is?"

Ragan nodded. "Before the night's over I believe we can cinch this case."

It was his duty, his duty as a police officer and as a friend of Ollie Burns, a good friend and a decent officer, but he felt like a traitor. It was late when he went to the place near the park and stopped his car. He had rented a car for the evening, and with Marcia Mahan beside him they would seem to be any couple doing a little private spooning, to use an old-fashioned term that he liked.

"What do you want me to do when you go in?" she asked.

"Sit still. If they come back, push the horn button."

The door of the apartment house opened and a man and a woman came out and got into a car. It was Al Brooks—hard, reckless, confident. He did not want to look at the girl, but he had to. It was Angie Faherty.

For an instant, her face was fully under the street light and Ragan saw her eyes come toward his car. She said something to Brooks. Ragan turned toward Marcia. "Come on, honey, let's make it look good."

She came into his arms as if she belonged there, and she did not have to make it look good. It *was* good. The first time their lips met, his hair seemed to curl all the way to the top of his head.

Brooks came across the street toward them, and turned his flashlight into the car. Ragan's face was out of sight against her shoulder, and she pulled her head up long enough to say, "Beat it, bud! Can't you see we're busy?"

Brooks chuckled and walked away and they heard him make some laughing remark to Angie as they got into their car. Then they were driving away.

Marcia unwound herself. "Well! If this is the kind of work detectives do . . ."

"Come here," Ragan replied cheerfully. "They might come back. I think we'd better give them at least fifteen minutes of leeway. They might have forgotten something."

"I think you'd better go inside and see what you don't want to see. I'll wait."

Opening the door was no trick. Once inside he took a quick look around. It was all very familiar, too familiar, even to the picture of himself on the piano. That picture must have given Brooks many a laugh.

His search was fast, thorough, and successful. The files were lying in plain sight on a shelf in the closet. He was bundling them up when the horn honked.

They came fast, because when he turned around, he heard the key in the lock. Ragan grabbed the files. One bunch slipped and he reached to catch it and the door slammed open. Al Brooks, his face livid, was framed in the door.

Slowly, Ragan put the files down. "Well, Al, here it is. We've been waiting for this."

"Sure." There was concentrated hatred in his eyes. "And I'm going to like it!"

Brooks had his gun in his hand and Ragan knew he was going to kill, but not without a fight.

Brooks fired as Ragan started for him, and something burned Ragan along the ribs. Ragan knocked Brooks back over a chair and went over it after him. They came up slugging, and Brooks was throwing them hard and fast. He caught Ragan with a wicked right that shook him to his heels, then brought over a left that Ragan slipped. Ragan had not been a fast light-heavyweight for nothing. Taking punches had been his line of business. He took the two going in, and smashed both hands to Brooks's body. Brooks backed up and Ragan hooked a left to the mouth that smeared it to bloody shreds against his teeth. Brooks ducked to avoid the payoff punch and took it over the eye instead of on the chin. The blow cut to the bone and showered him with blood.

Shoving him away, Ragan swung again and Brooks jerked up a knee for his groin. Turning to avoid it, Ragan turned too far, and Al got behind him, running a forearm across his throat. Grabbing Al's hand and elbow, Ragan dropped to one knee, throwing Brooks over his shoulder.

Al staggered up, his face a bloody sight. "What's the matter, chum? Can't you take it? Come on, tough boy! You wanted it, now you're getting it!"

Brooks came in again, but Ragan stabbed a left into his face, then belted him in the wind. Al stumbled forward and Ragan grabbed a handful of hair and jerked Brooks's head down to meet his upcoming knee. It was a neat touch, but hard on the features.

The door smashed open and Mark Stigler came in. Casey was right behind him. "Got him?" Stigler asked.

Ragan gestured and Stigler looked. "Man, oh, man! I've seen a few, but this!"

"There are the files." Ragan pointed. "You'll find the Towne, Chasen, and Upton files there, and a lot of others." He glanced out the door. "Did you . . . ? I mean, was Angie . . . ? What happened to her?"

"She's out there. Your blonde is with her."

Angie did not look as lovely as he remembered her. In

fact, her eyes were venomous. Her hair was all out of shape and she had a puffed lip.

"What hit you?" Ragan asked.

Marcia smiled pleasantly. "A girl name Mahan. She gave me trouble, so I socked her."

Angie said nothing, and it was not in Ragan to get tough. She had double-crossed him and helped to frame Mary Burns, but it was not in him to hate her. "Whatever made you pull a stunt like this?" he asked.

She looked up. "You can't prove a thing. You can't tie this one on me."

"Yes, we can, Angie," he replied gently. "It is all sewed up. You killed Ollie Burns, then smeared him with lipstick. With you, whom he trusted, he would have talked. It was Al who called, but you who met him after you got Mary called away. Mary thought you were in trouble, and when she came back and you were gone, she tried to cover for you. She never dreamed you had killed Ollie.

"You took the gun from their home. Al Brooks wouldn't have had access to it. You would.

"You had a good setup after Al came in with you. You were in it with Bayless or Bradford. You worked with Alice Towne and you wormed the information out of her that she was being blackmailed.

"On one of his vice raids, Al Brooks picked up some information and got hep to what you were doing, and declared himself in. Then he killed Bayless, and you two took over the business. He killed Keene when he caught him in your office after hours, then shot him to make it appear to be suicide."

"Got it all figured, have you?" Brooks said. "Wait until I get out!"

Stigler just looked at him. "They don't get out of the gas chamber, Al. We've got one of the bullets you put into Bayless. It checks with your gun."

"The information that led to your arrest of Latko, Al, came from your blackmailing racket. You had a good thing going there."

Ragan hitched his shoulder holster into place. That was the trouble with having been a fighter. When you were in trouble you used your fists.

"We checked some charge accounts of yours, Angie. Your bank accounts too. We have all the information we need. We know your brother did time with Bayless."

"My brother?" Her eyes turned wild. "What do you know about him?"

"We picked him up today, and his girl friend talked. Anyway, we found him with enough guns to outfit an army. He was using the name Valentine Lewis."

Later, when Al Brooks was being booked, he took a paper cup from the cooler and drank, then compressed the cup and pushed the bottom in with his thumb, an unconscious gesture. Seeing it, Stigler looked over at Ragan.

Marcia was standing beside Ragan. "Joe? Shouldn't we go see that officer's wife?"

"All right."

"She's a friend of yours, isn't she?"

"One of the best."

"Will she like me?"

"Who wouldn't?"

They drove in silence and then he said, "How about dinner tomorrow night?"

"At my place?"

"I'll be there."

There was no moon, but they did not need one. There was a little rain, but they did not mind.

WHAT IS LOUIS L'AMOUR'S LOST TREASURES?

Louis L'Amour's Lost Treasures is a project created to release some of the author's more unconventional manuscripts from the family archives.

Currently included in the project are *Louis L'Amour's Lost Treasures: Volume 1*, which was published in the fall of 2017, and *Volume 2*, which will be published in the fall of 2019. These books contain both finished and unfinished short stories, unfinished novels, literary and motion picture treatments, notes, and outlines. They are a wide selection of the many works Louis was never able to publish during his lifetime.

In 2018 we released *No Traveller Returns*, L'Amour's never-before-seen first novel, which was written between 1938 and 1942. Additionally, many notes and alternate drafts to Louis's well-known and previously published novels and short stories will now be included as "bonus feature" postscripts within the books that they relate to. For example, the Lost Treasures postscript to *Last of the Breed* will contain early notes on the story, the short story that was discovered to be a missing piece of the novel, the history of the novel's inspiration and creation, and information about unproduced motion picture and comic book versions.

An even more complete description of the Lost Treasures project, along with a number of examples of what is in the books, can be found at louislamourslost treasures.com. The website also contains a good deal of exclusive material, such as even more pieces of unknown stories that were too short or too incomplete to include in the Lost Treasures books, plus personal photos, scans of original documents, and notes.

All of the works that contain Lost Treasures project materials will display the Louis L'Amour's Lost Treasures banner and logo.

LOUIS L'AMOUR'S LOST TREASURES

POSTSCRIPT

By Beau L'Amour

Though never as enamored with underworld figures as many in Hollywood and the literary scene were, my father did know L.A. gangster Mickey Cohen fairly well. The two had lunch with some mutual acquaintances on a couple of occasions, and Dad patronized the Sunset Boulevard clothing shop that was Cohen's headquarters. In his Oklahoma days, Dad was also reported to have met with bank robber Charles "Pretty Boy" Floyd while trying to arrange an exclusive interview, and may have once had connections with infamous characters in Shanghai and New York, too.

However, Dad's closest criminal connections were of the type he wrote the most about, the small-time hoods who hung around the fight game. By the time I was born most of the crime-story characters who came in and out of our lives were men in law enforcement—local police officers and Border Patrol and FBI agents.

If Louis had any real-life model for Detective Joe Ragan and the other policemen in his fiction, it was probably Ray Gray, an officer with the LAPD. He and Dad occasionally had breakfast in coffee shops along Wilshire Boulevard's Miracle Mile and Dad occasionally helped out with the various youth groups Gray mentored in the late 1940s.

Below are several fragments of Joe Ragan stories that my father never completed. The first two exist in a subgenre that became sort of a specialty of Louis's: Western Noir. Usually these were set in a small town, often a mining town not too far from the modern metropolis his detective called home. The tension between life in these dusty mid-twentieth-century Western towns and the big city was often central to the conflict. That theme can also be found in *Sand Trap, Under the Hanging Wall, The Hills of Homicide,* and *A Friend of a Hero. Sideshow Champion* might fit that description as well, though it's certainly more of a sports story than a crime story.

Here is the first fragment:

Joe Ragan left the sidewalk and crossed the dusty street to the freight depot, glad when he reached the coolness of the shade under the wide eaves. The big door stood open and it looked cooler within, but

Ragan halted in the doorway, watching a man put the lip of a hand truck under a trunk, then break it back easily.

A bullet head topped with sparse reddish hair was set upon a thick neck and wide, powerful shoulders. The man wore a blue cotton shirt, now sweat stained, and his hands were large and covered with red hair.

"You the freight agent?"

The big man turned his head and stared back over his shoulder. He was bigger than Ragan himself, which was pretty big, and there was a hard, glassy stare in his blue gray eyes. He looked like a bulldog disturbed over a bone, no teeth bared but every sense alert for trouble.

"If I am, so what?"

"My name's Ragan. I've got a few questions I'd like to ask."

There were blotchy freckles under the skin of the man's face, tight drawn skin that made his cheek and jaw bones stand out. He looked tougher than a life sentence on Alcatraz. "Ask 'em," he said.

"Been on this job long?"

The big man let the trunk down easily and shook a cigarette from a crumpled pack. "Seven or eight years."

"Steady?"

"Mostly."

"You the only one who works here?"

"Who else would they need? This ain't no city, bud. This is a jerkwater town."

"You get many bodies shipped here for burial?"

Red's eyes lost some of their glassy look and the blue in them hardened even more and pin pointed. "Not so many. Like I said, this ain't a big town. Most people want to be buried where they die."

"Uh huh, and some don't have any choice. How many have been shipped in here in the past three months?"

"How should I know? I'd have to check."

Ragan lit his own smoke before he answered. "Figured you might recall, if there weren't many. A coffin isn't something a man forgets."

"I can forget anything. I often have."

"All right, Warneke. Suppose you check for me."

"You know my name, huh? What else do you know?"

Ragan smiled. "That you did four years in Joliet for armed robbery and that you've been arrested in Frisco, Los Angeles, Reno and El Paso."

Warneke did not like it. Not even a little. "So what? I'm clean. Nobody's got anything on me, one way or the other. I'm goin' straight."

Ragan shrugged. "Sure. So why worry? You asked me what I knew and I told you. I've no beef with you. If you're clean, then maybe we can work together. Me, I'm just looking around."

"Looking for what?"

Ragan shrugged. "Maybe I'm looking for money."

"I can smell a dick a block away."

"All right, so you can. It just happens I'm looking for something else and I happen to see that a lot of bodies are shipped here to Cadwall. Now I've been through here before, and I remember that it isn't a big place, so it begins to look funny. When things look funny to me I usually prowl around and see what I can turn up."

"Be careful it ain't your toes."

"It won't be."

"Anyway," Warneke commented, "this used to be a boom town. Lots of folks lived here or passed through, and some of them liked the place and wanted to be buried here. It isn't so strange. Also," he shrugged it off, "funerals here are cheap. Burial lots are cheap. It isn't a graft like in most of the cities where it is more expensive to die than to live. Burial here is a simple thing, not a lace trimmed production."

"Sure, I thought of that. Only some of these folks were young, and some of them never were anywhere close to this town, and sometimes there were other towns closer to where they died where it would have been cheap to bury them. I'm just curious, that's all."

Warneke finished his cigarette. "Don't let it throw you, bud."

"How about those records? Got your duplicate bills of lading?"

"Suppose I have? What right do you have to ask for them?"

Ragan shrugged. "If I have to ask for a court order, I'll have to give reasons. That's going to make a lot of people curious, it's going to start questions being asked. Let's save us both some trouble."

Warneke picked up a clipboard with high arched rings from a desk and tossed it on the scarred counter. "Help yourself, although what you're interested in a lot of bodies for is beyond me."

"Is it?" Ragan looked up at Warneke from under his brows. "You're making me wonder."

Warneke's face stiffened and whitened a little under his eyes. "You looking for trouble, Friend?" he demanded. "I told you I was clean, so don't think you can come in here and make me back up just because I've done time. You start nosing around and you're asking for it."

Joe Ragan checked through the bills of lading idly, then handed the clipboard back. "Thanks," he said, "you're cooperative. I'll put in a word for you with the boss."

Outside in the sunlight he walked slowly up the street, then when he reached the end of the pavement, he crossed and walked toward the hotel. He was asking for trouble, there was no doubt about it. Warneke was not dumb, nor was he soft. He was as tough as he was big, and anything he would have a hand in would be good and solid. Hard to crack.

Cadwall had one business street and a dozen residential streets with a number of residences scattered over the mountainsides on each wall of the canyon. That main drag was mostly motels and cafes to catch the passing tourists, but on a street back of the hotel there was a funeral home. There had been seven bodies consigned to this town in the past thirty days, and four of them for that home. Three had been signed for by individuals. He had made a mental note of the names.

Once back in his room he picked up a briefcase and took out a pair of binoculars. From one of his windows he could command a view of most of the main street, and perched there just out of sight from the street below, he waited and watched.

A dozen times he followed men down the street but in every case they turned off into a store or a side street before reaching the freight depot. He might be barking up the wrong tree, but he was confident that Warneke, if he was involved, would call someone else within a matter of minutes after he had taken his leave.

It was quite by accident that he happened to notice the tall man in the gray suit come out of a doorway leading to some offices across the street, and turn left along the shaded walk. He strolled casually, speaking to several of the people whom he passed, but continued toward the freight depot. Ragan studied the man carefully, and noted a Darwinian extension on his right ear. He wore glasses with a black ribbon attached, and might have been fifty or slightly more.

The man in the gray suit might not be his man, but Joe Ragan had a hunch that he was.

Again, he felt doubt, and

hesitated over the idea of wiring Merriam and having a meeting arranged. Certainly, he would be more than willing to listen, for unless Ragan was sadly mistaken, he had butted into the biggest insurance swindle in a long time, and one that had been operated safely and securely for at least two years.

Yet nobody needed to warn him that these men were playing for keeps. Warneke would play no other way, and he, Ragan, had stuck his neck way out. And he had no evidence, yet the ant hill had been kicked and now there was nothing to do but sit tight and let the ants race around. And from their racing might come just the evidence he needed.

Mopping his brow with his handkerchief, Ragan watched the man in the gray suit return up the street and to his office. The building was a dry goods and women's wear store downstairs, a collection of offices upstairs. The windows opposite his own were those of a doctor and a little beyond, an architect.

Ragan put away his glasses and went down to the street. At the filling station nearby a man was changing a tire, and three men loitered on a bench before the poolroom. Several people moved about in the warm morning sunshine, busy with their shopping. He glanced once at the building across the street, then walked down toward a café he had seen that morning.

There were few people in the café and he found a table near the wall. The waitress who crossed over to him was pretty, and had green eyes and good legs.

He tipped his head back and smiled up at her. "You recommend something," he suggested, "you know the food."

"Try the Swiss steak," she advised, "it's always good here."

"All right, and coffee." She hesitated beside his table, willing to talk. "Nice town," he ventured. "Been here long?"

"All my life except for two years in New York. It's all right if you like it. I'm thinking of moving to Los Angeles."

"I'm from there. Say, are there

any good doctors in town? I hurt my back yesterday."

"Sure, try Doc Mooney. He's about your age, but not as good looking. He's nice, though."

"Mooney? I'll try him. Somebody pointed out an older man; he wore a gray suit and glasses with a black ribbon. How's he?"

"That's Doctor Pegis. He's all right, I guess, but he hasn't been here long, and he charges so much few people can afford him. I don't think he wants to practice very much."

"Lots of money probably. Maybe he made it before he came here."

"He must have. He sure drives a swell car. The best in town, and he lives out on the old Gaynor Place."

"Nice place?"

"The best. Big house about a half-mile out of town with a park around it, and a stone wall around that. I used to go there when I was a kid and before he moved in. There's a swimming pool and everything. He never has anybody from around here out there, and that uppity daughter of his spends most of her time in Los Angeles."

When he had finished eating, he got to his feet and walked out into the sunshine. Pegis had come here about two years ago. He had a daughter named Margaret, and he had two servants, both men. The name of the waitress was Joyce Young and she hoped she would see him again.

She would.

Here is another version of the same story. In this variation there is a bit more information and you can also see that Louis was trying to figure out if Ragan was the right character to use, given the plot. As he worked out the details of the mystery it was likely he would have had to adjust either the case itself or his protagonist to justify the level of his detective's involvement and jurisdiction:

"You the freight agent?"

The big man turned his head and stared over his shoulder. He was a big man, bigger than Ragan himself, which was pretty big, and there was a hard, glassy stare in his blue gray eyes. He looked now like a bulldog disturbed at his bone, no teeth bared but every sense alert for trouble.

"If I am, so what?"

"My name's Ragan. Detective

Sergeant Joe Ragan, to be exact. I've got some questions."

The fellow had rust red hair and blotchy freckles under the skin of his face. His cheekbones were high and the skin tight drawn. He looked tougher than a life sentence on Alcatraz. "Ask 'em," he said.

"How long you been on this job?"

"Seven or eight years."

"Steady?"

"Mostly."

"You get many bodies shipped in here for burial?"

Red's eyes lost some of their glassy look and the blue in them pin pointed. "Not so many. This ain't a big town. Most folks want to be buried where they die."

"Uh huh, an' some don't have any choice. How many have been shipped here in the last three months?"

"How should I know? I'd have to check."

Ragan looked up from under his brows. "Figured you might recall, if there weren't many. A coffin isn't something a man forgets."

"You don't know me. I can forget anything. I often have."

"All right, Warneke, suppose you check."

"You know my name, huh? What else do you know?"

"That you did four years in Joliet for armed robbery. That you've been arrested in Reno, San Francisco, Los Angeles and El Paso."

Warneke's eyes were ugly. "Never leave a man alone, do you? If he has a record, you're right on him."

"Only if he asks for it. If you're clean you've nothing to worry about, Red. If you aren't, you'll do time. It just happens that I'm a right curious sort of man. Your records interest me. Seems that for the size of the town there's a good many bodies shipped in for burial."

Warneke shrugged. "People die all the time. Lots of folks lived here during the boom, and they want to be buried here."

"Sure, that's understandable. I thought of that one. Only some of these people were young. Some of them nobody knew anything about and they had no chance to choose this town. Now why were they sent here for burial? I'm just a curious guy."

"Ever get into trouble, nosing around? You could, Pal. You sure could."

Ragan smiled. "I thought of that, too, Red. But I'm still a curious guy. Let's have those records."

Joe Ragan had thought about it. He had been thinking of it all the way down here. If this deal was half as big as he believed it to be, he was sticking his neck way out. It was, he decided, a lousy way to take a vacation. Yet the Department had agreed when he asked permission to take over this job for the insurance companies. The investigation was official as well. He was killing two birds with one stone. Providing, of course, he didn't turn out to be the third bird.

Warneke now. He was tough. In a scrap he would be hard to handle. Not only big, but slinging freight around for eight hours a day he would be strong as a bull and in good shape.

Cadwall was a jerkwater town. It was a town with only one business street and a dozen residential streets. Mostly it was motels and cafés, but it had a funeral home. Ragan checked through the bills of lading. Seven bodies in thirty days in a town of less than three thousand. It was definitely out of proportion. Four of those bodies had been consigned to the funeral home, three to individuals.

Making a mental note of the names, he shoved the clipboard back over the counter. Red Warneke walked up and took it. "If any more come in, call me at the Central."

"I'm liable not to," Warneke said dryly, "you do your own work, copper. Don't make trouble for me."

Ragan walked back to the hotel and mounted the stairs swiftly. Once in his room he grabbed the briefcase from the bed and moved with it to a chair near the window. From the briefcase he took a pair of binoculars.

He had the old feeling in him again. It was in his chest and in the hair on the back of his neck. It was a feeling he always had when he was walking into trouble. He was a powerful man, himself. Starting life as a lumberjack, he switched to fighting in the ring, then back to a job as woods boss, and after returning to college, to police work. He was a careful, painstaking man with an eye for detail and a constructive imagination. Seeing everything in pictures or scenes as he did, it allowed him an almost immediate perception of the misplaced detail. He was quick to notice anything out of order.

A tall man in a gray suit and a black hat came from a building up the street. An office building, not a mortuary. He walked down the street, strolling casually and speaking to most of the people he passed. His hair was gray, and through the field glasses, Ragan studied him with care. He had a Darwinian extension on his right ear. He wore glasses with a black ribbon attached. He walked on down to the freight office and entered.

His lip reading did Ragan no good with Warneke. The man had a stiff lipped, convict's way of speaking. The newcomer was not so difficult. This man nodded, glanced out of the window toward the hotel, then asked, "Where's Meg?" Or was it Mag? Or Mug?

He was on a hot trail now, Ragan knew. He should wire Stigler and Merriam, too. Merriam was the insurance man who was paying for this. But first he would have to find out who the gray suited man was. He would have to check the mortuary and make a few inquiries around.

Nobody needed to tell him that these men were playing for keeps. Dealing in millions as they must be, and with the setup only started, they would brook no interference now.

Ragan had an idea that if they got the chance, they would kill him, and quickly. He lighted a cigarette and thought it over. As yet he had no evidence, but the anthill had been kicked, and the ants were racing around. Now things would begin to happen. He was going to have to invite trouble.

The man in the gray suit walked back up the street and returned to his office. Ragan studied the building. It was a dry goods and women's wear store downstairs, but upstairs there were offices of doctors and dentists. A doctor, probably. That was the most likely answer.

For an hour he watched first one place and then the other, but without learning anything. He got up then and locking his room went downstairs and out into the street. It was almost noon and the sun was bright. Down the street in front of a garage a man was putting gas in a car. In the other direction, on a bench in front of a poolroom three men loitered, enjoying the sunshine.

Ragan went down the street to a café and got a table against the wall. The waitress who came over to him was pretty, and had green eyes. He looked up and grinned. "What's good?" he asked. "I'll take your word for it."

"Try the Swiss steak," she told him.

"All right. And coffee." Then he said, "Nice town, been here long?"

"All my life. It's all right if you like it. I'd rather live in Los Angeles."

"That's where I'm from. Say, are there any good doctors in this town? I hurt my back yesterday. Not bad, but I'd like it looked over."

"Sure, there's Doc Mooney. He's about your age. He's nice."

"Mooney? Maybe I'll try him. Somebody pointed out a guy on the street. Older fellow, gray hair, gray suit and glasses with a black ribbon. How's he?"

"That's Doctor Pegis. Yes, I guess he's all right. He hasn't been here long. About three years."

"Pegis? The name doesn't sound familiar. When they pointed him out to me, I thought maybe I'd seen him before."

She returned with his coffee. "You might have. He used to live in Los Angeles, but he practiced back east somewhere. He doesn't do much business here. Doesn't even try, from what they say. But when you've got his money you don't have to."

Before he had finished his meal he knew that Pegis drove a six thousand dollar car, that he lived in one of the town's most beautiful homes, which was on the edge of town in a small grove of trees with a wall around them, and that he had a pretty daughter who lived in Los

Angeles but frequently came out to visit.

The name of the waitress was Joyce Young, and no, she wasn't doing anything tonight and would be glad to see him again.

Joe Ragan walked out on the street in the sunshine and watched a beautiful young woman in a green convertible roll up the street and stop not far away. Dr. Pegis came down the stairs from his office and met her, and together they started up the street, talking earnestly. Pegis did not see Ragan until quite near and then he glanced up, their eyes met briefly and Pegis looked down at the girl, smiling.

The slight change in his step was beautifully done, and his shoulder bumped that of Ragan so accidentally that had Ragan not been expecting something of the kind he would never have guessed its purpose.

"Oh, I beg your pardon, sir!" Pegis stopped abruptly. "Awfully clumsy of me!"

"Don't let it bother you!" The girl's eyes were blue, level and just a shade hard. She was pretty, Ragan decided, even more than merely pretty. "Father's always bumping into strangers!"

Ragan welcomed the meeting. "It was my fault," he said, "but I'm glad it happened. At least, I now know somebody in this town."

"Then you are a stranger?" Dr. Pegis looked at him over his glasses. "We must not allow Cadwall to be amiss in its hospitality. Won't you join us in a drink? Or a cup of coffee?"

It was very neat. It was neat to the point that Dr. Pegis suddenly recalled a phone call he must make, then returned to excuse himself, leaving them alone.

What next? Now that they had picked his pocket and discovered who he was the next move would be one of two things: to soft-soap him into having a good time and forgetting his investigation, or leading him to a spot where he could be carefully removed.

Next are two fragments from a different Joe Ragan story:

"Doc figures he's been dead for about four days," Daly suggested, "but you know how that is. You can't place the time of death too accurately in a case like this."

"What gets me," Joe Ragan commented, "is the setup. There's no sign of a struggle, no glasses out, no cigarettes in the ash trays. Hammond was a smoker, so if he had been at home long there would have been cigarette stubs around."

"Unless the killer emptied the trays." Daly looked around the beautifully appointed room with thoughtful eyes. "Maybe that was done, but the maid says no. She says she always placed those trays just exactly where they are, and she doubts if anybody else would think of being so careful."

"She's got something. She seems like a smart gal. Is she still around?"

"Sure. She's waiting in the kitchen. Want to talk to her?"

"Might as well." Ragan ran his fingers through his dark hair and scowled unhappily at the room. This was the second killing in two days, and not a clue. Of course, there was a lot of difference in the two jobs, and especially in the locale. This was a far cry from the untidy bedroom where he had found Al Dover with a knife in his ribs.

Heels clicked on the hardwood floor and he glanced up, then did a double take. For a maid this girl was something . . . in fact, she was a dish with a figure off of the line at Earl Carroll's.

"You the maid?" He was incredulous.

"Exactly," she said crisply, and her brown eyes flashed, "and just the maid! No," she added sharply, "extra-curricular activities!"

"Lady," he protested patiently, "I didn't accuse you of anything! I'm just here to ask questions."

"Then ask them," she replied shortly, "and don't start looking at me and wondering what I'm doing in this uniform! As it happens," she continued, "Mr. Hammond was very particular about his home and his food. I am a dietician and a homemaking expert!"

"Okay, okay!" Ragan waved a hand. "All right, then. You're a smart girl. You know the setup here. You've told Daly that you know of no enemies Hammond had . . . now take a look around and see if anything's wrong with this room."

Their eyes held for an instant, then the girl turned and surveyed the room . . . suddenly they froze. "Who hung up Mr. Hammond's overcoat?"

"Who?" Ragan's eyes sharpened. "Nobody. You didn't, did you, Pat?"

"No, it was hanging there when I first came in. Why, what's the gimmick?"

"Then if you didn't hang it up, the killer must have. Mr. Hammond always threw it over a chair or over the sofa. I always had to hang it up for him."

Joe Ragan rubbed his jaw. Then he glanced at the girl. "What was your name again?"

"Katherine Ryan," she replied, and waited for his next question.

There was none. Joe Ragan walked thoughtfully from chair to chair, then to the sofa, and finally to the coat itself. He did not touch it, but walked around it thoughtfully. Then, still without speaking, he opened the door and stepped out, then he came in, closed the door after him, noting the sound it made, and walked into the living room, making a motion to throw his coat on the sofa, then turned toward the library. Where the body had been found, he stopped.

For a moment he stood silent, and then he walked into the library and turned to face the living room. After a minute of pondering, he turned and glanced around. It was a room solidly walled with books, and only two windows, both high above the ground. The grounds outside, he remembered, were surrounded by a high iron fence.

When he came back into the living room the girl and Daly looked at him expectantly. "I got it," he said, "at least, I think I've got it." He walked across the room to a place directly opposite the library door and studied the wall, then with a sudden exclamation he lifted a painting from the wall, and began digging at the walnut panel with his knife. When he turned back to them, he was grinning. Between his fingers he held a bullet!

"Somebody is here in the house . . . probably alone. Hammond isn't home yet. He was still out to the opera, like Miss Ryan said. This guy is working the place over, or maybe he has a grudge against Hammond, anyway, he's in the library when Hammond comes home . . . maybe Hammond comes home earlier than he expects.

"Hammond walks in, tosses his topcoat on the sofa and turns toward the library. He either sees the other man in the door, or knowing he's going to be trapped, the fellow gets panicky and shoots . . . he misses his first shot and this," Ragan held up the bullet, "is it. His second scores a hit, and kills Hammond. Then he blows out of here."

"It looks good," Pat Daly said, nodding. He was a short, rather fat man with a round, thoughtful face. Ragan, in contrast, was over six feet and rugged. He looked like a halfback, and his hands were big, tight jointed hands that balled into hard fists. "Only, who was the killer? Was he looting the joint? Or was he, like you suggested, some guy who had it in for Hammond? Furthermore, who let him in?"

Daly's eyes swung to Katherine Ryan, and Ragan's followed them. She stiffened. "Don't look at me, you City Hall Sherlocks," she said sharply, "I wasn't here."

"Can you prove that?" Daly asked. "Have you got people who can say where you were?"

Listening with half his attention, Ragan turned and walked into the library. If his theory was right and the shot had come from here, what was the killer doing in here? What was it he wanted? So far as he could see there was nothing in the room but books. The desk invited inspection, and he strolled over, careful to touch nothing.

This fellow Hammond had connections. His killing would have repercussions, and those repercussions were sure to result in some heads rolling in the Homicide Bureau if results were not forthcoming. There wasn't a single lead on the Al Dover job, either. Wherever they looked in that direction they ran into a blank wall.

Dover was small potatoes; Hammond was something else again. They had worked fast, interviewing his friends, Judge Samuel Young, sportsman Gig Fields and Arnold Hale, the investment broker. And not a lead from any of them.

Whoever the killer had been, he had wasted no time. He had been quick to shoot. That did not argue a professional hand. Veteran burglars are hesitant to shoot for the gas chamber is so much more final than a prison sentence. Unless . . . Unless the killer already had a rap hanging over him.

It is possible this next piece is just a different version of the same story. After thinking about it for a while, Louis may have decided that he wanted to use a more eccentric victim and an atypical setting:

"The way I see it," Ollie Burns explained, "is that the murder wasn't intentional. I think it was a burglary that went haywire. Some joe figures the old man has a lot of scratch, see? So, when the old boy is gone, he crashes in and starts shaking the place down. Then the old boy comes home and the guy knocks him off."

Joe Ragan nodded absently, and

stared around. It was a gloomy place in which to live, merely a corner of the great loft over a warehouse, the corner partitioned off from the vast, empty room by a stack of empty packing cases and several large, old-fashioned trunks.

Yet it was a fit scene for murder, and the logical end to the strange career of Herman Scoblick.

A single light bulb suspended from the high ceiling offered the only light except for a reading lamp over the battered roll-top desk. The dead man lay sprawled on the floor and beside him was a burst paper sack and some scattered packages. A can of peaches had rolled under the edge of the iron cot.

There was a wound on the back of the old man's head, and he had been stabbed from behind. The murderer had known where to stab. Apparently, the blow on the head had struck the old man down and the murderer had then finished the job with the knife while he lay unconscious.

The desk had been rifled and there were papers scattered around.

The mattress had been rolled back and partly ripped open, all evidence of a hasty and not very thorough search of the premises.

While the photographer stepped around snapping pictures, Joe Ragan stood with his big hands on his hips and stared moodily about. Ollie was probably right in his guess that Scoblick had been murdered by a sneak thief. On the way over from Headquarters they had told him something about the old man. That he was reputed to be wealthy. That he owned the warehouse and would neither rent nor sell it. That his early life had been exciting and dangerous and then suddenly after an unhappy marriage he had become almost a recluse.

"The body was found an hour ago by Kitty Burleson. She's a waitress at the Porter House, and the old man always ate Sunday morning breakfast with her. When he didn't show up, she thought he might be alone and sick, so she came over and found him like this."

"Thoughtful of her," Ragan said grimly. "Oldish woman?"

"No," Ollie grinned, "young an' damned good looking."

"Good legs," the old man in the dirty shirt scratched his stomach and leered. "Mighty good."

"Who's he?" Ragan demanded, bobbing his head at the old man.

"Friend of the deceased. Named Harold Asbury. Used to play checkers with him."

"He doesn't look like a Harold." Ragan stared at the old man.

Asbury glowered. "You don't look like a cop, either. You look like a baseball player. Like a left handed pitcher."

"The way it looks," Ollie said, "he was killed Saturday night, sometime. Probably about nine o'clock. He used to go down to the diner for coffee, and Gus Fisher, the night counterman, says he was in Saturday night, and then he went shopping. He didn't come in Sunday night."

Ragan looked at the medical examiner who was getting up from his knees. "What about it, Doc?"

"Can't tell. Could have been Saturday night. Autopsy should give us a slant on that."

"We found a downstairs window jimmied open," Ollie added, "doesn't look professional, an' from the marks on the sill I'd say it was done with a hatchet, using the blade to wedge under the window and pry up. Pete found a hatchet down near the window, but no prints."

"Looks routine," Ragan admitted, "but we'll go over it. Where's this guy from the diner? He around?"

"Downstairs. We've got them all here. This Burleson dame, Fisher, Asbury here and Hale."

"Who's Hale?" Ragan stared at the mattress, peered under the bed, and looked curiously around the partitioned space. He glanced at the can under the edge of the bed, but did not touch it. Under the bed was a small wooden box, unopened.

"William Hale. He's the nephew. Only relative there is. We got him out of bed and had him come down here because he might have something to offer. You want to talk to them?"

"Pretty quick." Ragan looked over at Asbury who stood blinking like an owl in a hail storm. "You knew him well?"

"Nobody knew him well." The old man spat. "Queer duck, he was. We played checkers, an' he was good, mighty good. Never liked much else. Wouldn't spend a dime he could avoid. Thought people ate too much soft food. Pap, he called it. Too many sweets. Wouldn't touch them, himself. First, I heard about him eatin' at the Porter House," he added suspiciously. "He didn't like nothing, Scoblick didn't."

"What do you mean?" Ragan asked.

"What I say. He didn't like Republicans or Democrats. He hated cops and was afraid of crooks. He wouldn't own a radio or go to a movie. Hadn't voted since James G. Blaine. He was suspicious of everybody, an' his only living relative, he hated."

"The nephew? Hale?"

"That's the one. Works somewhere down in the theatre district. Scoblick didn't trust him an' wouldn't tolerate him around."

"Anybody ever come to see him besides you?"

"Me? I never come here. He wouldn't stand for it. Told me he'd come to my place. That's what he done."

"You know this waitress? Kitty Burleson?"

"No. Think probably she was the one I seen leavin' here once. I said something about her to old Scoblick an' he got awful mad. Told me to mind my own damn' business."

Ragan poked around the room, looking into this and that, but seeming to have nothing definite in mind. Finally, he straightened. "All right, Ollie, we'll go downstairs. Is there an office, or anything? Where I can talk to those people?"

"Sure. It hasn't been used in a long time, but it will do."

Joe Ragan walked into the little office, enclosed with glass but dusty, and brushed off a chair. "Let's talk to this fellow from the diner."

Gus Fisher was a big man with a red face and a thick red neck. He twisted his hat in his hand and stared at Ragan out of pale blue suspicious eyes. He looked strong enough to choke an ox.

Ragan looked up at him, his hands

in his coat pockets. "How are you, Fisher? Did you know the old man very well?"

"No, I didn't. Knew him sort of for all of three years. He was comin' around for coffee before I ever started to work at the diner, so naturally, I got acquainted with him. He never had much to say."

"How often did he come in?"

"Every night, regular as clockwork. He'd always come in between six thirty and seven o'clock. The last time was Saturday."

"What time did he leave there?" Ragan stared out of the office at the others, who waited, not talking. The girl _was_ pretty.

"Don't know for sure. I guess it was seven thirty or a quarter to eight. He always sat over his coffee for a long time, sometimes had three or four refills."

"What did he pay you with? Change or bills?"

"That night? It was a bill. A twenty. That was unusual as he mostly paid in change. He never left no tip, not any time. I'd say he left about fifteen to eight."

"Anybody around? Anybody follow him out?" Ragan asked. Fisher was wearing new shoes, very good shoes.

"No. No, nobody did. He got up all of a sudden, slammed the paper down and went out. Muttered something, sort of like 'Hell, he can't . . . ' That was all I heard. Then he went out."

Joe Ragan tilted his hat back on his head and looked up at Gus Fisher. "Gus, you know Dewey Smith?"

"Who?" The big man's face turned redder, then pale. He licked his thick lips. "I don't think I do? Should I?"

"Uh huh. He was your cell mate at Quentin."

Ollie Burns looked up, startled. First at Ragan, then at Gus. The big counterman cracked his knuckles, his face sullen.

"All right, so I was a con. That doesn't mean I knocked off that old man. I've been goin' straight."

"I'm not accusing you," Ragan said, shrugging. "And your being an ex con doesn't matter one bit. Maybe you are going straight,

Fisher, but maybe you aren't going *quite* straight."

"What's that mean?" Fisher demanded suspiciously.

"Well, Dewey Smith, for one thing. He's been around that diner quite a lot. Dewey isn't doing much of anything, these days, but he has more money, quite a lot, for him. Not that it would be much for an honest man, but a crook never makes much. He always thinks about the big take he's going to make and keeps risking his life or ten years in the pen for an amount of money an honest man could earn in a couple of weeks."

Ragan tipped back in his chair. "There's a couple of other guys been around that place, too. And there's been some jack rolling around the neighborhood. Could it be you're spotting for them? Tipping them off as to who has a roll and who hasn't?"

"I ain't talkin'," Gus said flatly. "You ain't framin' me, nor bluffin' me."

"Did you tell Dewey about old man Scoblick?" Ragan asked suddenly.

Fisher paled a little, and his

lips tightened. "I ain't talkin'!" he insisted.

Ragan looked up. "All right, Fisher, you can go."

Gus Fisher hesitated, staring from Ragan to Ollie uneasily. "Now listen," he protested, "I haven't--!"

"Forget it." Ragan looked up and smiled. "Only take a tip from me, Gus, and stay away from those ex-cons. If you don't, we'll be picking you up one of these days. Suppose you had tipped the boys off to Scoblick? You'd get that murder rap hung on you, too, Gus, and you're a two-time loser. You'd make the chamber."

The big man was sweating. He turned and ducked out the door. Ollie stared after him. "Want I should put a tail on him, Joe?"

"No, forget it. He didn't do it, anyway."

"But he'll go right to Dewey Smith, an' they'll both lam."

"He won't go to Dewey. He'll never go near him. Dewey's in the jug now. I had him picked up along with three others when I got the location of this job. Just for luck. We'll talk to him." He glanced at his wrist watch. "Send a car, we'll talk to him here." He looked out at the waiting people. "And send Hale in next."

Hale walked briskly through the door and closed it carefully behind him. He turned and faced Ragan, and Ragan glanced at him, then away. Pale featured, blue eyes, straight blond hair, rather attractive, and tall. Well dressed.

"Sorry to keep you waiting, Mr. Hale," Ragan said, his eyes friendly. "I know you're very busy, but I thought you might be able to help us. You were Herman Scoblick's nephew?"

"That's right, sir. My mother was his sister. Although I did not know him overly well. He was a peculiar man."

"He certainly was." Ragan stared moodily at his toes. What questions to ask? They always came so easily to some people, but to him it was always difficult. He had to study out each question, and then they rarely failed to elicit just the information he wanted. "Did you ever call on him here?"

"Yes, I did, but not often. I tried to convince him he should live elsewhere, and assured him that I would gladly help if he needed ready cash."

"You didn't believe that he had money hidden away?"

"I don't know. He may have had. Evidently the killer thought so, but it was always my impression that taxes kept him poor. This building he wouldn't rent at all, yet he paid taxes on it all the while."

"How did you two get along?"

And to wrap up, here are the few notes that still exist pertaining to the above fragment; they include the identity of the killer as well as some of clues:

Herman Scoblick was murdered on Sunday morning by his nephew, William Hale.

Hale brought a sack of groceries with him and spilled them on the floor in an attempt to indicate that his uncle had been murdered when returning from his Saturday night shopping.

Hale then pried up the window to make it appear that someone had forced entry, also he ripped open the mattress and searched the premises as though burglars had been active.

On the surface it appears logical that the old man has been murdered by someone who either followed him home, or more likely, lay in wait for him on his return.

There are four suspects:

Gus Fisher, counterman in the diner.

William Hale, nephew.

Dewey Smith, a small-time crook and sneak thief.

Kitty Burleson, waitress and heiress to Scoblick's estate, although this fact is unknown to Hale, who believes himself to be the heir.

First clue: *A can of peaches.* Scoblick hated sweets and did not believe in soft foods.

2nd clue: *A locked box unopened.* It seems obvious a sneak thief would have broken into it first . . . unless he knew it contains nothing.

These are minor indications that do not seem to fit the picture of Scoblick Ragan has received.

The body was found by *Gus Fisher*, on Monday night. When Scoblick failed to show up two nights in a row, he investigated.

Beau L'Amour
November 2019

ABOUT LOUIS L'AMOUR

"I think of myself in the oral tradition—
as a troubadour, a village taleteller, the man
in the shadows of the campfire. That's the way
I'd like to be remembered—as a storyteller.
A good storyteller."

IT IS DOUBTFUL that any author could be as at home in the world re-created in his novels as Louis Dearborn L'Amour. Not only could he physically fill the boots of the rugged characters he wrote about, but he literally "walked the land my characters walk." His personal experiences as well as his lifelong devotion to historical research combined to give Mr. L'Amour the unique knowledge and understanding of people, events, and the challenge of the American frontier that became the hallmarks of his popularity.

As a boy growing up in Jamestown, North Dakota, he absorbed all he could about his family's frontier heritage, including the story of his great-grandfather who was scalped by Sioux warriors.

Spurred by an eager curiosity and a desire to broaden his horizons, Mr. L'Amour left home at the age of fifteen and enjoyed a wide variety of jobs, including seaman, lumberjack, elephant handler, skinner of dead cattle, miner, and officer in the Transportation Corps during World War II. He was a voracious reader and collector of books. His personal library contained 17,000 volumes.

Mr. L'Amour "wanted to write almost from the time I could talk." After developing a widespread following for the many frontier and adventure stories he wrote for fiction magazines, Mr. L'Amour published his first full-length novel, *Hondo,* in the United States in 1953. Every one of his more than 120 books is in print; there are more than 300 million copies of his books in print worldwide, making him one of the bestselling authors in modern literary history. His books have been translated into twenty languages, and more than forty-five of his novels and stories have been made into feature films and television movies.

His hardcover bestsellers include *The Lonesome Gods, The Walking Drum* (his twelfth-century historical novel), *Jubal Sackett, Last of the Breed,* and *The Haunted Mesa.* His memoir, *Education of a Wandering Man,* was a leading bestseller in 1989. Audio dramatizations and adaptations of many L'Amour stories are available from Random House Audio.

The recipient of many great honors and awards, in 1983 Mr. L'Amour became the first novelist ever to be awarded the Congressional Gold Medal by the United States Congress in honor of his life's work. In 1984 he was also awarded the Medal of Freedom by President Reagan.

Louis L'Amour died on June 10, 1988.